Under the Shadows

Tony McFadden

If you purchased this paperback and feel like re-gifting it, go right ahead. Just do the author a solid and leave a review somewhere first. If you're interested in more titles by this author, a list can be found at the end of this book.

ISBN: 978-0-6456733-3-3

DEDICATION

For all of those who run into danger

instead of away from it.

ACKNOWLEDGMENTS

The journey I've followed over the past almost two decades
is on the back of the feedback I get from you, my readers.

Thank you so much.

One

I hate running. Have I mentioned that before? I barely made it through the physical part of the admission process of the Australian Federal Police, and that was well over a decade ago. Until recently I relied on my smarts.

Though you'd never know it today.

I was in Wyee, a small, no-stoplight town an hour or so north of Sydney.

Not by choice.

I ducked around a corner of a bottle shop and fumbled my phone out of my pocket. Still no reply from Lucy. Fuck. I sent her another text. *What's happening with Davie?*

It was late afternoon. This morning, I thought I had the case cracked. Knew everything. I was about to bring down a foe from my distant past. It was big. Things have gone to shit since then.

"Where da hell did he go?" A familiar voice yelled out behind me. One of the Finns. Big lads. Brothers, and I felt sorry for their mother. Either one of them could de-bone me like I was a mall rotisserie chicken. And both of them were on my tail.

They were getting close.

I continued around the corner of the bottle shop and tripped over an old guy sitting with his back against the wall, his face tilted up to take in what was left of the winter sun.

"Get fucked!" He tried pushing himself to his feet and failed twice before succeeding by sliding his back up the wall.

I dusted myself off, stood and held up my index finger. "Shh. Sorry, mate. Gotta keep it down, though. Someone's after me."

He closed one eye and squinted through the other. "Coppers? Whadya do?"

I put my hand on his shoulder and gently sat him back down. "Not coppers. Just a couple of pissed-off giants. Distract them for me if they come by, and I'll buy you a bottle of whatever you want."

He nodded. "Fair deal." He closed his eyes and turned his face to the sun again. "Something expensive, right?"

If I were lucky, they'd trip over him, too. "You got it. Top shelf." I slipped around the third corner of the building. My car was a thirty-five kilometre drive away in Gosford, I don't know how many mongrels were chasing me, and I regretted getting into this mess in the first place.

On the surface, just a simple missing persons case. Then, I had the stupidity to dig a bit deeper.

I heard the old drunk behind me. "Get fucked! He went thataway." Shit. They were getting closer.

I shook my head. If I lived through this, I'd be hitting the gym a bit more frequently.

I tried opening the map on my phone while I ran. Not as easy as it might seem. I knew there was a train station around somewhere. I had no idea exactly where, and I had no idea when the next train was.

A couple of dumpsters—skips—were against the side wall of the bottle shop. Their garbage smell made my eyes water, but the spot between them and the wall would have to be a good enough hiding place for now.

The map on my phone finally opened. The station was a bit less than a kilometre southeast of me. The next train was in ten minutes.

Shit.

More running. I wouldn't be able to outrun them without a head start. There was a plant nursery just west of me. Some of the plants were large enough for cover. And it was back in the direction of the highway, a likely place to try hitching a ride. A good place to draw my predators with a bit of misdirection.

I made a lot of noise as I headed into the nursery. And I heard the howls getting closer behind me. I pulled up short and ducked behind a stand of saplings, potted and ready for sale.

I could see the small parking lot off Wyee Road. A flatbed backed into a spot, and the driver jumped out, leaving her keys in the ignition. Maybe I would be lucky.

She reached the back of the truck, paused, then retraced her steps, leaned through the window and pulled the keys out of the ignition.

Shit. No luck this time.

The two (maybe three now) meatheads tracking me were making enough noise at the front of the nursery that I could leave the way I came in without being noticed. Hopefully.

Running, again.

My right ankle was killing me, my left knee felt like gravel was being ground between the bones, and my lungs were aching. All-in-all, a poster child for laziness.

I ran across the road through light traffic and over the railway bridge. I looked to my left, north up the tracks. The train was arriving. The road curved to the right, heading south toward the station. I redoubled my efforts.

In reality, there was no doubling. I increased my speed by maybe one km/hr. I risked a glance behind me. The two that I thought had become three were now four—all much fitter than me.

I took the steps up to the concourse two at a time, feet slamming into the pavement behind me, getting closer every step.

The train arrived as I made it to the platform. As it slowed, I ran to the end beside the front carriage and jumped in as it stopped. I sat in a seat facing the back and slouched.

The doors between the front car and the second car and between the second and third cars were open. I watched them get on the last carriage and walk down the aisle, looking for me.

The biggest Finn in front saw me and smiled. Even his mother couldn't love that face. He sat on one side of me, and his brother sat on the other. They stunk of old sweat.

I was fucked.

Two Days Ago

Two

Running cases out of my apartment made my job seem more like a hobby than a viable enterprise. I needed to move to a more professional environment. I needed signage on the door, meeting rooms for clients, things I couldn't afford with my current caseload. But it was a chicken-egg thing, right? I needed the business to afford a place and a place to generate the kind of business that brought in that kind of revenue.

So, I found one of those shared workspace setups. I had a small office, access to conference rooms by the hour and a secure printer. It would do for now.

A big advantage was that it was close to my childhood friend Davie's work. And even closer to where Lucy worked.

Davie and I were sitting at one of the outside tables of a cafe half a block from the bank that employed him and in front of my office space. He put his half-empty cup of coffee down, sloshing some on the table. He moved quicker than

I'd ever seen him, grabbing his bottle of water and dodging the fast-spreading pool of sugary mess.

He checked his trousers. Satisfied they were unblemished, he opened his water and took a healthy drink. "I need to get to work, mate."

I nodded. "Five minutes. Let me show you my new office." I looked up at the building above us. "Five minutes."

He pushed back from the table and sighed. "Sure. Why not." He winced as he stretched out his back. "I still hurt from that thing. I'm going to start sending you my physio bills. Tapped out my insurance months ago."

I chuckled and led him up to the sixth floor of an anonymous office building in Sydney's CBD. Floors four through twelve were short and long-term office spaces, small to large. Each floor was essentially the same: Common kitchen area and some meeting rooms you could book for client visits. Larger conference rooms. Very professional-looking and a hell of a lot cheaper than locking into a long-term lease.

The lift doors opened, and Davie followed me into the common area. "Your business is picking up, I take it?"

"Chicken and egg thing, right? I've banked a couple of bucks in the last few cases, but if I want to expand, I need to look more professional. Can't keep meeting prospective clients in cafes." I shrugged. "I've signed a six-month deal. See if it works out."

We stood in the middle of the common area—basically a large lunch room. A pool table took up the greater part of the centre. Café-style tables were spread along the walls. A small kitchen with an automatic coffee machine and a stack of generic coffee cups sitting beside a double-wide refrigerator filled with chilled bottles of water. A couple of young professionals were at the coffee machine chatting about something. A wealthy-looking middle-aged woman sat at one of the tables, scrolling through her phone.

"Which one is yours?"

I pointed, and he followed me down a hall and around a corner to a glass door with "Nick Harding Investigations" in a fancy font stencilled with stick-on letters.

The lock was a keypad. I entered the six-digit code and pulled the door open. I stood to one side, letting him enter in front of me.

It was crowded. There were two desks and a portable whiteboard. My laptop was in a dock, and the display was spread across two monitors. I pointed at the empty desk. "Room for you?"

"Oh, hell no." Davie swung his arm around, the other hand holding his sore shoulder. "I prefer non-contact IT work, thanks. The last job..." He shook his head. "Yeah, no." He cocked his head and looked at me. "How's Lucy doing?"

"Same as you. Keeping her distance from any cases. Don't blame her. You two got the brunt of the physical abuse on the last one."

Davie poked himself in the chest with his thumb. "I'm your guy in the chair. Nothing else."

"Got it." I sat in my seat, and he sat on the corner of the empty desk. I swivelled my chair to face him. "And if I need a guy in the chair, I can call you?"

He thought about it for a minute. I don't blame him for his hesitation. He got beat on pretty hard a year ago and was taking a while to recover.

I shook my head. "Hey, mate. Don't worry about it. I've only been looking at low-impact cases for a while myself. It's been a hectic few years."

"Like what?"

I spun back to the monitors and tapped the space bar to wake the screens. "Corporate background check stuff, maybe missing persons. Some divorce crap for rich people."

The door popped open as if on cue, like the intruder had been listening outside, and a head poked in. Angular and lean, short cropped thin hair and a furrowed brow over a smiling face. He pointed at Davie. "You Nick," he leaned back and read the sign on the door, "Harding?"

Davie pointed at me.

"Right-o. Private dick. We've got a thing for you. What are your rates?"

Davie smiled and stood. "I'll leave you to it, mate. Ping me if you need me." He pushed past the guy at the door with a nod.

I stood and held out my hand. "You've got me at a disadvantage."

He grabbed my hand and held it, not shaking. It was weirdly intimate. "John Ravenhill. I'm sales for CommTech, a small telecommunications consultancy on this floor. So what do you charge?"

"It's nice to meet you, John. My rates vary depending on the type of job I'm doing. And where." I pulled out the chair from the empty desk. "Have a seat."

"Variations based on *what,* I understand. How does *where* your job is impact your rates?" He sat, the furrow deeper and his smile gone.

"I'm going to charge a hell of a lot to find someone who has disappeared out past Broken Hill, but I'll do it on Hamilton Island for room and board."

The smile was back. The brow was still wrinkled like an underweight Shar-pei's face. "Got it. It's basically local. We want to partner with a PNG-based company for a project, but we need someone to check into it before we sign any papers with them. We've got a standard NDA, but that's only good for honest people. We don't know this mob." He held up his perfectly manicured, very soft hands. "We don't need you to go there. They're based in Port Moresby, but everything is online. Database searches, phone enquiries, that sort of thing."

"You're looking for an independent eye to limit your liability if things go to shit."

He laughed. "Hell yeah. You got it. I like you."

Lucky me. I handed him a freshly minted card. "Email me the details, and I'll send through a proposal. Are you the decision maker?"

He waggled a hand. "I don't sign the engagement letter if that's what you mean. I do influence the decision, though."

"I'll need to meet with the person signing the cheques. Are they available today?"

"She's out of town. Her name is Harriet Gosling." John looked at his watch. "It's Monday. She was supposed to be back from Port Moresby today, but the discussions went long. I expect she'll be back Wednesday."

I nodded and stood. Nothing more I could do today. "Drop me a mail, copy Harriet, tell me what the details are. Like the name of the company, any principles, their address, anything you've got. I'll reply with a proposal, probably before Harriet returns to the office." I held out my hand.

He didn't return the action.

"How 'bout you stop by *our* office and meet our solicitor? You can ask him any questions you might have."

"Not a good time right now. I'm still getting organised. Have them call me and set something up, okay? What's their name?"

"Raymond Tennyson. And no problem. I think he's around all day."

Fantastic. A new client and they immediately pull out their lawyers. I held out my hand again. "Email me the docs and include Raymond in the email. I'll contact him that way."

"Aces, mate. Expect something in your inbox imminently." He shook my hand this time. Now it was clammy. I was slightly repulsed.

I took the coffee mug from my desk. "Hey, how's the coffee machine work here?"

He laughed, and I followed him into the shared kitchen area. He showed me tricks to get a double shot out of the machine, then returned to his office.

A cloud of cinnamon fruit smell wafted past me, overpowering the smell of the coffee filling my mug. Followed by a dainty throat clearing. "Ahem."

I turned to an elegant woman in her, well, hell, I'd be guessing. Maybe 40s. Or very rich 50s. Or extremely rich 60s. I smiled. "Hi there. Can I get you a coffee?"

"Oh, I don't drink it. Are you Nick Harding, the investigator?"

Two clients on my very first day? This place was going to pay off. "I am. And you are?"

"Interested in hiring you."

The espresso machine delivered a final belch. My coffee was ready. "Let's sit over there." I nodded toward one of the tables along the wall. "And you can tell me your name and why you want to hire a Private Investigator."

She pulled out her chair like she was accustomed to having it done for her. "My name is Lyla Porter."

"Very nice to meet you, Mrs Porter. How could I help you?"

A flash of irritation crossed her face, and she cleared her throat. "*Miss* Porter. Call me Lyla. It's easier. My son is missing. I'm hoping you can find him for me."

To the point. This and her very expensive clothing increased my rates by at least 25%. Maybe. "Okay, but before you tell me about your missing son, Mrs - Miss Porter, have you contacted the police?"

She shook her head. "They're busy enough with real crimes. I think he just ran away. No foul play. No ransom demands. Calling the cops seems like overkill." She put her hand on mine. "But if you can't find him by Wednesday, I'll go to the police, okay?"

Two whole days. "Sure. If that's what you want. What brings you to *my* office?"

She waved that question away like it was a meddlesome fly. "Coincidence. I was here to visit an old friend and heard about a detective opening an office on this floor."

"Very fortuitous. Who is your friend?"

"You wouldn't know her. Harriet Gosling. An old friend from way back. She owns a small consulting company." She frowned. "Waste of time, though. She's out of town until Wednesday."

I really hate coincidences. A couple of years ago, two cases that turned out to be connected almost got me killed. I probably wouldn't have minded so much if I knew they were linked from the outset. I took a deep breath, exhaling through pursed lips. "I haven't met Harriet yet, but I've been asked to do some work for her company. Some corporate background checks. I'm not a big fan of coincidences. Your son hasn't pissed off to PNG, has he?"

Lyla chuckled. "No. He's fifteen. Smart kid, but poor at school. I think he bores easily. I'm not sure he'd even know where Port Moresby is."

Probably okay. I would be pissed later if I had to be, and I'd add a healthy surcharge to her bill. "Okay. Are you sure I can't get you anything to drink?"

I caught movement out of the corner of my eye and looked up at John. My other new client.

"Hey, Nick. Sorry to interrupt, mate. Your email bounced." John handed my business card back to me. "Is it wrong on the card?" He nodded at Lyla. "Hey, Lyla. Sorry for the interruption."

She sat back in her chair and crossed her arms, looking at John and then at me. I handed John my mobile and opened the mail app. "Put your email address in here, and I'll mail you. You'll have my correct address then."

John nodded and took my phone, holding it out at arm's length and squinting. I took it back. "Give me your card, and I'll email you. You can reply to my email with the details. And maybe get your eyes checked." I smiled. He was still a potential client. I typed in his email address, put 'It's Nick' in the subject line and sent it to him.

His phone chirped in his hand. "Aces, mate. I'll get back to you today or tomorrow." He wandered back toward his office.

"He's a fool." Lyla sniffed.

"It is weird that you know them, and they hired me before you found me."

"They've hired you? Doesn't seem like they've hired you yet."

"Close enough. They approached me about engaging me before you found me. And for accuracy's sake, you haven't hired me yet, either. Why do you say he's a fool?"

She shook her head, like talking about the sales guy was a waste of time. But she talked about him anyway. "He's the son of one of Harriet's friends. He's not totally useless, but he's lost business before. Business any competent teenager could keep."

"I'm in this place not even an official hour, and I'm getting the good gossip. How'd that happen?" No, I shouldn't. I held up a hand. "Never mind; it's none of my business."

"They had a good engineer working inside a large company. Good daily rate. Very good margin on him, and John missed the fact that the kid's contract came up for renewal. Not the contract with the client, understand, but the contract with the kid. When the kid didn't hear about an extension, he went to one of Harriett's competitors. Harriet lost the business, and the competitor got a new client. John doesn't do well checking his emails. You're going to have to follow up with him."

"Thanks for the heads up." I looked at the card. "I'll give him a call tomorrow." I slid it under my phone and smiled at Lyla. "So tell me about your wayward son."

Three

Lyla pointed her nose toward the coffee machine. "Do they have tea over there?"

I shrugged. "Probably. My first day here."

"You're new at this?"

I shook my head. "Not my first day as a P.I. I'm not a novice. First day in this office." I stood. "Let's check."

There was indeed tea. It would be foolish to think there wouldn't be. She chose a lemon infusion type, dropped the bag in a cup and filled the cup with hot water. "How did you get into this business? Are you any good?"

"Two completely different questions." We sat back down at the table. "I used to be with the Australian Federal Police, working mostly on financial crimes. I got really good at tracking money trails around the world. Almost as good at finding people who didn't want to be found. I burned out after fifteen years and started working for myself three years ago."

She frowned while she sipped her tea, thinking about something. I waited. I had nothing else to do. "I googled you. I've seen your company website. You need to update your contact details to include this address."

"I'll keep the PO Box. I don't think my corporate neighbours would appreciate angry ex-husbands showing up here."

"Have you taken a missing persons case before?"

"A few." I still hurt from the last one. An occasional stabbing pain along the scar on my back.

"Successful?"

"You mean, did I find the person I was looking for?" I nodded. "Every single time. Tell me about your son." I started typing in the Notepad app on my phone. "What's his name, how old is he, who are his friends? That sort of thing."

She smiled, sat back in her chair and crossed her legs. "We should talk about your rates first, maybe sign an engagement letter, I think you called it?"

I told her my rates. Inflated a bit to account for her obvious wealth. It works the other way, too. I lower them for people who are obviously not well off.

"Those numbers sound reasonable."

I knew they would. Her shoes cost more than I *ever* made in a month. "I'll email you a retainer agreement once I get your email address." I handed her one of my cards.

"The address on this is correct. Send me a note so I have yours."

She took out her phone and sent a quick message. My phone chirped, and a notification showed her incoming email.

"Tell me about your son." I re-opened the Notepad app.

"Okay. Lachlan is fifteen. I told you that already. Very athletic. Forward on his school's AFL team. Smart, but not good at school."

"Can you tell me about his friends?"

She mentioned the name of the school he attended. I should have quoted double the rate.

"He's in Year Ten. I don't know their names, but I'll contact the school and let them know you'll be by."

"And you haven't contacted the police?"

Something strange flashed across her face. I wasn't sure what it was. In hindsight, I should have been more alert.

"Like I said, he's a teenager. They think he'll show up on his own in a couple of days." She shook her head. "This is out of character for him."

"How long has he been missing?"

"He went out Friday night with friends." She stopped herself. "No, that's not correct. He told me he was going out with his friends, but he didn't."

"How do you know? You talked to them?"

She shook her head again and took out her phone. "We track each other's phones. His disappeared shortly after he left the house. He disabled the GPS or something." She had opened the phone tracking app and placed the phone on the table, facing me. The 'Last Position' shown for Lachlan was in the very exclusive suburb of Vaucluse the previous Friday.

I should have quadrupled my rates.

I tapped the screen. "Near your house?"

"About a block away. He'd have to disable tracking on his phone intentionally, right?"

It sure seemed so. "Was he picked up, or was he walking?"

"He left on foot." Lyla took her phone back and tapped her screen a couple of times. I got another notification on my phone. "His picture. It's current." She opened another app on her phone, but didn't show me. "His last bankcard transaction was about an hour after that."

"How long has his father been out of the picture?"

She scoffed. That same strange look on her face. "We split when Lachie was one. He's not in the picture. Hasn't been since then." She glanced at her phone, then back up at me. "We were thick as thieves before Lachie came along. Barry, Dom and myself. Ran riot." She shrugged. "Ancient history."

"Dom?"

"Nobody." She sounded wistful. "Old friend. Barry got him in the divorce."

"Anybody else in your life?"

She arched an eyebrow. "Is that important?"

I shrugged. "Who knows? Any seemingly trivial thing might be key."

She sighed and pocketed her phone. "Nothing ever serious. It's been Lachie and me through thick and thin."

"Looks like you've been doing okay for yourself. Nice neighbourhood, expensive school."

"Are you interrogating me?"

I held up my hands. "Just trying to get all the info. Any problems at home?"

She contemplated me for a few seconds before shaking her head. "The usual teen stuff. It was rough a couple of years ago, but he came around." She chuckled. "His grades were always a subject of discussion. A sore point. I really hoped the private school would help, but it seemed to make things worse." She closed her eyes, took a deep breath, and then opened them, staring at me intently. "You'll help, right?"

I nodded. I wasn't 100% sure, but I was leaning toward it. It shouldn't be too difficult to track down a fifteen-year-old, even in this sprawling city. Of course, I'd need some help from Davie. He'd get a slice of the fee. And I shouldn't have to worry about her ability to pay. A typical house in Vaucluse went for around $10 million. More if on the water. "Certainly. I'll email you the agreement. If you think of anything else, please give me a call."

"How frequently will you update me?"

"I'll email you a daily summary." I collected our cups. "I'll get the agreement sent to you immediately. But first, I need to nudge John. I would have expected something from him by now."

She remained seated as I stood. "Certainly. I look forward to hearing from you."

I smiled and returned the cups to the sink. I wasn't sure of the office protocol. I rinsed them and left them in the sink. Maybe I was supposed to put them in the dishwasher. Maybe not. I'm sure I'd be told at some point.

I found John at the end of a few minutes of wandering around, working in front of a standing desk in a small office at the far corner of the floor. A young woman was at the desk next to him, typing something official-looking on her laptop. Their corporate logo was on the office door and the door of the larger but empty office beside them. Peons sat here in the small office, and important people sat in the larger one.

I knocked on the door frame. "John, mate. I found you."

He pulled out his earbuds and smiled. "Nate, right?"

"Close enough. How's it going with the details of the company you want me to investigate?"

He nodded at the young lady sitting beside him. "Maria is putting it together as we speak. Aren't you Maria?"

She gave me a terse nod and a brief smile before returning to her work. She didn't like him much.

"Great. No rush. Harriet's not back until Wednesday, right? It would be good to get a feeling for the breadth and depth of the case before we talk."

"He'll have something for you by the end of the day," said Maria. Strong emphasis on the 'he'll'. She really didn't like him.

"Fantastic, Maria. I appreciate your hard work." I tapped John on the arm and headed back to the coffee machine.

It was a different route, taking me past a large, industrial-sized printer. It reminded me that I had to catch up with whoever ran the IT department around here. I wasn't going to buy a printer if I didn't have to.

I studied the controls. A keypad sat to the right of the usual buttons you see on a printer. An LCD screen showed jobs in the queue, with the document title, originator name and document size. Top of the list was one from Maria.

She arrived to collect her print job while I stood there trying to remember where the IT team lived. I smiled and stepped out of her way. She entered a code into the keypad and waited while the pages churned out.

She looked at me looking at her. "Nick, right?"

I nodded. "I was going to ask you about where the IT team lived, but I've got a different question for you. Did you point Miss Porter my way?"

"No, that was Ray Tennyson. I hope that wasn't too much of a problem."

"Oh, no. Not a problem at all. What can you tell me about her?"

The printer stapled the pages, and she took the stack. "I don't know her that well. She pops around and grabs lunch with Harry every couple of weeks. They've been friends for since I started with the company. Since before—" she paused. "A long time." She pointed to an office in the far corner of the floor. "Look for Claude, the balding guy with a ponytail in the far corner. He can help you with your computer stuff. It's pretty straightforward. Has to be if John can figure it out."

I chuckled and thanked her.

I wandered until I found a room with an excessive number of computers and routers that looked, felt and smelled like an IT shop. But it was empty—a later problem.

Lucy called as I was returning to my office. "Hey, how are you doing?"

"Mondays," she said. "Like every Monday. Since you're in this neck of the city now, let's meet for coffee."

"I would like that very much. Fifteen minutes, downstairs?"

"See you then."

She hung up before I could say anything else. Anything. She was still upset about something. I think. Honestly, I struggle to read her mind.

Fifteen minutes, downstairs. Still, one thing to do.

Maria was alone in the office, and John was off doing something sales-related, I assume. It was Maria I wanted to talk to. "Can I bug you with one more question?"

"You can ask. I reserve the right to refuse an answer."

"That's fair. Earlier, you said Lyla had known Harriet since before, then stopped. Since before what?"

She smiled. "It's not relevant to you finding Lyla's son." She nodded. "It's not really any of your business at all."

So, that was that. "All good. Thanks for your help. Let John know I was by, okay? I'll see you around the floor." I turned to leave, then pulled a Columbo. "One more thing—can you send me Harriet's email address? I will probably have to line up a meeting for when she returns to town."

"I'll make sure to copy her with the information I'm sending you."

Maria, not John, would send it. Good to know the office dynamics. "Excellent." I checked the time on my phone. "Gotta run. I've got a coffee appointment downstairs."

She waved goodbye as I left. I saw ponytail guy heading to his burrow from the coffee machine on my way out and flagged him down. I handed him a card. "Hey, I hear you're the guy to talk to about connecting to the printer. I'm Nick Harding."

"The new guy. Right." He examined the card. "I'm Claude. I'll email you the instructions. You on the wi-fi yet?"

"I am."

"Mac or PC?"

"Mac."

He flicked my card with his thumb. "Instructions in your inbox before you're back in your office."

"I'm grabbing coffee, so you've got a couple of minutes, Claude." I jabbed the lift button. "Much appreciated."

The lift descended and opened to the building lobby, and there was Lucy, talking with the building concierge, a young woman just starting her career. I've never been in an office that had a concierge. That's what they called themselves. I'll have to test them someday. See if they could get me tickets to something.

"Hey there, Nicky. Let's get some coffee. I think I'm going to enjoy you being this close."

Smiling was easy around Lucy. "I'm buying."

"You are." She said goodbye to the young woman at the reception/concierge area and slipped her arm into mine. "Have you found a favourite coffee place yet?"

"Adjacency beats quality, sometimes. The place just outside is pretty good. Besides, any caffeine is good caffeine. The closer, the better."

Four

We sat at the same table Davie and I had sat at not an hour earlier. They had done a good job cleaning up. Lucy had a blueberry muffin and a cup of black coffee. I reminded myself again to ask her how she kept her teeth so white.

Some other time. She looked happy.

"You look happy."

She nodded. "You've set up shop for real. No more working out of your living room. A way to," she held her hands out and moved them apart as she spoke, "separate work from life." She took another sip of coffee and eyed the muffin, then split it in half, took the top and offered the inferior bottom to me.

I accepted. It was blueberry, after all.

She cocked her head, her pony-tailed red hair dropping off her shoulder. "Are you happy?"

I puffed my cheeks as I exhaled. "Sure. I guess so. A little nervous about the new thing."

"That's normal. I feel the same way."

That's right. I forgot. How could I forget? "So how's the gig going at the new place?"

"It's a bit more than a gig, don't you think? Private banking, high-end—very high-end—customers. A whole raft of new AML compliance regulations." She grinned. "I haven't had so much fun in I don't know how long."

"Is what's his face—Nigel—still there?"

"He says hi." She took the bottom of the muffin back from me. I hadn't touched it yet. "Are you settling in upstairs?"

"I've already got two cases." I took a quick glance at my phone. No notifications yet. "I *think* I've got two new cases."

Lucy sat back in her seat and chewed on her lip. "Vanilla?"

"Oh yeah. An independent corporate assessment of a potential business partner for one of the companies upstairs. All computer work. Right up my alley. The second one is a missing teen. Rich kid. Took off a few days ago. Very rich mother wants to pay me top rates to find him."

My phone chimed. "Okay, definitely have the lost teen case. She just sent through the signed agreement." I scrolled through the email. "And some useful details." I put the phone face down on the table. "Sorry about that."

"Don't worry about it. New business."

"I'm definitely going to do the background check on the business, but the missing kid—not really in my wheelhouse." I am good at it, though. It just comes with unexpected events sometimes. It is something I should have given more consideration to, I guess.

That's called foreshadowing.

But bathed in the beauty of lovely Lucy was killing off my short-term memory.

She raised her eyebrows. "It's good money, right? And a rich kid? How hard could it be?"

"Thanks for reminding me." I made a quick note to check Miss Porter's credit. Just a gut feeling. "If you've finished mutilating the muffin, want to see my new office?"

She checked her watch. "I've got a couple of minutes. And it's only two minutes to Martin Place, so sure. Why not?"

Claude and his ponytail were getting on the lift as we got off. "Your email working?"

"It was the printer, Claude."

"I know. The instructions are in your email, and I haven't seen you set it up yet." He held the closing door with his hand. "Let me know if you have any problems."

"I will. Thanks, mate."

The doors slid closed, and Lucy looked up at me. "He's the local Davie?"

"Davie's better." I waved my arm, encompassing the common area. "Pool table, coffee machine. Large refrigerator in which to store your lunch in the vain hope it won't get stolen by somebody."

"Or you could join me for lunch."

"Or I could join you for lunch." I led her down the hall and around the corner to my office. That still feels weird to say. The last time I had an office, I was with the Australian Federal Police, working in a team taking down ginormous money laundering rings.

Times change.

I held the door open for Lucy to enter.

"Cozy."

'Small, you mean." I sat at my desk and pulled the chair from the other desk over for Lucy. "Have a seat."

She perched on the corner of my desk instead. Just like Davie. "Take the missing kid. It's good money."

"I'm going to check her credit first." I held up my hands. "Probably off the charts, but I've got the ability, and good governance says check every time." I blew out a puff of air. "The last missing kid I looked for, that got you beat up." I watched her expression. "Remember?"

She got off the desk and smoothed out her dress. "Wasn't a kid, but yeah, I painfully remember. So, don't get me involved in any of your cases, right?" Lucy smiled. "I've got a diagnosed case of PTSD from helping you."

I stood and must have had an incredulous look on my face because she nodded and poked me in the chest. "I'm serious. You thought those nightmares were fake?"

I didn't. I took her hands. "Jesus. Sorry about that. I had no idea."

"You must have had an inkling. You started looking for a place like this as soon as they started. Anyway." She checked the time and kissed me. "I really need to go. Check the woman's credit before you take the missing kid case. Play it safe." She held up a finger. "And get some business insurance that covers on-the-job medical."

The faint smell of strawberry remained in her wake. I had no idea. No, that's not entirely true. She held her own in that other case, but I guess the lumps she took were more than just physical. Shit.

I trotted after her and got in the lift before the doors closed on me. "I had no idea it was that bad. I'm so sorry."

"Oh, I'm tougher than I look, Mr Harding. I'll work through it. Maybe we can head back up to the lagoon over the weekend. I'll start applying SPF 1000 now."

She was making fun of me. "Dinner after?"

"Your treat."

We stepped out to the hum of a busy city. She kissed me again and gave me a light hug.

I watched her walk up Martin Place. She glanced back at me, smiled and waved before she entered her bank.

That bank was the place where I helped disburse ten million dollars stolen from a very bad man to a host of anti-human trafficking organisations around the world. A small private financial institution catering to very wealthy clients. And now Lucy ran their compliance department.

She was smart. The missing teen would put a couple of bucks in the bank if mum could pay.

I scrolled through Lyla's email on the lift back up to the office. Her address, phone number, and a couple more pieces of information I could get from judicious googling would be enough to get a credit score.

Claude was standing outside my office with a tablet in his hand and glasses on the end of his nose, blocking my entry. He was engrossed in something on the tablet and didn't notice me.

"Claude, can I help you?"

"Oh, jeez, sorry, mate. Let me get out of your way. I was just stopping by to make sure you're all set up."

I scratched my chin and nodded at the door. "What have I done to get the VIP service?"

He tucked his tablet under his arm and chuckled. "Same service for everyone. Truth is, I'm bored stiff. This place runs itself. A lot of work the first couple of months to set everything up, then easy goings. I'm bored, frankly. Need some excitement. Unfortunately, the only kind of excitement I get usually results in the rest of you lovely people network-less and pissed off." He looked at the lettering on the door. "So what kind of investigations do you do?"

Jesus. I had to nip this in the bud, and fast. The guy never stopped talking. "The private kind. I hate to be rude, but I can't talk about my clients, and I've got one I've got to get back to." I clapped him on the shoulder. "Thanks for understanding."

When he left, he looked a little confused and maybe a little hurt, but I did have work to do. I read through his email and set up the printer. He was right. It was stupidly simple. The guy knew how to make things easy.

Back to Lyla.

I logged into the credit portal and entered the information I had. Her name, address and phone number were enough to narrow her down. Vaucluse was a relatively small suburb. I requested a current credit report, and while it was being generated and sent to my inbox, I strolled to the kitchen to get a glass of water.

A fresh-faced young professional was brewing a cup of coffee. I nodded at him as I grabbed a glass from the cupboard.

"You wouldn't be Nick Harding, would you?" The young guy was holding his cup of coffee with both hands.

"I am. And you are?"

He smiled and stuck out a hand. "Ray Tennyson. No relation."

What the hell was he talking about?

"The poet. I'm not related to the poet."

I didn't think he was. I shook his hand and picked up my water. "John mentioned I should talk to you about the PNG company, and I look forward to that, but it'll have to be tomorrow, okay? I'm chockers today." I fished a card from my pocket and handed it to him. "Drop me a note with your number, and I'll give you a call later?"

He examined my business card before sliding it into his shirt pocket. "Fair enough. It's good to get eyes on you. Welcome to the floor." He saluted me with his cup and headed back toward his office.

I was starting to understand the benefit of an office arrangement like this. Networking was easy. The pool of contacts was limited, but it was a start. These contacts would have other contacts, and if I travelled the six floors in this building hosting small companies, I should hit critical mass.

I returned to my office. It looked a bit stark. I needed plants. A couple of pictures. It was plain-looking.

I checked my e-mail. The agency had delivered Lyla's credit report. I double-clicked on the file and sat back in my chair, shocked.

Her credit score was 573. I double-checked the name and address and then checked again. She had horrible credit. She'd be lucky to get a pre-paid mobile phone contract with this score.

Damn. Christening my new office with a deadbeat client. "Shit."

The woman was missing a child. He was her only child. It was just them.

Dammit again. This was going to be difficult. I needed advice. I'm growing as a person, right? I ask for help when I need it. I hate it, but I do.

I called Lucy.

"Miss me already?"

"Luce, I've got a problem."

"I've got five minutes. I hope it's not a big problem."

I looked at the time on my monitor. "You tell me. I ran the woman's credit as you suggested. Five seventy-three. Below deadbeat territory."

"She must be running everything through a company. Afraid you won't get paid?"

"You think I should go ahead? I want to go ahead, but I don't want my third case out of this office to be tracking down my deadbeat first case."

"It's her only kid, Nick. Based on what you've told me, she seems desperate. Get a retainer from her. You figure it's an easy job?"

"It's a kid. Should have him by the end of the day."

"Then get a couple of days retainer in advance. Easy-peasy."

"Good point. Thanks. Is it possible to check the financial activities of a user from another bank? Do I need to go to the financial institution directly? It was a lot easier as a cop."

"You have to go to them directly. I'll email you the form. If it's the kid's account, you'll need the mother to sign it. I've got to run. Mwah." And the call was over.

My computer chimed with an incoming email almost immediately: a blank request form. I saved a copy and emailed it to Lyla's address. I opened the agreement Lyla signed, printed it and retrieved it from the printer. I gave her a call.

"Mr Harding?"

"Nick. Good morning. I got the signed agreement. Thanks. I apologise, but I failed to mention that I have to work on retainer for individuals. If you were a business, I could bill in arrears, but unfortunately, for my financial peace of mind, I'll need a couple of days of my fee upfront."

She hesitated briefly before speaking. "Certainly. To the same bank details as in the contract that I just sent you?"

I raised my eyebrows. Maybe this wouldn't be that difficult. "Yes. Exactly."

"I'm transferring the funds as we speak. Just a second."

I heard a muted chime from her phone, and then, a couple of seconds later, she spoke. "It should be in your account."

I checked. The money was there. "Thank you, Lyla, and I'll be starting on your case immediately. I'll review the info you've sent. There's a permission form in your inbox. Can you populate it, sign it and send it back to me? It will give me access to your son's bank transactions."

"I already told you his last transaction was about an hour after he left the house."

Jesus, I thought she wanted me to find him. "I can learn a lot from the transactions made by your son in the days leading up to his disappearance. If he ran off on his own, it's very likely he didn't run on the spur of the moment. He would have planned in advance."

She hesitated even longer. "You don't have to go to the bank. They'll take forever. I'll send you the transactions from the account for the past couple of weeks. Is that sufficient?"

"Thank you. It should be. Is there anything else I should know?"

"No. I think I've told you everything relevant. Thank you for doing this. I'm very concerned about my Lachie."

She sounded strange.

"I'll keep in touch as I proceed, okay? Don't worry. He's probably just taken off with some friends."

"That's not like him, though."

Of course it isn't. If it were, she wouldn't have contacted me. "This is what I do, Miss Porter. Have you contacted his school yet?"

"Just before you called. Mr Edwards, the Headmaster, is expecting you. Let them know at the gate who you are and that you're to see Mr Edwards.

"Let me get to work, and I'll touch base with you tonight. If you think of anything else, you've got my number."

I signed off and stretched. Made a note to look into her financials. Weird to be living in that neck of the woods with a crap credit score.

I looked at my watch. The school was about a ten-minute drive, and it was almost lunch.

Five

It was probably the most expensive Grammar School in the Greater Sydney area.

They waved me through at the gate. It was almost a kilometre through rolling hills from the front gate to the parking spots in front of the main building.

I backed my Mazda into a visitor spot and stepped into the crisp spring air. It had been a cold, wet El Nina-type of winter, and the warm sun was welcome.

The building was substantial. Giant rust brick with arched windows, a terra cotta slate roof and a spire housing a large clock that doubled the height of the building. I checked the time on my phone. Their clock was five minutes fast. Strategic, no doubt. Keep the little rich snots on their toes. It wouldn't surprise me if they varied it daily.

The broad granite steps led into an expansive lobby. The Administration Department was to the left. A long way to the left. I was halfway there when I was intercepted by a very well-fitted out man in his sixties with a thick head of grey hair and matching handlebar moustache. His demeanour was simultaneously genial and concerned. He'd been practising that particular look for decades, I imagine. Useful when managing a large school filled with the spawn of the overly wealthy who expect to get their own way in all instances.

He stuck out his hand. "You're Nicolas Harding, I expect."

I shook his hand. Firm for a man his age. "And you're Stewart Edwards. You've spoken to Miss Porter, I understand."

He nodded toward the 'Staff Only' door. "Best we do this in the office."

I followed him through the door into an anteroom reeking of muted wealth. In comparison, the school lobby was a shopping centre parking lot. The carpet was thick, the wood panelling was burled walnut, and the lighting was subtle. I was way underdressed.

Edwards opened the door to his office and stood to one side, inviting me to enter. The office didn't disappoint. It was just as opulent as the room leading to it: dark, supple leather furniture, solid mahogany desk and bookshelves, and a massive window overlooking a large green pitch. My god, the money.

He waited until I entered and followed me in, closing the door behind him. He motioned to the chair in front of his desk. "Please. Sit." He moved to his side of the desk with the grace of a man decades younger. The positioning was intentional. A massive slab of well-polished timber created a very effective barrier between us. He clearly wasn't pleased with a P.I. wandering his hallowed halls.

"Thanks for taking the time to meet with me, Mr Edwards. This shouldn't take too long." I checked the notes on my phone. "Lachlan Porter is a student here, correct?"

"Of course he is. And he didn't show up today, and his mother is panicking." He shook his head. "Helicopter parents are a pain in the behind, excuse my language. He's a young, smart man, and I'm sure he's just off with some friends."

"So you know him personally?"

Edwards shook his head. "There are over 2000 students at the school. I know of him, certainly. His athletic feats reach even me. And I've met the mother a couple of times. Lyla. Lovely woman, despite her hovering presence. She has done very well for herself. I'm not sure what I can tell you."

"Who did he associate with? Was he on any teams?"

Edwards' brow furrowed. "Sports? Of course."

"Or chess. Math. Acapella. Doesn't matter. Who'd he hang out with?"

Edwards opened the file on his desk and perched his glasses on the end of his nose. "He's a very active student. Let's see, shall we?" He flipped pages over while looking at me, not the file. "I trust you will be discreet with your inquiries, Mr Harding."

"Are you looking or not?" I leaned forward, placing my elbows on his desk. "I'll be as discreet as I need to be. My obligation is to my client. She wants her son found." I pointed at the file. "So, to that end, what have you found?"

"Yes." Edwards slowly, deliberately, took off his glasses, folded them and slipped them into his inside suit breast pocket. "He's on the footie team. I'm sure his mother told you that. Barely average marks." Now, he leaned forward, breaching my personal space. Old Spice and peppermint breath mints. "You will keep any negative information in the family." He raised an eyebrow. "His family includes this school. Let me know if you find anything out, and keep it out of the press, okay?"

I got the distinct impression the question mark he put at the end of that sentence was politeness. It wasn't a question.

I sat back in my chair and rubbed the end of my nose. "I need to talk to his teammates now." I stood and headed to the door. "I'm assuming they'll be in the cafeteria or whatever you have here." I went to a public school. The 'cafeteria' *there* was the paved area outside the demountable, poorly air-conditioned classrooms. I opened his door and pointed up the hall. "That way?"

Again, agile for an old man. He was at the door in seconds. "Follow me. They will be in the fitness centre. They're in a recovery session after yesterday's big game."

He said 'big game' as if I'd get the reference. I didn't.

The labyrinth he led me through ended at a facility most professional teams in Australia would kill for. The benefits of incredibly wealthy alumni. The reason people pay the money to put their kids in schools like this isn't for a better education. The education wasn't that much better than you'd get in a well-run government school. It was the contacts made here that would set you up for the rest of your life. That's why their well-connected parents forked over the fat stacks to gain admission.

Pops could have afforded this.

And I'm fucking glad he didn't send me to a place like this. It reeked of entitlement. Undeserved, in most cases.

The fitness centre stank of Lynx body spray and privilege. The student-athletes were all superbly fit. Whatever they were doing didn't look like recovery. Their warmup was more than I did as a complete workout. I pulled a hammy just watching them.

Edwards pulled the trainer to one side and whispered something to him. The trainer chuckled, then stopped himself when he saw I was watching. He cleared his throat and got the team's attention.

"Lads, pay attention. This is Nicolas Harding. He's a private investigator. He wants to talk to you about Lachie. Co-operate."

They gathered, towels around their necks, sponsored sports drinks in their hands, murmuring among themselves. It's ridiculous, but even in my forties, I hated these guys. The jocks and I never got along in school. "Nick, not Nicolas. I've been asked by Lachlan's mother to find him. I understand he missed the game on the weekend, and the last any of you saw him was in class on Friday."

"His mummy is worried about him?" The lanky shit with a freshly styled mullet had a smirk on his face. "Poor little Lachie's mummy."

Twat. "He's two years behind you, right, champ?"

He nodded, still smirking.

"You still live at home? Or have you moved into your own place? Do *you* still live with your mummy? Do you think this is funny? His cards haven't been used since Friday noon. His phone hasn't pinged. Does this sound like the normal actions of a fifteen-year-old *champ*?" I fucking despised these entitled shits. At least the smirk had disappeared. "Tell me about him. Tell me about the things you'd know that his mother doesn't." I'm afraid I may have raised my voice a bit.

I had their undivided attention. One of the smaller ones raised his hand. I pointed at him. "Go."

"He hasn't used his phone at all?"

"Assume what I said is established fact, and let's move forward. He hasn't used his phone or accessed any funds."

The kid nodded. "Okay. Fair call. He's always on that phone."

I looked at the rest of the team; all of them were mute. "Nothing? I guess he wasn't a good teammate. I expected a bit more from you. All of you." That seemed to piss them off just the right amount.

"Not cool, mate." This seemed to be the captain of the team. A little more confident than the rest, better haircut, broader shoulders. "He was one of us."

"Was?"

"Is. Is. Shit. He *is* one of us. What do you want to know?" Definitely not made captain because of his brains.

"Mate, like I said. What do you know about Lachie that his mother wouldn't?"

They opened like a spillway at the Warragamba Dam. All talking over each other. I was ready. My voice recorder was on. I let them spew for a few minutes before I held up my hands for them to stop. "I hope you play with a bit more teamwork than this. One at a time."

The trainer tapped on his watch. "Look, this is all well and good, and I hope you find Lachie. He's a good kid. But these boys need to cool down in time for their next class." He looked to Edwards and shrugged. "Sorry, boss."

"He's right. These lads don't know anything that can help you, and I can't have you disrupting class any longer." He held open the door and waved me out. "If I hear any scuttlebutt about what's happened to Lachie, I'll be sure to give you a call."

I looked at him expectantly. I hope it was expectantly. I definitely expected something from him.

He didn't pick up on the cue. He raised his eyebrows and said, "What do you want? Do you need someone to help you find the way out?"

"I want you to ask for my number so you can call me with scuttlebutt." I took out a card and stuck it in his suit breast pocket behind the tidy little folded pocket square. "I await your call with eager anticipation." Dickhead.

I found my way out. I had to dodge kids in school uniforms trudging to their post-lunch class, all of them carrying backpacks that looked as heavy as anything I'd be comfortable lifting in a gym.

It was warming up. The sky was a deep blue, and the sun was cranked up a notch. It was the start of melanoma season. Third-term school holidays were a week away, and today's high was forecast to be in the mid-twenties. Summer was going to be hell.

The inside of my car already was. I shouldn't have parked in the sun. I cranked the AC to the lowest temperature it would go and opened all my windows. It was counter-intuitive, but I needed a few minutes of air conditioning cycling through the car to get the hot air out. I sat sideways in the driver's seat, door open and feet on the ground.

This case was stalling. I had no idea what a 15-year-old would find enticing enough to run away to, and without some kind of help, I wouldn't be able to find enough determinative evidence of a snatch-and-grab to get the cops involved.

I was probably going to have to get Davie involved. The homeowners in Vaucluse would universally have security cameras, and some of them would be lax enough, security-wise, that he would be able to access them.

I needed lunch first.

The car had cooled, and the map on my phone said there was a chicken place half a kilometre away, in the general direction of the office. I waited for traffic to clear, my mind on a chicken wrap, when a convertible passed driven by a man I thought had been dead for a decade.

A man I had helped ensure was dead. A man whose actions had killed one of my colleagues. Back in a different life. I glanced to the right to make sure no traffic was coming and accelerated after him. I was almost 100% sure I wasn't imagining it. There wasn't any reason for this guy to be on my mind. I'd forgotten all about him years ago.

But there he was.

My phone rang. It was Jackson. I punched the button on my steering wheel. "Hey, mate. What's up?" I craned my neck to keep an eye on the convertible.

"I'm going to need you in a couple of days."

"Does the AFP want to pay for my services? I don't know, mate. Are you guys financially viable?" The convertible abruptly turned left down a side road.

"This is going to be a freebie for us. The prosecutor wants to call you as a witness for the thing we did at the go-kart track last year. The trial is in a few months, but he wants to chat with you first. Won't take more than an hour."

The convertible had disappeared.

"Yeah, no problem. Email me the details. Hey, do you remember Huang Leung?"

"Sounds familiar. Provide context, mate. I'm getting old."

"You're the same fucking age as I am. The drugs arrest that went bad almost ten years ago. The warehouse blew up. Curtis was at the front of the stack, and all his wife had left of him to bury were his feet."

"Oh, shit. Yeah. I remember now."

"He was inside with an enormous amount of cocaine, fentanyl, some other shit. It took the team weeks to clean that up. I just saw him." I'm positive I just saw him.

"Who? Curtis? Have you been drinking?"

"Are you okay, mate? Leung. I just saw him drive past me in a convertible. Fiat, I think. Red. Late model." I told him the street he had turned up.

"Bullshit. The guy is dead. We have incontrovertible DNA proof that he's dead."

"Then I saw a ghost. It was him. I'd bet lunch on it."

I heard him sigh. "I need you to be a credible witness. Making up shit about seeing ghosts isn't going to cut it."

I laughed. "I won't bring it up on the stand. We should get together for a drink sometime. I've got an office in the city. You're only a tram ride away."

"That's impressive. Send me the details, and I'll definitely buy you lunch. Gotta run. Stop chasing ghosts. It's not healthy."

I signed off and continued to section the neighbourhood where he had disappeared. It wasn't a ghost; I saw him.

Six

I spent far too much time driving around the neighbourhood looking for a red Fiat. Every house had a garage. I was wasting my time. And the more time I spent driving, the less time I spent looking for my client's son.

It's like she was reading my mind.

My phone rang. It was Lyla Porter. "Good afternoon, Lyla. I've just left the school. Picked up a thread. Is there something more you've remembered??"

"I was hoping you had more information for *me.* How did it go at the school?"

"I committed to giving you an update every evening. Micromanaging doesn't help either one of us." I wasn't charging her enough.

"I know. But next time *your* fifteen-year-old is missing, see how well you sit on the sidelines while someone else does all the looking."

I could only imagine what that would be like. "The headmaster is a stuffy, distrustful arsehole, and the students I talked to had no idea what might have happened to your son. They seemed to like him, though. I don't think there's much info to mine there. Edwards has my card. He didn't seem too pleased to get it or eager to use it."

"The amount of money I've forked over to that school, he should be crawling across glass to help. I'll call him again."

I was back on the main road now; Fiat hunting was finished for now. "If you think that will help. He seemed pretty intractable. I'm checking out the shopping centres now."

"Thanks, Nick. I look forward to your call tonight."

"Email, Layla." I hung up on her.

She had listed three shopping centres he and his friends liked to hang out at. The largest was Westfield Bondi Junction, not far from home. I'd hit it first. If I was there near the end of the afternoon, then had to head back to the office before heading back home, it would piss me off. I'd work my way back toward the city.

I needed my man in the chair, though. And he was just a quick phone call away. "Davie, buddy, can you talk?"

"For a couple of minutes. Buddy. What do you want now?" He sounded flat. He needed to inject more excitement into his life.

"Getting into unsecured security cameras isn't a big deal for you, right?"

"Home systems?"

"Yeah."

His voice got quieter. "It's a big deal if I do it from the office. I'll have to do it from home tonight."

"That'll work. I'll send you the starting address, and the time I last saw this kid I'm looking for. I'll cut you in on the fee."

"That you will. I've got a meeting coming up. Talk later."

He disconnected before I could answer. Smart guy. Weak in the interpersonal skills area. And he seemed a little off his game lately.

The Bondi Junction shopping centre was massive. Fortunately, I didn't need to walk all of it. I headed to the security office and showed them my credentials. "I need your help tracking down a missing fifteen-year-old."

The woman on duty, whose name tag read Lauren, was all smiles. I had the distinct impression that the smile was surface only and a heart of over-cured cynical darkness lay beneath. "Haven't had an alert about any missing kid."

"He's rich, fifteen, and the mum thinks he's run away. No foul play. The mother has hired me to find him. Give it a few days, and the cops will be involved."

She snorted with contempt she didn't even try to disguise. "He's rich *and* white? The cops will be all over this by coffee break."

She wasn't wrong. "Be that as it may, I've got my marching orders from the mother." I showed her Lachlan's picture on my phone. "Do you have any way of quickly scouring video to find a face in a crowd?"

She barked a laugh. "This isn't CSI, mate. No facial recognition here."

I really needed Davie. "If I buy a thumb drive, can you copy footage from the past weekend? I've got a guy who is pretty good at the analysis side of things."

"I probably need some kind of court order or something."

I let out a puff of air, trying to present myself as a guy between a rock and a hard place. Which wasn't entirely untrue. "I need your help, Lauren. A fifteen-year-old boy is missing. The mum is trying to keep the police out of it because he's almost an adult. He really likes hanging out here. If he had been grabbed, it would have been here. And if I can find evidence of it on those tapes, I can get the police involved immediately." I smiled. "So what do you say? Between security professionals."

She thought about it for a bit. The 'security professionals' line didn't hurt. She slowly nodded. "Get the thumb drive. But be quick. I've got rounds in fifteen minutes." She chuckled. "And that'll take a couple of hours."

There was an electronics shop close to the security office. I splurged on a 1 TB drive and got back before Lauren went on her stroll around the mall.

"Did you buy a big enough one? There's a lot of video in a day." She opened the packaging and inserted the drive into the laptop on her desk. "Oh yeah. That'll do." She opened a folder, selected a dozen files and dragged them to the thumb drive. "Two minutes, luv."

"I appreciate that, Lauren. His mother appreciates it."

She waited until the progress bar hit 100%, then ejected the drive and handed it to me, briefly holding my hand. "If you ever need anything else, anything, let me know."

Jesus. Well, more work for Davie. I smiled and beat a hasty retreat.

I hit the other two smaller shopping centres. Security in the first one wasn't as accommodating, and I spent an hour talking to shop employees, showing them a picture of Lachlan. Some had seen him, but weeks ago.

The second one also copied video files for me. And he hit on me, too. I let him down easy.

So now I had a thumb drive full of footage and no additional information. Not useful information. I grabbed a coffee, sat at a sidewalk table and called Davie.

"What's good, Nick?"

"Not this coffee. They need to clean the machine more than once a year." I held the thumb drive up and looked at it. "Your facial recognition software still works?"

"Why wouldn't it work, Nick? What do you have?"

"Hours and hours of security footage from a couple of shopping centres and a photo of the kid I'm looking for. I'll bring pizza and beer."

"Does it matter if I had other plans tonight?"

I smiled. "Did you have other plans tonight?"

I heard him take a resigned breath. "No, Nick. I did not have other plans tonight. As usual." I heard him tap some keys on his keyboard. "Bringing Lucy?"

Well, that was a good question. "I don't know. She still has dreams."

"*I* still have dreams. And my shoulder clicks when I lift weights above my head."

"Above your—how often does that happen? The lifting weights thing." I sipped coffee and winced. "Seriously."

"Admittedly, not that often. Bring Lucy with you. Insist on it. Appeal to her better nature. You're looking for a young kid. Helping put a family back together. I think that'll hook her."

Dammit, but the big guy was smart sometimes. I pushed the mostly full cup of coffee as far away from me as I could on the small table. "You're right. I'll give her a call. I'll be by around 7. *We'll* be by around 7."

"Good man. Now, let me get back to work."

I looked at the coffee. The overwhelming need to feed my caffeine addiction was in a death battle with the aversion to the burnt taste. The addiction won. I pulled the cup closer and took another horrible sip before I called Lucy.

"Hey, big guy. I appreciate the call, but I'm about to head into another in a never-ending stream of compliance meetings."

I loved hearing her voice. "I'll be super quick, then. Davie's tonight. Pizza, beer and a little video surveillance fun."

"I don't know, Nick. Seems like a case to me. I'm trying to keep away from that part of your life, remember?"

I did. "This is my life, Lucy. I really can't apologise enough for the mess I got you into."

"There is absolutely no need to apologise, Nick. I willingly took part. I just didn't realise how crazy your job got."

"Getting grabbed in a parking lot wasn't a big enough clue?"

She laughed. What a laugh. "I really need to go to this meeting. I'll call when I'm finished, and you can try to convince me to join you two tonight."

"It's a deal. I love you. Be good."

I took a deep breath and checked the email Lyla had sent me. The shopping centres were covered. Or they would be tonight.

The next suggestion from Lyla was the skate park at Bondi. He frequented the place a lot, she said. Parking at the beach was bad, even on shitty days. And today was not shitty. It was turning into a beautiful spring day.

I parked outside my apartment in Bondi Junction. It was an easy walk to the beach and skatepark, and I needed to stretch my legs. It had warmed up. A lot. I stopped in the apartment and grabbed a bottle of water from the fridge.

I could smell the ocean before I could see it. A nice, salty tang in the air carrying the *skree* of the gulls. As I got closer, the availability of empty street parking spaces dwindled. It wasn't a bad idea to walk. Just uncomfortable. Damn, it was going to be a hot summer.

I was expecting an empty skate park in the middle of a Monday afternoon. I should have known better. Half a dozen kids—actually, kids may be a bad descriptor. Half a dozen people, aged early teens to mid-twenties, were skating, mostly male, with a couple of females. They were good. Tony Hawk would be pleased. I know. I'm showing my age. There are younger, excellent skaters, but I do not know their names.

Anyway.

I watched for a while. Sipped some water. Cooled off from the walk. Let the salty ocean breeze wash over me.

One of the girls was adjusting the trucks on her skateboard, sitting off to one side. I squatted beside her, my knees cracking as I descended. She looked up at me and laughed.

"Mate, that sounded like you're falling apart. You skate?"

"Only in video games, and rarely even then. I wonder if you can help me."

"I don't do training. Especially for someone as old as you. You might get hurt." She finished an adjustment, slipped the wrench into a pack, and dropped it with her other stuff. She stood and waited for my knees to let me do the same. "You probably shouldn't anyway. Your bones get brittle at your age, right?"

"I'm going to ignore that blatant ageism." I opened the picture of Lachlan on my phone. "Do you know him?"

She took the phone from me and turned to block the sun from shining on the screen. "Yeah. Lachie." She looked up at me, worried. "Is he in trouble?"

"When was the last time you saw him?"

A couple of the older kids joined the conversation. "What's going on, Kelly?"

"Dude here is looking for Lachie." She turned back to me. "He was here a week or so ago. What's going on?"

"He's been missing since sometime Friday afternoon. His mother hired me to find him."

The guy who asked Kelly what was going on started laughing. "Holy shit. He's done it. I can't believe it."

"What are you talking about Ger?" Kelly handed the phone back to me. "Wait. You think so?"

I locked my phone and slid it into my pocket. "One of you want to clue me in?"

Gerry crossed his arms. "And why aren't the cops involved?"

I sighed. I get tired of repeating myself, but I hadn't told this mob yet, so... "The kid is fifteen. Mum doesn't want the cops to get involved. Yet. She hired me to find him, and if I run into anything suss, the cops *will* get involved."

"Define suss."

"What information do you have, Gerry? His mother is worried. Would you want *your* mother worried?"

He shook his head, took his board and dropped in, laughing as he went. "Bit of a dick."

"That's just Gerry," said Kelly.

"So what do you think is going on? You seemed to think Gerry was on to something."

She shrugged and picked up her board. "Long shot. But Lachie was talking a lot about running away and joining the circus."

Seven

"Circus? You're fucking kidding me. Why in the hell…"
Well, on reflection, what kid wouldn't? "Did he sound
serious about it?"

Gerry was back. "Why the fuck should we tell you?"

"Ease up, champ." I extracted my credentials and
passed around the wallet. "Licensed Private Investigator.
Nick Harding. Engaged by young Lachie's mum to find him.
And that's what I'm trying to do. I would greatly appreciate
your help, but if you don't, I'll follow other leads." I stared
at Gerry. "And I'll remember your face." And then at the
others. "Faces."

I retrieved my identification billfold from Kelly and slid it
back into my pocket. "So." I clapped my hands together.
"Let's start again. The circus? Really?"

"Sorry, mate, we're kinda protective of the kid. Yeah, the
circus," said Gerry.

"We gave him shit about it, and he didn't drop it. So I'd say so," said Kelly. "Kind of a weird kid. Mad rush, and he wants to join a circus? Crazy. Good luck finding him."

"You wouldn't know where there's a circus around here, would you?"

"The only one I know about is the one set up in the reserve in Warriewood. Northern Beaches." Kelly nodded and got back to skateboarding.

I checked the maps on my phone. The reserve in Warriewood must have been Boonah Reserve. Like an hour's drive. After I walked half an hour back to my my apartment and my car. Shit.

An hour and a half later, pushing close to 3:30, I parked on Boondah Road in Warriewood alongside the field. A couple of trucks were still there, loading up the tail end of what once had been a circus. It was gone. The secret to successful PI work was tonnes of legwork and persistence. It got tiring, honestly.

I pushed myself out of the car and walked to one of the men who was strapping down the canvas on the back of his truck. He was grossly overweight, taller than me and pasty-looking. His shaved-bald head was wrinkled like a Shar-Pei's face.

He looked at me and wheezed. "We are getting out of here. Enough with the hassling. Fucks sake."

He was pissed at me, and I had no idea why. And I didn't care, except pissed-off people are not cooperative. "It's okay, mate. I'm not from the Council. Or whoever's been giving you a hard time. I'm a PI, looking for a kid." I help up Lachie's photo. "Have you seen him around?"

He was shaking his head before I finished talking. "I do not know anything. I just set things up and tear them down."

"You didn't even look at it, mate. There's a missing kid." I held my phone up in front of his face. "Look at it."

The Asian guy loading the second truck must have heard my raised voice and sauntered over. He was wiry. His pock-marked face was further blemished with what looked like old burn scars. "Everything okay here?"

I gave up on the big guy. "I'm Nick Harding. I'm a Private Investigator." I showed him Lachie's picture on my phone. "I've been hired by this lad's mother to try to find him. His name is Lachlan Porter. Have either of you seen him?"

"My name is Kai," said the Asian. And the unpleasant gentleman to your right is Karl. With a K. He must not like you. That's more than he usually talks in a day." He gently took the phone from my hand, looking at Lachie's photo. He examined it carefully and then showed it to Karl. "I have never seen him before. What about you, Karl?"

"Already told him I never seen him."

Kai handed the phone back. "Don't mean much, though. Karl and I are just roustabouts. Setting up and-"

"-tearing down. Yeah. Got it." I stowed my phone. "Where are you off to now?"

"What makes you think this kid is at the show?" Kai was the inquisitive type.

"He's missing. His mates mentioned he'd been talking about running away to join the circus." I looked at the battered field. "Why, is beyond me."

"Kids don't really run away and join the circus, mate. That's a movie thing. And we don't take just anyone. Does the kid have some kind of talent the circus might want? Trapeze? Juggler? Maybe an animal act?"

"Damned if I know. I'm just following leads. Any other circuses you know about, competitors of yours?"

Karl growled something and started tying equipment down to the back of the truck. I wouldn't be getting any more information from him. I turned to Kai. "Any?"

He slowly shook his head. "Don't pay much attention to the competition. I just do my job."

"So helpful. Nothing you can tell me?"

"Nope. Good luck. Hop to it, Karl. Time's wasting."

Karl was already halfway into his truck. It rumbled to life and left a muddy rut behind him as he left. Kai trotted to his truck and followed him, rooster tails of mud coming up from both back tyres.

Shit. I forgot to ask him. I yelled after his receding truck. "Where the fuck are you off to now?"

Kai stuck his hand out his truck window and waved as he headed up the road. I ran back to my car with the intention of following them to the next location. The trucks had disappeared around the corner ahead of me, and unfortunately, a four-exit roundabout was just around the bend. By the time I got there, I couldn't tell which one of the exits they had taken. I pulled into a fast food restaurant parking lot and opened a web browser. I sat in silence for a minute, eyes closed, trying to remember the name plastered on the side of the truck.

No luck.

I searched for circuses in the Northern Beaches. No circuses at all mentioned a stop in Warriewood.

I had a bit more luck on social media. A couple of posts were about the cold popcorn and lame trapeze act. Not a lot of positive reviews.

And a mention of them moving to Gosford for the rest of the week through the weekend.

Gosford was an hour away. Worse, since I'd be hitting traffic.

Lucy called. That made things a lot better. "How was the meeting?"

"Weird."

That threw me. "How can a banking job be weird?"

"I said I don't want to get involved in your detective stuff, right? Well..."

"You don't want me butting into yours. No problem."

"Except I'm going to tell you because of how weird it is." But then she stopped talking and *didn't* tell me.

I'd reached the main road that led to the motorway north. Traffic was stop and go. "Well?"

"We were notified today about an influx of dirty cash that needs laundering. Not so much notified as there's scuttlebutt from reliable sources. You used to do that at the AFP, right?"

"Launder money? No. The opposite." I smiled.

"Smart-arse. We need to implement new AML compliance guidelines, but nothing is perfect. How did you do it?"

"So I'm sliding into your work. It's interesting work though, isn't it? And from both ends. You and your colleagues are trying to keep it from happening, and in my old role, I was trying to catch the people doing it once it did happen. I promise I won't bug you about it, interesting as it may be. Are you still up for pizza and beer and watching Davie run facial recognition tonight?"

"Why not? I haven't seen him in a while. No olives on the pizzas, okay?"

"Looking forward to catching up tonight."

"Me too." She blew a kiss through the phone line. A poor substitute. "Later, love."

I relaxed into my seat. There were still forty-five minutes of driving left to go. It would take as long as it took.

I could kill more time talking to Davie. He answered on the third ring.

"What illegal shit do you want me to do now?"

I eased onto the motorway north. "You're old enough to buy beers?"

"For over a decade."

"Then nothing illegal. I'm going to be running late tonight. Grab the beers, and I'll order the pizza delivered to your place. No lite beer, though." Office noise increased, then lowered in Davie's background. "Am I keeping you from something?"

"Betty's 50th birthday. She's got cake. Trying to convince myself to have some. What's keeping you late? Got a line on the kid?"

The first stretch of the motorway, near Mount Colah, was a long run up a big hill. I was stuck behind a VW Beetle with too much traffic on my right to pass. "Fishing, mostly. Some of his friends said he talked a lot about running away to join the circus. I'm on my way to Gosford to check it out."

"You're shitting me, right? Who runs away to join the circus?"

"A bored fifteen-year-old kid with no direction in his life? I don't know. It's a lead I have to run down. I'll get there, check it out and should be back by 6:30, but if someone goes sideways on the bridge, I might be late." I didn't have to mention which bridge. The Mooney Mooney Bridge was infamous for the number of multi-vehicle accidents it hosted. It crossed the Mooney Mooney Creek and, probably because it was at the bottom of a long hill in both directions, was a magnet for smashes.

"No problem. Don't be too late, or there might not be any left."

"It's a work night, mate. And I'm paying you."

"Right, right, right. Facial recognition on some video."

"At least that. Some security cam stuff, too."

"If we have time. I gotta run, Nicky, I've got work to do."

"And cake?"

"I'll try to convince myself. Later."

Everybody's having birthdays. I pushed the button on my steering wheel to drop the call. I checked my mirrors. There was a gap coming up, just behind a Lexus. The Beetle in front of me was struggling up the hill, and I was tired of sitting behind it.

As soon as the Lexus passed me on my right, I floored it and pulled out just at the crest of the hill. From there, it was an easy ride.

Gosford is a small seaside town on the NSW Central Coast. A vibrant community but a bit, well, rustic. One of the local professional football (soccer) teams, the Central Coast Mariners, was based there. The bulk of the town (we can't kid ourselves and call it a city) was focused on the waterfront.

The place was the jumping-off spot if you wanted to visit the Central Coast of NSW. Half an hour in any direction to nice beaches, well-marked hiking trails, and great places to kayak. And if you were really energetic, horseback riding and mountain bike trails.

I was here for none of that.

It was pushing 5 pm when I found the circus in Gosford. It had already been set up in one of the waterfront parks. I hadn't been to a circus since I was a kid. A very young kid. I have no idea how these places made money. I had suspicions, but nothing had ever been proven. Gosford was a small town. The percentage of residents wanting to go to a circus couldn't be that large. And for a week? There wasn't enough free money among all the residents to justify setting up one tent, let alone three. Something was fishy.

But that wasn't my problem any more.

A temporary parking lot was set up in the grass just off the road. It was starting to fill. The draw was universal, I guess. The costs to run a place like this, well, maybe another time

The smell of popcorn and fairy floss brought back latent memories—most of them good memories. I still had a thing about clowns, though. They didn't frighten me so much as annoy me. There was too much fake happiness.

A section of the paddock was marked off for parking. Less than half full, which probably was normal for a Monday afternoon. I didn't really know. They seemed to be in a money-losing state at the moment. Maybe they made it up on the weekend. The losses could be written off as advertising, the lights from the rides reflecting off the water at night, promising a good time, would entice the locals to show up on Thursday night, or the weekend.

I turned off the car and listened to the raucous sounds of the attractions. A muffled announcer was setting something up inside. Lights from the rides were dim in the late afternoon light, but once the sun went down in an hour or two, they'd dominate the skyline.

There was a queue of families waiting to enter. I couldn't tell much more in the parking lot.

It was time to head in.

Eight

The circus was made up of three large circular tents laid out in a triangle, joined by covered paths between them. Outside, tearing up the paddock, were the rides: Tilt-a-Whirls, a Ferris wheel. One of those giant pendulum ships that people inexplicably liked.

The queue snaked through an airport-style maze, disgorging the eager locals to three different payment windows. After paying, they moved to the right and presented their tickets to the man holding the fort at the entrance to the main tent. He looked something like Karl, but younger and meaner.

The line was long.

The popcorn smell was strong.

I had no intention of waiting in line or paying to enter. I approached the guy I thought was Karl's younger brother with my ID out. "Hey there. I'm Nick Harding, a Private Investigator. Wonder if you could help me out?"

His pig eyes stared at me like drops of tar on a sandy white beach.

"You speak any English? No? Is there anyone here who *can* help me?" I tried stepping past him and was met with a large, meaty hand on my chest. I held up my hands, phone in one and ID wallet in the other. "Okay, already. I'll get in line."

"You again?" Kai appeared from behind Karl Jr. He didn't look that pleased to see me. "I see you found the place." People who state the obvious irk me. Of course, I found them.

I held out my phone. "Still looking for young Lachlan. You've seen the picture. Have you seen this face around here? Doesn't look like he'd fit in." I glanced at Karl Jr. "Is that Karl's brother?"

Kai nodded. "Mika."

"Doesn't talk much."

"As much as his brother. You wouldn't want to have a conversation with him. What is it you want me to do? I've already told you I haven't seen the kid."

I pocketed my phone and ID. "So let me walk around the place and look for him. Satisfy my curiosity. Let me tick that box."

Kai considered the suggestion for a minute, then tapped Mika on the arm and nodded at him. "Get rid of this guy."

Mika smiled. "Hurt him?"

Kai gave a quick shake of his head. "No. Too many witnesses. It'll come back on us, and Dom will have my head. March him to his car."

My hands were up. "I surrender. No need to escort me. I'm leaving."

I was lying. I pointed myself toward my car and walked away from the tent, around the back of a panel van in the parking lot, and out on the other side. I stood at the back of the line. Blended in with the other locals looking for animal acts and trapeze ladies in sequined tights.

The line moved at a good pace. I paid for entry and kept the receipt. I loitered until Mika was distracted by something on the far side of the tent before I entered the Big Top.

Acrobats were doing something with the trapeze and a giant wheel that looked interesting the first time you saw it. Lachie didn't strike me as the type. I walked through the tunnel to the next tent. A lot of pre-pubescent girls with their parents in here, soaking up the dozens of dogs doing tricks in the centre ring. Too cute. I scanned the faces of the team managing the dogs and the helpers. No sign of Lachie.

The next tent was no better. It was actually worse. A shit-tonne of clowns. Juggling, honking shit. It was horrible. I didn't see Lachie, but it was possible he was in a clown get-up. I scanned them. Lachie was tall. None of these clowns looked like footie players. It was unlikely that he'd be part of this crowd.

So I moved to the outside attractions. A heavily tattooed meth-skinny man was the only person manning the Ferris Wheel, inspiring no end of confidence.

Beyond the Ferris Wheel was the huge pirate ship. It was one of those things that acted like a giant swing. I never saw the attraction. If you're going to go on a ride at a circus, at least ride one that is a bit more exciting.

Lachie was manning the controls. He was taller than I expected. Height is not easily determined from a headshot. I'm not sure what I was expecting. He played on the school's footie team, so I shouldn't have been that surprised.

I watched him while he ushered one group of passengers off the giant ship and the next batch on. He seemed to be managing it okay. He caught my eye a couple of times, frowning each time. I waited until the ship swung back and forth in ever-increasing arcs before approaching.

"You're Lachlan Porter, right?"

He was quick. "Ah, shit. My mum?"

"She's worried about you. You should come with." I nodded for him to follow.

"Yeah, nah. I'm good. They need me here."

I stopped and looked at him, impatient. "Come on, kid. I've got shit to do tonight."

"Yeah, mate. So do I, don't I? Tell mum I'm fine. I'm set." The little shit turned his back on me and focussed on the swinging ship.

I grabbed him by the shoulder and spun him around. "You're a minor. You've got two choices: Come with me, or I'll hang here while we wait for the cops."

"There's a third option." The vaguely Scandinavian voice came from behind me. I forgot about the big guys. I turned to see Karl and Mika standing with their arms crossed. "I thought I already kicked you out. And the kid stays here," said Mika.

Standing beside each other, the brothers were massive—well over three hundred kilograms of fatty muscle. "Don't get involved, lads. He's a kid, and he should be in school." I took out my phone and started calling the police when Karl grabbed it from my hand. Very nimble for a big guy.

"You piss off." The accent was stronger with this one.

I reached for the phone, and his brother stuffed a hand in my chest, pushing me back. Karl held my phone at either end, winked at me, grunted, and bent it in half.

Fuck. Message received.

He handed back my deformed phone and leaned close. "You contact the cops, and I'll make sure your head matches your phone, *ja*?"

"Are you Finnish?"

"Yes, we are done. Go before I do that to you."

"No, idiot. Are you from Finland?"

"Get out of here, now, *mate*." Mika grabbed one arm and Karl the other and marched me out.

No, that's not quite true. I didn't technically march. My feet didn't touch the ground until I was well into the parking area. They dropped me unceremoniously on the dirt and returned to the circus before I finished getting back to my feet. I dusted off my trousers and, for about a third of a second, considered going back in.

A thought I quickly dismissed. I pulled my t-shirt sleeve up to look at the rapidly forming bruise. Those two wouldn't go down easy even if I knew how to fight properly.

I tried pairing my phone to the car, unsuccessfully. It was properly dead. The dash clock told me it was 5:45. I couldn't order the pizza or call ahead. It is remarkable how dependent we are on our smartphones. Fuck Steve Jobs' ghost.

The in-car navigation got me to the highway. I knew my way from there.

I got to the heart of Sydney an hour later. Traffic was heavy in the other direction. Most people on the Central Coast worked in the city, and those who didn't take the train home clogged the M1 Northbound.

Fortunately, I was going southbound.

I stopped at a pizza place close to Davie's, bought a couple, and got to his apartment just after 7:00.

Lucy opened the door as I approached. "I've been calling. Your phone die?"

"It's great to see you, too." I slid the pizza boxes onto the counter and kissed her.

Davie held up his hands. "A handshake is good enough for me."

"You're not even getting that, mate." I extracted my bent phone from my pocket and dropped it on the pizza boxes. "I've had communications issues."

Davie picked it up and whistled. "Get it jammed in something? Or did you run over it?"

"A very large, very angry Finn bent it. But I found the kid." I tossed the thumb drive at Davie. "If you want to look through these, fine, but I don't know what value there is in it anymore."

He handed the phone back and smiled at the memory stick. "I've been calibrating the facial recognition. This'll be a good test."

Lucy took the phone out of my hand and tried to bend it back into shape. "How big was the guy?"

"There were two of them. Brothers. Finnish, I think. They sounded like they come from that part of the world." I took the phone back from her and stuck a pin in the side to extract the SIM card. "They were huge. I thought it was mostly fat. I thought wrong."

I held the SIM in my hand and followed Davie to his computer. "You've got an old phone I can borrow until I get a new one?"

He pulled the top drawer of his desk open. "Help yourself." He slid the thumb drive into a USB port.

I picked a new model for the half dozen in there. "Charged?"

"You want everything?"

"I do. Do you want some pizza?"

He dragged files from the thumb drive to the main computer. "I'm not feeling that shiny tonight, mate. Something wrong with that cake, I think. Maybe tomorrow." He smiled, but it was a wan smile. "For breakfast."

Lucy called from the kitchen. "Double pepperoni and what looks like a supreme. No olives?"

"No olives," I said.

"Help yourselves. I'm not your mother." She walked into the living room with a bottle of beer in one hand and a plate with a couple of slices of pizza in the other. "What does this do, Davie?"

He selected video files and dropped them into his program. "Do you have a picture of the kid?"

"In my email. Give me a couple of minutes." The SIM card was inserted, and the phone rang as it powered up. "It's got 80% battery. Cool."

"Who's calling?" asked Lucy.

"The mother." I put the phone on speaker. "Good evening, Lyla."

"I've been trying to call you. For hours."

"Phone problems. All resolved. I'll invoice you for the one that was broken. I've found your son." Davie chuckled, and Lucy gave me a thumbs up.

"Invoice me for—you found Lachie? Where is he? Why haven't you brought him home? Is he okay?"

"He's in Gosford. Your son ran away and joined the circus." I twisted the top off a bottle and picked up a slice. "They're there until Sunday if you want to go get him."

The line was silent. I thought the call dropped for a second, and then she answered. "You talked to him?"

"I did. Told him you were worried about him and wanted him to come home. He said to say hi." That last part was a lie.

"He's just a kid. You should have forced him to come with you."

I picked up my bent phone and laughed. "Yeah, I tried that. Two of his extra-large co-workers convinced me not to. I'm sure if you call the police, they'll find some time in the next day or so to pop up and sort it out. In the meantime, those guys destroyed my phone and literally threw me out of the place. My invoice, which will only be for one day, will include the phone cost. I'll take it out of the retainer."

"He's okay, right?"

"He seems to be. Thanks for calling, and I'm sorry I couldn't deliver him to your door, but I did what you hired me to do. You know where he is now."

"I'll pay double your rate to return and bring him home."

Davie and Lucy stopped what they were doing and looked at me, eyebrows raised. I shook my head and made a horizontal slicing motion with my hand. "I'm afraid that's not the kind of service I provide, Miss Porter. You know where he is, and he's okay." I looked at Lucy and shook my head. "I have to go now. Good night." I poked the red button on the screen and dropped the call.

"Poor woman," said Lucy. "I can't imagine what it's like for her."

"You got the kid's photo, Nick?"

I scrolled through my email until I found Lyla's message with her son's picture and forwarded it to Davie. "Should be in your inbox."

I sat beside Lucy. "You think I should have taken her up on the offer?"

She wallowed her mouthful of pizza and laid a hand on my arm. "Oh, hell no. If one guy did that to your phone, I'd hate to see what a couple of them could do to your face."

"You like my face?"

She smiled. "It suits you. Your nose is a little bit bent, but I like it." She kissed the end of my nose, then turned to Davie. "You got it going yet?"

"You're leaving me for Davie?"

"I like his toys. Facial recognition could come in very handy at the bank. It's hard to spoof and perfect for ID.

Imagine a customer walks up, the camera identifies them, and the teller has all their information on their terminal before they open their mouth."

I nodded. It sounded like the bank would be risking potential privacy violations, but I'm sure, as a compliance person, she'd figure out a way for it to be used properly.

Davie dragged the photo I had sent him into the program he was running. "How's the algorithm?"

He looked up at me and back at the monitor. "What can you tell me about the video files?"

"Westfield Bondi Junction. The past couple of weeks, from all of their cameras. Another smaller file from a plaza about a klick west of it. I'd focus on Westfield."

Davie nodded. "This kid is definitely in here?"

"You tell me, mate. He frequents the place a lot, according to his mother. His friends back that up. How long does this take?"

"Shouldn't take too long." He tapped the laptop. "The Beast will make short work of it." He tapped a key, and a progress bar started crawling across the screen. A timer estimated five minutes to completion.

"Not bad for that amount of video."

"If it works."

"Oh, I have confidence in you, Davie," said Lucy.

The bar continued to creep across the screen. "When that's done, there are some security cameras I'd like you to look at."

Lucy flopped onto the sofa. "I thought you found the kid."

Nick sat beside her. "I did." I took her hand. "I think I saw a ghost."

"Someone from your AFP past?"

I nodded. "This guy was the head of a giant drugs enterprise. Big organisation. Huge. They moved literally tonnes of products into the country, most from China and less from the Golden Triangle. We swept up almost a hundred of his lieutenants and minions. He and a couple of his closest were presumed dead when they blew up with their product almost a decade ago. I didn't find his finance guy, and I never did figure out who was the head of his Australian operations. Stopped looking when he was declared dead." I took a mouthful of beer and wiped my lips with my sleeve. "Except I'm positive I saw him today."

"You're not with the agency any more, Nick. Call your buddies and let them know about it."

"I have. They don't believe me. They've got other more current things to worry about."

"So you're going to track this guy on your own?"

I knew what she wasn't saying. I was being an idiot. Again. "I just need to get a good picture of him to convince my former colleagues. I'm not an idiot."

"I didn't say you were." She crossed her arms. Ouch. "I'm worried you'll get in too deep again."

Davie's laptop saved me. It bleeped, and Davie spun in his chair. "We have results."

Lucy stayed on the sofa. I stood behind Davie while he opened a folder containing three small files. "How does this work?"

"It produces clips that are twenty seconds long. The clips start ten seconds before the face is recognised and run for another ten seconds. We've got three hits." He pointed at the three thumbnails on the screen.

Lucy got off the sofa and joined us. She glanced at me and crossed her arms again.

"When were these clips captured?"

"Two are from eight days ago, one from last Saturday."

"Hit the old ones first."

Davie clicked the first of the thumbnails. Video from the food court filled the monitor. The time stamp in the top right corner identified it as Saturday, the previous weekend, just before noon. After ten seconds, a group of kids walked in, a green box highlighting Lachlan's face. He had a bag of fast food in his hand. He and his friends sat at a couple of tables and laughed and joked while they ate. I recognised a couple of them from the skate park.

"Skip to the next one, Davie."

The next one was similar but from the following Sunday, roughly the same time. "Oh, to have the metabolism of a teen athlete."

Lucy patted my stomach. "You're not doing too bad for your age."

Double ouch. "Play the last one, Davie. Your software works great."

"It does, doesn't it?" He was very pleased with himself.

The third video was timestamped two days ago, on the Saturday after he disappeared. It wasn't at the food court, and it was later in the afternoon. The camera faced a bank of escalators. Lachlan's head appeared first, coming up the escalator. A second later, Kai's head appeared. Kai, the circus guy who definitely wasn't a roustabout. They were standing beside each other, talking. When they reached the top, they turned left and walked off-screen.

"That lying shit."

"Who?"

"The Asian guy Lachie was walking with is named Kai. Works at the circus. He told me he'd never seen the kid before." I patted Davie on the shoulder. "This is great work, mate. You need to commercialise this."

I had half-turned from the monitor to say something to Lucy when another face coming up the escalator caught my eye. "Hang on. Back that video up a couple of seconds and slow it down."

I leaned forward and stared at the screen. The face I'd seen earlier driving a Fiat convertible came up the escalator almost ten seconds behind Lachlan.

No question.

Huang Leung was alive.

Nine

I pointed at the monitor. "Freeze that, Davie. Grab that face."

He tapped the spacebar as Huang Leung looked up at the camera. He was wearing a baseball cap and sunglasses, but I did not doubt it was him. "Can you do anything with that?"

"Come on, Nick," said Lucy. "This isn't a case. Send that picture to your AFP friends and let it go."

She had a point. I won't get paid for this. And the subtext of her comment was that it was dangerous. Not a missing teen. An assumed dead man with a wealth of resources at his disposal.

The image, cropped to show just Leung's head, was on the monitor now. The resolution was crap; the picture was grainy. I shook my head. "Email that to me, Davie. I'll send it to the feds and be done with it." Maybe.

My phone rang. Dammit. It was the mother again. "Lyla. What can I do for you?"

"I need you to accompany me to Gosford and get my son."

"No. You engaged me to find him, and I did. My apologies, but I'm not a kidnapping service." I held a finger up to Lucy. *Just a second.*

"I don't want you to kidnap him. I need your help to get through to him. Tonight."

I looked at my watch and put my phone on speaker. "Tonight? Really? It's almost eight. They'll be closing by the time we get there."

"Perfect. He'll be facing the prospect of sleeping another night, not in his bed. He's just a kid, goddammit."

I closed my eyes and tapped the Mute button. "Shit."

"She wants you to go back and get him?" Unlike me, Lucy wasn't an idiot. Her most attractive trait.

I nodded. "Wants her and I both to go."

"I'll go too."

I grimaced. "You emphatically said you don't want to get involved in the actual in-the-field stuff. This is actually, really, getting involved in the field stuff. And these guys are huge."

"That's why I should go."

"What?"

"I think this is what they call female logic, Nick," said Davie. "Right in front of our eyes."

Lucy glared at him, then looked back to me. "Don't piss me off, Davie. I'm serious. Those tough types are usually reluctant to be that way in front of women they don't know."

"Really? I think you should stay here."

"And two mother figures pressing this young kid to go home will help, too."

"Insanity." I wasn't going to win this fight. "Okay, you win. Davie, can you look through the video—or get your computer to look through your video—and see if there's a better picture?"

"Maybe I should go too."

"Two guys showing up will be too threatening. Nick and I will be fine."

Davie raised his eyebrows at me and shrugged. "I'll man the fort, as they say."

"This is a bad idea, Luce." I held up my free hand. "But yeah, sure. Why not. Let's go." I took the phone off mute. "I will pick you up. Fifteen minutes."

She was waiting outside her house. Lucy rolled down her window as we approached. "Lyla? I'm Lucy. Nick's partner." She opened the door. "Let's chat in the back seat while Nick drives."

She seemed flustered—Lyla, not Lucy. Lucy hasn't been flustered once in all the time I've known her. "Oh, okay. Sure. I guess two women are better than one."

"Always." Lucy closed her door and walked to the other side of the car. "You can tell me about Lachlan on the way there."

I waited until both doors closed, and I heard the clicks of their seatbelts. I yawned and pulled from the curb, an hour from the circus.

Lyla and Lucy started talking. I listened in.

"Lachlan is fifteen?"

"Just turned. I thought he'd finally calmed down. We had three months of relative peacefulness after a couple of years of typical teen angst."

I wonder what happened when he turned thirteen.

Lucy asked, "What happened when he turned thirteen?"

Great. Now she can read my mind.

Lyla sat in silence for a few minutes. "I don't know for sure. I think his father reached out to him, but I can't be positive. Lachie said he hadn't, but," I saw her shrug in the review mirror, "I have my suspicions."

"Who is his father?" asked Lucy. I was wondering the same.

"No." Lyla took a deep breath. "We split just after Lachie was born. I haven't heard from him in well over a decade."

I hit the motorway north. The conversation in the backseat shifted to the Melbourne Cup and whether Lyla would go again this year. Lucy made a couple of unsuccessful attempts to steer the conversation back to family. I tuned them out after a few minutes and focused on the drive north.

Parking was full. It was 9:00 p.m. on a Monday night, and all of Gosford was at the circus. *Jesus, there really is nothing else to do here.*

I found a place to park about half a kilometre away. Lucy had decent walking shoes on. Lyla, not so much.

"That was the closest?" She winced as her foot rolled on a loose stone. "No, never mind. I shouldn't complain." She put her shoulders back and limped the rest of the way to the circus entrance.

"We're going to have to buy tickets if we want to get past the gatekeepers. I burned that bridge already." My arms still hurt, as did my pride.

"I'll get them," said Lyla. "You'd mark them up when you charge them back to me."

Lucy covered a smile and elbowed me in the ribs. "Your reputation precedes you, love."

Mika took the tickets, glaring at me while he handed them back. "You are back."

"You are right," I said, echoing his intonation. "Nothing gets past those little piggy eyes." The last part was under my breath. Despite what my girlfriend thinks, I'm not a complete idiot.

Lyla wrinkled her nose as we passed Mika. "So where is he in this place?" She headed toward the entrance to the main tent.

I tapped her on the arm. "Not in there. He's out by the swinging ship."

"Oh, dear god, I don't even want to know what that is. He's a child, dammit."

I couldn't tell if she was serious or joking. "Not that kind of swinging, Lyla. It's a giant pendulum. For some reason, people like it."

"It gives the passengers the sense of being in free fall while a safe environment." Lucy chimed in.

"Safe? It's managed by a fifteen-year-old. Sure, he's *my* fifteen-year-old, but still." Lyla picked up her pace and got in front of us. "Are these people complete morons?"

"She moves good in those heels," Lucy laughed outright. "Too bad all your jobs aren't this fun." She hustled to keep up.

Lachlan was still at the ship. He looked tired and bored. It took him a few seconds for his brain to catch up to his eyes and recognise that the woman running toward him was his mother. "Oh, fucking hell, mum. What are you doing here?" He looked at me. "You, mate, are an arsehole, bringing my mother up here." He glanced back at the ship, probably ensuring nobody was falling out.

"Your mother twisted my arm." The ship slowed to a stop, and the bell jangled to let everyone on it know they hadn't died. "You should probably attend to them. One more time."

He sneered at me. His glance over my shoulder before he turned to the ship should have warned me.

A meaty fist, the worst kind, grabbed me on that spot between my shoulders and neck and squeezed. Hard. "Told you to fuck off and not come back, pal."

I tried to twist free. The grip tightened, and I looked over my shoulder at Karl. "Could you let go? That hurts."

"It's meant to, Nicky. I google you. You stick your nose into all kinds of shits. Not here. Not now. Get your arse out of here." His Nordic-ish accent was getting stronger.

Lyla put her shoulders back and fronted up to him. "Let him go. And I am leaving tonight with my son."

He let go. "So you are the mums."

I rubbed my—whatever it's called - trapezoid?—and kept an eye on Lachlan. He looked pissed off as he ushered one batch of customers off the ship and another one on.

"I am his mother. He is a minor. He is coming with me. Are you smart enough to understand my English?" She poked him in the chest. "And you or nobody else will stop us."

He looked at where she poked him and chuckled. "There are half a dozen people here who could snap Nicky like a herringbone. So the three of you," he pointed at Lucy, "I'm assuming the redhead is with you, can get back in your car and be fucking all the way off."

Lucy's eyes narrowed. She looked at Lachie, then at Karl. "You tell him, Lyla. This guy isn't going to stop us."

"Shut up, Red."

"Up yours, fatso." At the time, I thought she had lost her mind. And maybe she did. But it had the right result.

"What did you say?" Lyla was between Lucy and Karl, and Karl's face was turning red. "I don't give a fuck who you are, the three of you are leaving now."

"Like you could fucking stop us." Lucy stuck her chin out and gave him two fingers. "You're just a fat bully."

That did it. Karl pushed Lyla to one side and lunged after Lucy. Lyla fell on her knees in the mud, letting out a yell that got Lachlan's attention.

He abandoned the ship, and Lucy ran to avoid Karl.

Lachlan helped his mother up and grabbed Karl by the arm, stopped him, and got in his face. He wasn't as beefy as Karl, but he was much taller. "What the fuck, mate? That's my mother. Keep your fucking hands off of her."

Karl snarled and raised a fist, took a deep breath and lowered it. "Your post." He pointed at the slowing ship. "Now."

Lachlan took his mother's hands. "Sorry about that. Karl is an oaf."

This was remarkable. Karl would use my head as a football if I had said that. Karl was ready to kill, but he lowered his fist, pulled Lachie to one side and whispered something in his ear.

The kid looked at him, scowled, and then nodded. "They said I should go back with you and talk in the morning. They said this is a good apprenticeship for me, for business-related stuff."

Lyla looked past her son at Karl, then grabbed her son by the arm. "An apprentice minding a stupid swinging ship? Get in the car."

He looked at me with a scowl but obediently got in the back seat. His mother pushed him over, so he was behind my seat, and she sat behind the front passenger's seat.

I held the door for Lucy, then got behind the wheel. I pulled up Lyla's address from the list of recent destinations and left Gosford.

An uneasy silence settled over the car for the first half of the journey. I could see Lyla glancing at her son, about to say something, then sitting back in her seat, crossing her arms and staring out the window into the night.

The dam broke as we crossed the Mooney Mooney Bridge. "What were you thinking, Lachie?"

He sat in silence.

"I asked you a question. Your future is limitless, and you run away to join the *circus*? What were you thinking?"

I wondered the same. But it wasn't my business. I had to get clear of this mess before I got dragged into a quagmire of family shite.

Someone else's family. I had enough family shite of my own.

Lyla leaned forward and stuck her head between the two front seats. "Tell him, Nick. The circus is a stupid idea."

Lucy covered her mouth and stifled a chuckle. I tossed an exaggerated scowl at her and looked at Lyla in the rear-view mirror. "That's a discussion between you and your son. I've more than done my part. I'll drop you both off at your house. The two of you need to have a family sit-down."

Lachlan snorted. "Just trying to do my fair share, Mum."

I watched Lyla glare at her son, her lips drawn tight. She sat back and didn't talk again until I dropped them in front of her house.

"Send the invoice to me for tonight. I'll pay it promptly. Thanks for your efforts; they are appreciated."

The car doors closed before I answered. Nothing much I *could* answer. Lucy yawned and adjusted her seat so she could lean back. She closed her eyes. I thought she had drifted off, but she opened her right eye and looked at me. "Easy case? Easy money."

I watched Lyla and Lachie walk back to her house. She linked her arm to his and seemed to have a necessary heart-to-heart with her son—not as angry as I expected her to be. I looked at the time on the dash. "It's pushing midnight. This isn't easy. Are you okay?"

"I'm confused."

"About?"

She flicked the handle on the side of the seat and was sitting upright again. "The encounter at the circus was strange."

"I know, right? They didn't manhandle me."

She shook her head a bit impatiently. "No. Well, yes. They didn't manhandle you, but stranger than that, they seemed to treat young Lachie with more deference than a fifteen-year-old deserves. I wonder what that was about. And his mother wasn't as furious as I expected her to be."

She reclined the car seat again, closed her eyes and seemed to fall asleep.

I should have paid more attention to her observations.

Ten

"Hey, Red, time to wake up." Lucy's hair obscured her face.

"I am. And please don't call me that." She stretched in her seat. "Just thinking."

I pulled to the kerb in front of Davie's apartment block. "What about?" I turned off the car. "Anything I should be worried about?"

"She's going to come back to you to extricate him from the circus. Maybe next week. Maybe the week after. Let the cops do it."

"You think?"

She unclipped her belt and opened the door. The dome light reflected off her red hair. "I do. He'll be back there sooner than later." She got out of my car and walked to hers. "I'm serious, Nicky. Call the police if she calls you again. Those guys scared me."

No kiss, not even a peck on the cheek. Into her car, and she drove away without even a wave. She was truly worried. And she was pissed off. And she wasn't wrong.

Davie was still in front of the monitor, a half-empty, 2-litre bottle of water beside the keyboard, four windows of CCTV footage spooling by at accelerated speeds. He looked up at me briefly and returned to watching Keystone Kops-like characters running through the Westfield Bondi Junction.

"What are you looking for?"

He tapped the spacebar and stopped the videos. He swivelled his chair and yawned as he rubbed his eyes. Made me yawn too. "A better picture of your ghost." He scratched the stubble on his chin. "There isn't one."

"Only one picture of him?" I pulled a chair up beside his. "In all of this footage? Is your program working?"

"Piss off. My program works just fine. There's no better picture than the one we first found. I think I've found him in almost a dozen places. There are a couple of more hours to go through manually. I haven't found anything that *my program* didn't already find."

I chuckled. "Easy, lad. Did *your program* find anything interesting?"

Davie smiled as he clicked a file on his desktop. A video clip opened, and he maximised it to fill the monitor. "Most were either him walking past a camera or sitting in a coffee shop nursing a green tea." He poked a finger at the screen. "Then these two guys joined him, and they talked for about ten minutes before going their separate ways."

One of the guys who joined my ghost was middle-aged, hard-looking, with a skin full of tattoos. His head looked like it was shaved. Maybe naturally bald. Maybe a bit of both. Like yours truly. Tatts were common, but tattoos up the throat, not so much. "Any other pictures of the big bald guy?"

"I haven't looked yet."

The second guy was the exact opposite of Baldy. He had a thinning head of long hair tied back in a ponytail and a chest full of thatch poking through the opened buttons at the top of his shirt. He was whippet-lean and looked like he'd give Baldy a run for his money in a scrap.

"What about this guy?" I tapped on the Baldy's head.

Davie used his sleeve to wipe the smudge off his monitor. "No, Nick. And it's way too fucking late to look tonight. I've got a real job tomorrow. I'm kicking you out. We can reconvene tomorrow evening."

"Fair call. It can wait." I wanted to keep going, but it wasn't my apartment, and it wasn't my software.

Davie walked me to the door. "I'll give you a call tomorrow."

"Thanks for the help, Davie. I really appreciate it."

"I'll let you flatter me tomorrow. I need sleep."

I chuckled as the door closed behind me. I sat in my car, smelling lingering hints of Lucy's perfume. I wanted to call her, but she had work tomorrow, too.

I woke early. Strange dreams meant I must have hit the REM stage of sleep, but I was exhausted. The siege on the warehouse Leung was holed up in kept getting replayed in my dreams, Rashomon-style. The last version, the one that woke me, had me in Curtis' location, at the front of the line, about to enter when the building exploded.

I know. Technically incorrect. The building didn't explode. The chemicals inside the building exploded. I jerked awake. It took a second to settle. My heart was pounding.

At least I didn't have to go to the office. Running my own shop was good. Not having a nine-to-five was liberating. I made my own rules and worked my own hours.

And typically, the rules were actually made by the client who was paying the bill, and the hours were always longer than nine-to-five.

I put off shaving and had a quick shower. Got dressed in comfortable clothes and filled a travel mug with strong coffee.

By seven, I was walking the neighbourhood where I'd last seen Huang Leung, with my coffee in one hand and his photo on my phone in the other. I was going to get my steps in.

Fortunately, it was a weekday. Most people were getting up and ready for work.

My first stop was delayed when I opened the gate to walk up to the house, and a little rat-dog bolted from nowhere across the lawn and onto the street.

"Trixie! Get back here!" An older woman in tracksuit pants and an ABBA t-shirt sprinted out of the front door after Trixie. She glared at me. "Don't just stand there. Help me. You caused this."

Trixie was an uncooperative player in this game. I didn't do much. Blocked access when I could. Kind of helped shepherd the little rat back into the yard.

The owner slammed the gate shut with me on the outside. "I'm not interested in joining whatever religion it is you're flogging."

"No, Jesus, no. Not flogging religion. I'm a PI, looking for this guy." I held up my phone. "He drives a red Fiat convertible. Have you seen him around?"

She narrowed her eyes and crossed her arms. Trixie yapped like an invasion was imminent. "Is there a reward in it for me?"

"Your reward would be the swell of pride you feel when you know you've aided in the apprehension of a very bad man."

That didn't impress her at all. "Never saw the man."

I made sure my screen hadn't locked and held my screen closer to her. "You haven't looked."

"Not interested. And I highly doubt 'very bad men' live in this neighbourhood."

"What about the car? Little red convertible. Sporty looking."

"Be off with you." She turned back to her house. "Come on, Trixie."

"Thanks for all your help," I called after her. I hope my sarcasm wasn't subtle.

Her neighbour was out on his front step, drawn, no doubt, by Trixie and her incessant yaps. He nodded as I approached. "Who ya looking for, mate?"

He was well into his retiring years, short grey stubble on his head and a freshly clean-shaven face. Reading glasses were perched on the end of his nose.

I held out my phone, showing Leung's picture. "This guy. He was spotted driving into this neighbourhood in a red Fiat convertible."

He took my phone and peered down his nose at the screen. He considered it for a moment, then shook his head. "Nah, mate. It doesn't look like anyone I know." He handed my phone back. "I saw the car, though. Red Fiat 500C. 2016, I think. It's in good nick. For a Fiat."

He slid his hands in his pockets. "What's he wanted for?"

"I'll get to that in a minute. Where did you see the car, and when was the last time you saw it?"

"It's gone past the house a couple of times. Most recently, a couple of weeks ago. On a Thursday."

I nodded. "Any idea where it was heading?"

He pointed to the right of his house, in the direction I was walking. "He turned left at the T-intersection at the end of the road. After that, who knows? Who is he?"

"Thanks for your help. He's a guy the cops have been looking for. For years, actually." I handed him a card. "Could you call me if you see him again?"

He read my card. "Nick Harding. Private Investigator. Huh." He slipped the card into his shirt pocket and stuck out his hand. "I'll keep an eye out for you."

I shook his hand, thanked him and skipped ahead a few houses.

After an hour of this, I was nowhere, had sore legs and desperately needed a piss. The coffee seemed like a good idea at the time. I found my way back to my car and called Johnson.

Jackson answered. "Mr Harding. I thought you private eye types slept until noon."

"Where's Johnson?" I started driving, looking for a McToilet.

"Tied up. You rich yet?"

"No such luck, mate. Tell me about Leung."

"Oh, Jesus. Still this? The old man is dead. D-E-A-D. Blowed up. Blowed up real good."

I found one. The Golden Arches to the rescue. I stopped in the parking lot. "Then I must have seen his twin at the Bondi Junction Westfield this past weekend."

Jackson paused on the line. "Mistaken identity. Has to be. We confirmed his death."

"You saw the body?"

He laughed. Hard. "You know we didn't. The place was reduced to dust. He would have been atomised in that explosion."

"If there's no corpse, there's no confirmation of his death. He could have slipped out somehow."

"We scraped his DNA off the pieces of brick. He's dead, Nick. I think you might need an extended vacation. Tilting at windmills."

"Hang on a sec." I found Davie's email with the screen grab. It wasn't a great shot, but it was all I had right now. I forwarded it to Jackson's address. "You should have a screen grab from the security cameras at Bondi Junction. Tell me that's not him. Show it to Johnson and anyone else in the office still around who knows Leung."

"Now you're wasting *my* time."

"Look at it. Tell me that isn't him."

I heard tapping on his keyboard. "It can't be him because he's dead. Is this what you're like now?" There was another single tap of his keyboard. "Okay, I've opened the picture. It looks a little bit like him, I'll grant you that. But, and I've said this before—"

"He's dead. Right. And I'm making shit up just for the hell of it. Look, mate, I've got enough going on I wouldn't be asking you about him unless I really thought it was him.

Did I strike you as an idiot when I worked with you? Be honest."

"Honestly, no. Maybe it's something in the water. Are you living near a tip?" Jackson was laughing out loud by this point.

"Arsehole." I tapped my steering wheel, thinking. Something that is very hard to do when your bladder is about to burst. "I'll be there in half an hour."

I hung up before he could tell me not to. I really had to go.

Eleven

It had been a few years since I'd been in the AFP offices in downtown Sydney. I didn't miss the place. The people, sure. I miss them a lot. There wasn't a single person I'd worked with who I'd want to toss off a bridge.

Jackson, and his partner Johnson, were getting close, though.

I missed the employee on-site parking, too. It was a long half-kilometre walk to the building from the closest parking space I could find.

Two duty officers sat behind a Perspex screen in the ground floor lobby. I didn't recognise either of them. Both of them were young. Well-armed. Attentive.

The lobby was separated from a bank of lifts by electronic gates that opened with a pass card. If you tried jumping the gates, the two duty officers would make sure you wouldn't get to the lifts. I slid my Driver's Licence through the gap at the bottom of the security screen.

A young Senior Constable extracted it, looked at it, and then at me. "How can I help you, Mr Harding?"

"Could you call Inspector Jackson and let him know I'm here? He's expecting me."

"One minute."

There wasn't a place to sit. This wasn't meant to be an inviting waiting area like a doctor's office or the service department at the car dealership. This was a reception area that said, 'You better have a reason to be here. And you better not even think about loitering.'

I wandered aimlessly while she contacted Jackson. After a minute, she knocked on the Perspex and slid through my licence and a visitor's pass on an AFP lanyard. "Pass number 13. Sign the book. He'll be down in a minute."

"Thanks." I populated the sign-in form with my particulars and threw the lanyard over my head as one of the lift doors opened and Johnson exited, a pissed-off look on his face.

He approached the gate but didn't open it. "I should have told them to march you out at gunpoint."

"Good to see you too, Johnson. I thought Jackson was coming down. Are you going to let me in? I've signed in and everything." I held up my visitor's pass. "Even got one of these."

"That'll get you through the gate. Hurry up, and let's get this over with."

I tapped the reader, the gates slid open, and Johnson held the lift for me. He took us to the third floor, entered codes to get from the lift lobby to the floor and turned to me. "Remember the rules? You have to be escorted everywhere. If you walk around with that thing on and aren't escorted by someone like me, you'll be booted out."

"There's no one like you, mate. Except Jackson. Can't tell you apart some days."

His glare intensified. "You walk around *without* it on, and you'll be lucky if you're not shot."

I laughed.

He didn't.

I followed him to a pod of desks. Jackson was at one, Johnson sat at one near him. Jackson looked up at me, nodded, and went back to whatever he was doing.

Johnson rolled a chair from an adjacent empty desk over to his. He pointed at it and sat. "How can I convince you the old man is dead?"

"How can I convince you he's not? You've seen the photo, right? I saw the guy. Twice. It was him. I'm not going to forget him."

Jackson rolled his chair over. "Billy's been telling me you've been seeing ghosts."

I held up an index finger. "Just the single one. And he is corporeal." I watched as Jackson tried to figure out what that word that sounded so much like 'corporal' meant. "Physical in form, mate. Not a spirit."

"Yeah, I know what it means. So the guy has a doppelgänger. You know what that means, right?"

I did. "He wasn't a double. It was him."

"Show him, Johnson." Jackson reached for Johnson's mouse and had his hand batted away.

"He doesn't work here anymore, Jackson." He moved the mouse out of the way. "We can't."

"He's going to keep bugging us."

"He's not bugging you, he's bugging me."

"When he's tired of bugging you, he'll start bugging me. He tag teams us."

I watched them go back and forth, a well-honed act. "You two been practising this schtick? The guy is alive, and he's back, and if you choose to believe he's not, the consequences will be on you. I warned you."

Johnson's eyebrows were rock-climbing up his forehead. "*Warned* us?" He looked around and lowered his voice. "You're only here because we were recruits together, and you're mostly reliable."

"And I helped you get a money launderer and international criminal off the street last year."

"How's the back?"

"Cool scar." I nodded at his monitor. "Show me what Jackson wants you to show me."

He opened a case management system and navigated to a file from my past: Operation Snowball, the single largest drug importation in Australian history at the time. Multiple ports of entry were used, and isolated cells of mules were employed to transport the drugs to the central staging area.

Which blew up with Huang Leung and most of his lieutenants.

"I've seen all this before. So what? The warehouse was obliterated. Body parts were found, but none of the head of the snake. Not implausible that he found a way to sneak out before the ka-boom."

Johnson tapped a key and brought up DNA results. "See this one? The son. Confirmed DNA from a leg we found inside. Actually, just outside." He tapped another key. "DNA found with parental linkage to the leg found in a gooey mess from inside the blast zone. Male parental linkage." He closed the program. "That's all I can, or am willing to, show you. Evidence that he's dead. Leave us alone. We've got our own problems. Don't need a PI getting in our face telling us we don't know what we're doing." He didn't look happy. "You know this shit, mate. You worked beside me when this was closed."

Yeah. Don't believe my lying eyes. "So, what are you guys working on now?"

"Chatter about a new—"

"Shut the fuck up, Jackson." Johnson shook his head. "You're going to get us fired."

"Fair call. " Jackson smiled, patted me on the back, and then pulled his hand back. "Sorry. Was that where he got you?"

An unhinged Russian human trafficker, by way of Miami, tried to cut me open a while back. I ended up with twenty-seven stitches diagonally across my back. It didn't hurt anymore. And it wasn't really that deep.

I twisted away. "Yeah, that's exactly where he got me." I adjusted my shirt, piling on the guilt. I nodded toward Johnson's monitor. "So he's incontrovertibly dead." Not a question.

"You and all the big words," said Johnson. "Yes. Dead. Incontrovertibly dead. Satisfied?"

"Not hardly. You'll answer my phone call when I corner this guy, right?"

"Sure. Whatever makes you leave." Johnson stood and held his hand out toward the door, offering to let me go first. "Leave."

"Champs. Later. Don't block my number." I got to the door and pulled it open. Nope. So I pushed it—still a nope. I turned around to see Johnson, arms crossed, a smile on his face.

"Allow me."

He tapped the card reader with his ID and pushed the door open. "Can't have riff-raff letting other riff-raff in. It doesn't work without a card. A real card, not a visitor's card." He held the door open and followed me out. He used the card in the lift and took us to the ground floor. In silence.

He carded the security gate open and sent me through. "Hand in your visitor's pass. We know where you live."

"I've recently moved."

"We know."

I had no idea if he was joking. I slid the pass through the gap under the security screen and signed myself out.

The pair I was just with, as well as Vinod, Bruce, Eugene and all of the others I worked with were good—extremely good. If they said Huang Leung was dead, they were convinced he was dead.

Except I saw him. With my own two eyes.

If I wanted to convince them, I'd need something a bit better than a grainy photo. DNA would be good.

I started the car and called Davie's mobile number.

"I'm working, mate. I'll continue the facial recognition work tonight."

"I'll only be a minute. You can keep running that tonight if *you* want. But that's not what *I* want." I checked the time. "I'll be back in my office in ten minutes. Can you take an early coffee break and set my system up to query civilian security cameras?"

Davie's voice got quieter. "That's on the shady side of the legal line. Are you sure? You're all legit and everything. Would hate for you to get into trouble."

"I'd just claim ignorance and blame my IT guy."

"I'M NOT YOUR IT GUY."

"No need to yell, mate. Give it a couple of weeks. Can you do it?"

"The kid case is over. He ran away to a circus. Living the dream. You're going fuck it up. What's the CCTV snooping for?"

"I'm almost there. You coming or not?" I was stuck at a red light just outside the AFP offices. I was not even close to being back in the office. Should have taken the tram.

"Tell me the case. If I'm going to be an accomplice in potential felonies, I want to know it is worth it."

He had a point—sort of. "It's to track the guy you found on the mall footage. There should be lots of cameras in the neighbourhood where he disappeared. These are high-end houses, no fences, and doorbell cameras on every porch. I've got to track him to a source.

"Sounds a lot like something your AFP friends should take care of."

Don't I know it. "I just left their offices. They've modernised the place. They showed me some evidence. Stuff I already knew. Case closed as far as they're concerned."

"So what in the hell do you think *you're* going to do?"

I accelerated through an old amber light and hoped I didn't trigger the red-light camera. "I'm pulling into the parking garage under my building. Are you showing up, or do I have to fumble through this myself?"

"Are you buying me a coffee?"

"Don't I always?" The machine in the communal kitchen would have to do.

"Okay." He sighed extra loud. "I'll be there in five minutes."

"Many thanks, friend."

"Right." He hung up. I was going to pay for this at some point down the road.

Claude was at the lift waiting to enter as I exited. "You get the printer working?"

"Been kinda busy, mate." I clapped him on the shoulder. "But I have. Thanks." I grabbed two mugs from the communal pile and brewed a couple of long black. 'Brewed' as in, put the cups under the spouts and pushed the necessary buttons.

I had an invoice to get out. Now was as good a time as any.

Lyla got a daily rate for the day, double the daily rate for the trip to the circus and bought me a new phone. I subtracted the retainer, added GST, saved it as a pdf and emailed it to her.

My office door swung open, and I looked up, expecting Davie.

It was John Ravenhill, the sales guy. I motioned for him to take a chair. "Harriet back in town early?"

"Nah, mate. Wanted to know if you wanted to grab lunch later. There's a Bahn Mi up the road we hit on Tuesdays."

"I'd love to, and appreciate you asking, but I have a full day today. Rain check, and it'll be my treat."

"Understood. All good. You're still on to meet Harry tomorrow?"

"Harriet? Sure. As scheduled."

"Excellent. I'll leave you to it. You know where we are. You've got my number?"

"I do. Thanks." I realise salespeople exist to sell for their business, but it's a personality I don't work well with. I stared at him, a smile fixed on my face, until he backed out with a smile of his own. I swear he was spray-tanned. "Something off about that guy," I muttered.

"Who, me?"

I looked up, a flash of panic that I might have said that out loud in front of the sales guy. I didn't. "Hey, Davie. Thanks for helping out."

He had a laptop case in one hand and a brown bag from the local pastry shop.

"Where's my coffee, and something's off about *what* guy?"

Twelve

"So what nut job are you worried about now?" Davie dropped the bag of pastries on my desk and motioned me out of my chair. "You take these. I've lost my appetite." He sat and opened his laptop while I took the bag of goodies.

They weren't pastries, as such. Two bran and sultana muffins. "What the hell is this? Are you okay, mate?"

"I've been feeling like shit, so I thought I'd try eating healthy." He looked tired.

"Maybe take a couple of days. Rest up. " I gave him the muffin with a paper napkin. "Get it in you. You need to eat."

He smiled and placed it on the table beside the keyboard. "Sure thing, mate. I'll take it with me." He copied an internet address and pasted it into an email he was composing. "Same email address, or have you set one up for your new fancy business?"

"Same." I looked at the muffin he took. "You're not going to eat that, are you?"

"You can have it if you want."

He transferred to my laptop and checked my mail. "Hey, you've got a remittance email. Your second day on the job, and you've already been paid for something?"

I leaned over and opened the mail. She paid already. Fuck. Lucy was right. She's going to call me when the kid takes off again. "Mind your business, and what did you mail me?"

The mail he had sent me was at the top of the pile. He opened it and clicked on the link. His CCTV surveillance setup appeared on my monitor. He looked up at the glass office's glass walls and angled the monitor so casual strollers-by couldn't see it. "Nicky, I'm not 100% sure of the legality of grabbing video from unsecured cameras. And I don't want to test it in court, right? So if you could kinda keep this to yourself, I would really appreciate it." He exited my chair, pulled the spare one beside it, and sat. "And if you *do* get caught, forget my name."

"What a friend." I rested my hands in front of the keyboard. "Remind me how to drive this thing."

Davie was gone in less than ten minutes. He left his muffin and grabbed a bottle of water from the communal fridge.

He'd improved the system since I last used it, looking for an Irish money launderer and a Russian mobster. With the added feature of facial recognition, it should make short work of the search. But the pissy-arsed monitor the office centre provided wouldn't do the job. And Miss Porter just paid her bill in full.

The advantages of working in the city. I locked up and walked across the street to an electronics shop, picked out an extra-wide monitor, HDMI cables, and lugged the booty back to the office.

By the time I'd wrestled it through the door and into my office, rearranged the real estate on my desk and had it functioning alongside the original monitor, an hour had elapsed. Time well spent. It was a decent setup.

I re-opened his software and panned the map until I was in the general area where the Fiat had disappeared. Over a couple of minutes, camera icons appeared on top of houses. Green ones had accessible cameras, and the red ones were secured. The grey ones weren't powered. Technically, Davie could probably bypass the typically flimsy security on doorbell cameras, but I wasn't feeling lucky enough to try that.

Maybe later, if I had to.

I searched the internet, found a Fiat very similar to the one I saw Leung in, and used it for the facial recognition reference. It was just maths, right?

The computer chugged away at the problem, looking for a red convertible Fiat in an area about 5 km in diameter, spanning thirty-six hours—eighteen hours either side of the time I spotted him.

The program was faster than I thought it would be. Davie is good. I stepped out of my office to the central kitchen, grabbed a glass of chilled water, and by the time I'd returned, the map was spotted with little images of the Fiat, like measles, scattered across it.

Davie had programmed a time slider across the top of the map. I slid it back to the beginning of the time window and slowly stepped it forward. The car mapped its journey through the neighbourhood, past Trixie's house, left at the end of the street and into a cul-de-sac where all of the cameras were secured. Somebody with some IT smarts had helped their neighbours. Every one of the home security systems in that cul-de-sac was actually secure.

One of the cameras picked up part of the car's registration number. The first three letters. JBE.

I had thirteen houses to check, a lot less than the hundreds I started with. It was time for a road trip.

"Hey. You look hard at work." Lucy laughed when I jumped. "Did I startle you?"

I leaned back in my chair. "I was engrossed. What brings you here?"

"Thought I'd buy you lunch."

I checked the time on my monitor. "Crap. Already?"

"It's that kind of enthusiasm that endears you to me. There's a nice place across the street. My treat."

I had canvassing to do. But lunch with Lucy? No contest. I'm not an idiot. "Sure, but it's my treat. The rich lady has already paid me. Tell me about this place."

Her eyebrows skittered up her forehead. "Already paid you?"

I smiled. "Yeah."

"No complaints?"

"Not even for charging her for a brand new phone."

"She's going to call you again when the kid pisses off."

"My thought as well." I locked the office door, and we walked to the lift. Claude waved as we passed his office.

"Who's that?"

"My local IT guy. Set up the printer."

Lucy waved at the lady manning the reception area and took my arm. "Exciting night last night."

"Are you okay? You seemed a bit off after it all. Kind of disappeared really quick."

She hugged my arm a little tighter. "I was tired. And the adrenaline was still bleeding off after facing those giants." She looked up at me and grinned. "I worked up a hell of an appetite."

We walked across the street to a small cafe. Tables inside and outside. It was an outside kind of day. "What's good here?"

"They make a Portuguese chicken thigh, with a salad, on a bed of rice with a poached egg perched on top." She chef-kissed her fingertips. "I could eat it every day."

Like-wise. "One each? Grab one of those patio tables, and I'll order."

"They do fresh-squeezed OJ. A large for me, please."

She grabbed a two-seat table at the railing. I ordered and joined her, putting a wooden block with our order number in the middle. "It's not cheap."

"I did say it was my treat." She smiled. "Next time."

"Sure thing, Luce. Why did you really want to catch up? You usually take your lunch break an hour later than this. What's up?"

Lucy raised her eyebrows. "I keep forgetting you're good at this." She leaned back as our orange juices were served. She waited until the server left, then leaned forward conspiratorially. "I did some research on that Huang Leung guy. He's not nice."

"The feds say he's dead." I sipped. The juice was incredible. There was a very slight hint of ginger in it.

"You don't believe the feds, though. And I know you. You think he's still alive. And I believe you." She smiled. "The juice is good, though. Right?"

I nodded. "What research did you do?"

"First, the internet. There's a tonne of information about him and his crime family. The massive importation of drugs a few years back." She smiled. "There was mention of an AFP task force that tracked his money to expose him. I'm assuming you were part of that."

"Guilty as charged. Did you get to the part about the explosion?"

"Where he, his son and half of his lieutenants blew up with his product?" She nodded. "Very descriptive writing in the local papers. And the international papers. I had one of my colleagues at work, originally from Hong Kong, translate the editorial in the Beijing Daily. They were low-key pissed about the whole thing."

"I heard." I shrugged. "Except he's not dead. They shouldn't be pissed." I wiped my mouth and took another mouthful of OJ. The chicken was spicy. "He's not dead."

She looked at me over her glasses while shoving rice around her plate. "I'm worried, Nick. You've got to give this guy a wide berth. He's bad news."

"Oh, I know."

"I don't think you do. The Beijing paper has a couple of recent articles about his legitimate businesses on their mainland that seem to imply he's still alive. Which means he doesn't care if he's found. And he'll be looking to avenge the death of his son."

"He absolutely is alive. And he'll be getting a wide berth from me. I just need a couple of good pictures to convince Johnson—actually, Jackson seems more open to the idea— that the case needs to be reopened. And, if possible, a DNA sample from a discarded coffee cup, or something." I held up my hands. "I'm not going to tangle with him. He won't even know I'm around."

She seemed to relax a bit. "Good. You're good at what you do, as long as what you do doesn't include the physical bits. All brain, only a modicum of brawn."

She wasn't wrong. But I didn't have to like it. "So I'm a weakling?"

Her laughter was like the peal of a bell. She waggled her hand. "Eh. How's the back?"

The scar still itches. Lucy rubs vitamin E oil into it. She says it helps to reduce scarring. I'm unsure if that works, but it usually leads to better stuff, so I'm not complaining. "My back? My agility and fleetness of foot kept that from being much worse." I took her hand. "But keep an eye on it for me, okay?"

"I'll watch your back if you watch mine, Nicky." She took her hand back and returned to her lunch. "Any interesting people in that office share space you work at?"

"A bunch of small businesses trying to make it work. Like me."

"Ten to one, none of them put their lives on the line like you do."

"It's never intentional, Lucy."

Her smile was sad. "That's the problem. It's never intentional." She shrugged. "If it were intentional, that would be a different story. As it is, you could go for months without somebody trying to kill you. I'd be lulled into a false sense of security. Then," she snapped her fingers, "you're in the emergency room getting your nose set or twenty stitches to hold your back together. You have an uncanny knack for finding really bad people and making them want to hurt you." She leaned forward and lowered her voice. "Or kill you."

I didn't know how to respond. I didn't go looking for these arseholes. Actually, I *did*, but I had no idea they were arseholes when I started looking for them. I sighed.

"You have a funny look on your face, Nick."

"I'm trying to rationalise what I'm doing. For you. For me." I rubbed my scalp. It needed a shave. "I was successful at the AFP. Had a great career tracking money laundering activities, locating the bad guys, and letting other people bring them in. It wasn't a challenge after the first couple of years. These guys aren't the smartest. Not the dumbest, but definitely not the smartest. There are only so many ways to launder money, and all of them are easy to find if you're looking. I had to get out of there. I would get old, grey and soft sitting behind a desk. Slowly slog my way up the career path of a federal government employee until they held a retirement party for me, and I shuffled into a retirement community in the Hills District."

Lucy wrinkled her nose. "Eww. Sounds horrible. Steady paycheque. A solid set of work friends. Nice pension." She fake shuddered. "Horrible."

I laughed. "So here's my promise."

She shifted forward in her chair. I think she was still mocking me. "Ooo. Tell me."

"You're getting a bit cheeky, Luce. Here is my promise. I'll look, but I'll call for actual police assistance instead of engaging." I held up my right hand like I was being sworn in for something. "I swear."

Her eyebrows raced to her hairline. "You promise? Really?" she nodded. "Okay, I'll take your word for that." She pointed at my plate. "Eat, before it's cold."

My next steps were going to be awkward. "Thanks for letting me know about this place. Right after we eat, I'm going to canvass the neighbourhood I saw Leung drive into." I held up my hands. "And as soon as I see him, I'm letting my former colleagues at the AFP know."

"Nick, he has to know what you look like. If you see him, he'll see you. You think that's—"

"He probably doesn't. I was the equivalent of Davie, back in the day. Anyway, I'm going to do my job carefully. I'm always careful. I'm an investigator. I investigate."

"You should go in disguise."

I laughed and almost immediately realised she was serious. "Really?" I shook my head. "No. Really? Like Fletch?"

"Who?"

"Nobody. Never mind."

She was dead serious. "Leung will try to kill you. Be safe." She stared into my eyes until it got really uncomfortable. "Okay. Now let's eat and stop talking shop."

I got back to the food. But as soon as we were finished, I had canvassing to do.

Thirteen

Lucy finished her food, checked the time, pecked me on my cheek and told me to be careful. I watched her walk away. She waved over her shoulder without looking and walked into the bank where she worked.

She had me in a bind.

Her idea of a disguise was ridiculous, right? Fake moustache, maybe a hat and sunglasses. But if I *didn't* canvass in disguise, and Leung caught on to who was looking for him, and I were to be on the receiving end of a punch-up, well, I'd never live it down, would I?

Fuck.

While I was finishing the orange juice, I used my phone to search for party shops near me. What was I becoming?

I pulled over at a servo on the way, almost in the suburb Leung had driven his Fiat into. I pulled a cap out of the shopping bag on the passenger's seat and shook my head as I looked at it. Some American baseball team I didn't know, and inside the back was stitched a fake mullet. I sighed and pulled it onto my head. It was too tight. I took it off, adjusted the plastic strap on the back and put it back on. A little too loose, but better than cutting into my scalp.

The second item in the carry bag was a pair of Clark Kent-styled glasses with non-prescription lenses. I put them on, looked at myself in the rear-view mirror, and chuckled. "Lucy, if you could see me now."

I found the cul-de-sac the Fiat had entered, the one with the locked-down doorbell cams. I wound through the suburb, backtracking a couple of times until I found it. Google Maps didn't do it justice.

It was a deep cul-de-sac. Five houses on each side of the street to the circle at the end. The three houses that arced the end of the street were the largest. Well over 500 square metres each. The others were almost as nice. All lawns mowed. Hedges trimmed. All in all, a very schmick neighbourhood. A Baker's Dozen of upper-middle-class luxury.

I pressed the doorbell at the first house on the left and stepped back so they had a good view of me. Fake me.

"Who is it, and what do you want?" A gruff voice for a tony neighbourhood, modified by the cheap speaker in the doorbell cam.

"Good afternoon. I'm—" Shit. If I was in disguise, I couldn't use my real name. "I'm looking for this man." I held up my phone, showing a media photo of Huang Leung from a decade ago.

"Sod off, mate. Or I'll set the dogs on ya."

Okay. One down, twelve to go.

I crisscrossed the street, working my way toward the bulbous end of the cul-de-sac. It wasn't much different at the other houses—a very tight-lipped group. Getting my steps in would be the only thing I got out of this endeavour.

I was at ten down, three to go. A white panel van was parked arse end in at the next house. 'Karen's Kleaning' was stencilled on the side. A 'For Sale' sign was planted on the front lawn with a local real estate company promising an executive-level property for those who chose to buy. I stepped aside to let who I assumed to be Karen get a bag of cleaning rags from the back of the van. I smiled and nodded and followed her into the house.

It was Tardis-like, much larger inside than it appeared from the street. Much of that had to do with the fact that it was built into a hill. The front of the house looked like it was a single-story home. But from the back, it was two and a half. A large foyer opened to six steps down to a large lounge area. A flat-screen TV took up most of the right-hand side wall.

Walking through the lounge led to sliding doors onto an elevated patio overlooking a small river. The kitchen, a large space with an island in the middle and a double sink extending out in a bay window, also overlooked the river.

I was intercepted in the kitchen by the agent responsible for getting someone to buy this executive-level dream home.

"I'm sorry, but the Open House isn't until this Saturday." She slipped a business card from her folio and pressed it into my hand. "Please come by then if you're interested. The owner is looking for a closing price between 1.8 and 1.9 million dollars." She tilted her head and looked at me like she knew there was no way I could afford that.

She wasn't wrong. Her card said her name was Fiona Parker.

I showed her Huang Leung's photo. "I hope you can help, Fiona. I'm Nick Harding, a private investigator. I'm looking for this man. I know he lives in this cul-de-sac somewhere. I tracked him into this street and didn't see him leave."

She handed the picture back. "He left. Do you have any identification?"

I looked around the interior of the empty house. "Here? He lived here?"

She crossed her arms. "Identification?"

I fished my wallet out and opened it to my Private Investigator's license. I removed my cap and fake mullet and rubbed my head while she examined my credentials. "I won't be needing this." I looked around for a trash bin.

She handed my wallet back. "You'll be taking that thing—that cap, with you. Yes, Mr Huang owns this house." She dipped her head and corrected herself. "His company owns it. He had everything packed up yesterday. It hits the market on the weekend. And no, he didn't leave a forwarding address. Why are you looking for him?" She gestured at the wigged cap. "And why the disguise? Those glasses are fake, too, right?"

I felt like an absolute tit. I'd forgotten I had them on. "Yeah. Dammit." I took them off and folded them. "Was the disguise any good?"

Her stern features finally cracked. "Oh, hell no. I hope you're a better detective than a disguise artist." She tipped her head again. "So you must have some kind of history, old history, with Leung if you're trying this kind of thing."

"What do you know about him?"

Fiona placed the folio on the counter. "Not a lot. Chinese, obviously. Owns this house and some warehouse properties. Why are you looking for him?"

"I used to be a member of the AFP. Financial crimes. I had tagged him for money laundering, and my colleagues linked the money and him to a massive drug importation operation. We tracked him for months and finally located him in one of his warehouses. One of the few times I got away from my desk. I went with them on the raid. We had the place surrounded. We knew he was in there with his son and half a dozen of his men. Didn't know how well-armed they were. I was there, but back in the surveillance van. The lead man—Curtis, a good friend—threw a flash-bang through a broken window, and the place went up like a bomb went off." I hadn't spoken this much about that day since then. "Curtis was obliterated. The guy behind him was out of commission for almost six months. We assumed Leung died in there, along with his son and crew. After weeks of clean-up, the case was closed. DNA found at the scene confirmed the deaths." I was on a tear. Pent-up frustrations, I think. I wiped the build-up of spittle from the corners of my mouth. "Then I saw him drive in front of me in a Fiat convertible."

She seemed a lot more interested now. "Not the most reliable car. But that's him, yeah. A little red one. He's gone now, and I really don't have any way of contacting him. Sorry."

I waved at the various parts of the house. "So, how's this supposed to work for you, then?"

"Shells companies. His solicitor signed a Power of Attorney for all matters related to the house sale to a solicitor we work with. There's a local account the money goes to after closing." She shrugged. "A dead end for you, I'm afraid."

This wasn't going to be as easy as I hoped it would be. But it never is, is it? "You can absolutely confirm you've met the man, though?"

She nodded. "When I first met him, he had some colleagues over to take pictures of the house."

"Not family? It's a large house."

"Not unless he adopted. A woman, middle-aged, well off with a Kiwi accent and a bogan type man, hard, 50s with a shaved head. Neck tatts, both sleeves. Looks like he could flip Leung's Fiat single-handed."

Interesting. "Give me a second, and I'll be out of your hair."

I stepped out of the kitchen and called Davie. "Mate, did you listen to me and go home?"

"What now?" I heard office noise behind him. Not at home. Good for me, not so good for him.

"There's a photo on my laptop. I was hoping you could pop over to my office and send it to me."

"You don't store your photos on the cloud?"

"Wasn't you who told me the cloud is just someone else's computer? No. Not on the cloud."

There was a longer pause from Davie than usual. No quick retort. No sarcasm. Then he sighed. "So, I'm going to tell you something that might piss you off. Don't be pissed off, though. It's going to help you."

I glanced at Fiona. She was waiting but checking her watch. "You change my settings? They're actually on the cloud now?"

"What?" Indignant Davie was a treat. "Hell no. You were unequivocal in your opposition to 'the cloud'." I could hear the sarcastic air quotes over the phone. "I, um, I set up remote access on your machine." He scrambled to make an excuse before I could say anything. "It's specifically for times like this. I can disable it once I get whatever photos you need."

"Nah, mate. It's all good. Show me how to access it from my phone tonight, but for now, can you get the screenshot of Leung with the bald guy in the shopping centre and email it to me?"

"So we're cool?"

"Very. Thanks. How long?"

"Mere seconds." He hung up, and ten seconds later, my phone chimed with an incoming email. I opened the picture and approached Fiona. "Thanks for waiting. Is this the bald guy?"

She took my phone and used her fingers to expand the picture. The best shot of Baldy was 3/4 face from the left. She considered for a minute, then nodded. "Yeah. Who is he?"

"Another piece of the puzzle. Thanks for your time." I started to turn away, then did a Columbo. "One more thing. If he contacts you again, could you let me know?" I handed her one of my freshly minted business cards. "And could you tell me if he calls from a local or international number?"

She frowned and slipped the card in her folio. "If it doesn't violate any privacy laws."

"Thanks. It's a beautiful house. It should sell quickly. Thanks for your time."

I left and handed my hat and fake glasses to Karen. "Can you dispose of these along with all the other trash?"

She looked at them, shook her head and handed them back. "No." She pointed to the red bin at the end of the drive. "You can put them in there yourself."

"Fair enough." I tossed them and got into the car. I put Davie on speaker and pointed my car toward the office.

He answered on the first ring. "You got it?"

"I did. Many thanks. I'm on my way back to the office to do some paperwork. You free tonight?"

"I can't. Work. It's my work, not your work. There's a cyber security conference coming up, and I need to have the first draft of my presentation ready for an internal review tomorrow. I shouldn't have left it so late."

"Where is it this year?"

"Here. Fucking Sydney. At the convention centre. I finally get a chance to present, and I don't get the enjoyment of expensed travel. It's bullshit."

"That it is. Not a problem. I need to do some more security camera facial recognition tracking. You've set me up well enough that I don't need your help."

"I'm hurt."

"As well you should be." I laughed. "Good luck with the presso, and I'll catch up with you tomorrow. And for god's sake, get some rest."

"Thank you, mate. Stay out of trouble."

"I always do." I hung up on his laughter and called Lucy.

"How are you, Nick? Any luck?"

"Not really. Found his house, but it's empty. He's moved on. It's for sale."

"Did you—"

"Yes."

"—wear a dis—what was it?"

"Cap with a fake mullet and fake Clark Kent glasses. Really naff."

"Oh, nice. You'll have to wear them for me."

That was a side of Lucy I hadn't seen before. "I binned them. Very uncomfortable." I rubbed my head. "The wig-slash-cap was very scratchy."

"That's too bad. What now?"

"I'm going to spend the evening tracking his progress from the house to whatever his next destination was. Want to join me?"

"Oh, as enthralling as that sounds, I think I'm going to have a quiet evening. You stay out of trouble."

"You sound just like Davie. How much trouble can a guy get into in front of a monitor, burning his retinas while looking for faces and cars on CCTV?"

She grunted a chuckle, if you know what I mean. "Knowing you? Lots. Give me a call tomorrow. We should have lunch again. There's another place I want to show you. I'll buy this time."

"You find the places, I'll pay. Have a nice, quiet night."

Her background noise increased. "Hey, I've got to run. It's Lara's birthday, and there's cake. Loveyoubye." And she hung up.

All that free cake and I was missing out. And I was on my own tonight.

At first.

Fourteen

I ended up working from the office. There was no point packing everything up, moving it to my apartment and setting it all up again—it was a waste of an hour. I ordered a pizza to be delivered to the office and started Davies' program.

Pizza and chilled water don't bring the same joy as pizza and beer, but it had to do.

Claude popped his head in, handed me the pizza that had just been dropped off at the front desk, made some noises about building security and left a slip of paper on my desk with the alarm code. Ravenhill stopped by on his way out and offered to buy me a beer at the nearby pub. Not a hope in hell I'd spend more time in his presence than I had to. I begged off, lots of work for an independent contractor, an always ready excuse.

Once the office traffic slowed, I took my laptop to one of the conference rooms and HDMI'd it to the large wall-mounted monitor. I set the parameters to find either the Fiat or Leung.

Since I had no idea which direction he headed when he left his house, I had to expand the search area greatly. That meant an expanded number of potential cameras to both find and search.

But I could assume he wasn't actively on the run. He wouldn't know that I knew he was in town. So he wouldn't feel the need to stay off the main roads.

So, I selected the main road out of the suburb. It travelled, generally, east-west. I selected properties a couple of kilometres in each direction and let the program run. Roughly half the cameras were accessible—better than I expected.

No faces were recognised, but three cameras heading west picked up a red Fiat. I extracted the video from those three cameras and put them up on the big screen. Froze them each in an attempt to catch the rego. No luck so far. The first three letters were 'JBE'. Unless it was a vanity plate, and I doubt a vanity plate would start like that, the next three characters would be two numbers and a fourth letter. Still no joy.

But he was heading west. That was something.

I extended the search ring another kilometre west, beyond an intersecting motorway. Not as many cameras were available. And I had a Schoedinger's Fiat situation. A camera southbound on the motorway, as well as a camera half a kilometre beyond the motorway, picked up the red Fiat. It couldn't be in both places at the same time.

I put both videos up on the monitor, side-by-side and scrubbed through them until the Fiats were clearly visible. The one on the motorway was directly from the back, facing south toward the city. The rego started with an EBZ.

Not Huang.

The Fiat westbound wasn't as identifiable. There was no clear shot of the driver and no rego, but it was all I had to go with.

"Mate, this is cool. What is it?"

Ravenhill. What a dick. Scared the shit out of me. I slowly turned in my seat. "John. You came back."

"Gotta grab my shit before I head home to the ball and chain."

Fucking hell. I closed my laptop, cutting off the feed to the wall monitor. "No rest for the sole proprietor." I disconnected the cable. Shit.

He grabbed one of the chairs in the conference room and sat across from me. He pointed at the monitor. "What was that? Looked cool. Chasing a bad guy?"

I sighed. I closed the top of the pizza box and slid my laptop under my arm as I stood. "Client confidentiality, John. I can no more talk about this case than you'd want me to talk to someone outside your organisation about whatever Harriet engages me for. Right?" I slid the pizza box across the table. "I've had enough. Take it home with you if you want."

He gathered the pizza box and followed me out. "Yeah, got it. Makes perfect sense. No worries. Catch you later."

He followed me to my office. I really didn't have time for this idiot. "Mate, go home to your wife. And kids, I assume?"

He groaned, shifted the pizza box and held my office door for me. "Two."

I slid my laptop into its case, added Porter's case file and pushed past him. I closed my office door and blocked his view while entering the code to lock it. "I'm gone. And if you keep following me, I'm going to have to ask you to buy me dinner first."

He chuckled, then stopped when he saw the look on my face.

I thought about the next steps on the way home. All I really needed was a good face-on picture of Leung. I'd hand it off to my AFP friends and wash my hands of it. I just had to find him.

My TV wasn't as large as the monitor at the office, but it would do. Tracking the car got progressively harder as the houses became more spread apart in the semi-rural areas northwest of the city, but by the process of elimination, I tracked Leung to a house in the Hills District, just outside of Arcadia. The house east of his destination had an active camera, as did the house to the west. His Fiat passed the house to the east, and didn't pass the house to the west.

Elementary.

It was close to 8:00 pm. I could leave it until tomorrow.

Or I could get it over with and start tomorrow fresh.

It would just a drive-by. I'd see the place, verify that the Fiat was present, pass some info on to my fed buddies and move on.

Easy, right?

No point bothering Davie. He had work. Or Lucy. She had things to work out.

It was a nice night. Dinnertime traffic had eased, and it was smooth travel up the motorway until I exited onto the main artery I'd tracked the Fiat to. GPS had me into SUV country in no time. Not the *I need an SUV to roam the outback culling roos* SUV. More the *I need an SUV to pick the kids up after they spend a day at their outrageously expensive private school* SUV.

The countryside was beautiful. Houses sat on large plots of land. Massive lawns. A waste of good arable land, if you ask me.

I approached from the west and rolled past the house where Leung had landed. The gate blocked a clear view of the house, which sat on about twenty-five hectares of land—not farmland, not an orchard, just seven hectares of lawn.

I would have to jack my day rate up if I ever wanted to afford a place like this. Maybe I should franchise.

I stopped about half a kilometre up the road, near the corner of the property. I opened a map app and tracked the property line. It was closer to 9:00 now. No moon. I got out of the car and leaned against it, looking up at the cloudless sky. Without city lights, the sky was amazing.

I turned to walk along the fence line and spotted the small camera in the tree across the road from the property. I continued walking, pretending not to notice. I didn't remember seeing that camera on Davie's tracking software. There had to be others.

And I'd be stupid to think they weren't infrared.

It was a slow walk along the road. I had no idea if I was being tracked, but not being a fast-moving target might keep me below their radar.

I was deluding myself. I was smoking hopium, hoping to be lucky.

The property was close to a perfect square. The house was offset from the centre. If the road in front of the house ran east/west along the property's south side, the house was closer to the southwest corner than the centre.

If there was a security room in the house, and if there were people monitoring the cameras in that security room, they'd expect people to sneak in from the back or north side of the property, right? It backed into the bush. If I were stupid, I'd come in that way.

I walked along the side of the road, facing traffic, just a normal guy, minding my own business. I affected a slight stumble, the local who had a few too many at the pub, being the responsible guy walking home.

I saw three more cameras facing the house. These guys were locked down.

I got to the southwest corner of the property—another camera. I fell into the shrubbery on the side of the road and pushed myself out on the other side. I kept close to the ground and crawled along the barbed wire fence line. I checked the ground as I crept. It didn't look like the ground had been turned any time in the past decade. I hoped there were no ground sensors, but I knew what these pricks did for a living. I wouldn't put it past them.

The west side of the house had a single window, which was probably the best way in. I reached for the barbed wire and stopped. The front door had opened.

Two guys stepped out with flashlights, their beams crisscrossing the space between them and me.

Son of a bitch.

I stepped backwards into the bush, timing my moves with their talking, hoping to mask the noise.

"You hear that?" The one on the left was shining his light to my right. "I heard something over there. You hear it?"

I turned my face away. Grabbed some dirt and rubbed it on my bald scalp.

"I didn't see him on the cameras. What did he look like?" The other guy was talking.

He sounded closer, and he also sounded huge. His voice was deep, and he had an Islander accent. I wasn't small, but he'd pull me apart like a croissant. I tried to burrow deeper with little success. I wasn't a wombat.

The fence creaked as someone, probably the big guy, leaned on the top wire. An animal north of me scurried through the bush. About a hundred metres north of me. My saviour, whatever animal it was.

"Up this way," exclaimed the Islander. The lights moved away from me. The holders of the lights moved with them. Cool.

They abandoned the search fifteen minutes later.

"The drunk kept walking, I guess. This security system pisses me off."

"Pays well, big guy."

"How long is the Chinese dude staying here?"

They were in the house before the Islander guy answered. Leung was in the house. That was all I needed to know. I waited a few more minutes before I dared move.

And then I moved extremely slowly.

I got this far, and leaving without proof didn't make sense. Leung was acting like he was leaving town. I had to get in.

I needed to get past the fence—the big guy leaned on it, so it wasn't electrified—then across a broad expanse of lawn and into the house.

I needed help. A lot of help.

I crawled further into the bush and got to the far side of a large eucalyptus. I took out my phone and dialled the brightness down to almost nothing, then called Davie, cupping my hand over my mouth.

"I just got home, mate, and I'm beat. I'm about to open a beer, watch an episode of Firefly, and then crash. I'm not going out."

"I don't want you to go out," I whispered. "But I do need your help."

"Why are you whispering?"

"Long-ish story. I'm outside the property where Leung disappeared. Out past Glenhaven. I think I'm technically in Arcadia. Big-arsed piece of land. Cameras all over the place. I almost got nabbed on the way in."

"Jesus, mate. Let it go. Get out of there."

"If I stand up, I'll be seen on one of the many cameras surrounding this place. I need you to get into the system. Take them out or find me a blind spot or something."

He sighed. "Where are you?"

"Flat on my back west of the property. About 20 metres west of the fence line. I'll drop you a pin." I took the phone away from my head and sent him my coordinates. "Get it?"

A bottle clunked on his desk, and I heard him tapping at his keyboard. "I got it. The cameras are going to be a bitch to get into. Why don't you keep crawling west for another fifty metres or so? You should be clear by then."

"Well, that kind of defeats the purpose of calling you, doesn't it?"

"How do you mean? I won't have to hack my way in and disable the cameras if you just head west, young man."

"You think I want you to help me *leave*?"

"Well, yeah." Davie sounded genuinely confused. Then the truth dawned on him. "No way."

"Yeah, way. Find me a way in."

Fifteen

"Are you fucking kidding me? Jesus." I don't think Davie's voice was this high since before he hit puberty.

I closed my eyes and leaned my head against the tree trunk, hoping whatever animal that distracted the muscle twins didn't come back around. I liked cities. You could see the lethal inhabitants of a city coming at you. "I don't like this any more than you do. Less, even. This guy is bad, mate. He can't get away again. Can you get in?"

"You in any kind of rush?"

I looked around at my surroundings. Are snakes nocturnal? Spiders? I'm not sure what else was out here. What if the Kenthurst Panther was real? "I mean, the sooner the better. I like cities. This is not a city."

"A side of you I've never seen before. Okay. I've found the place, IP address-wise. It's going to take me a couple of hours to get in and get enough information to be of any use to you. Have a nap. I'll buzz you when I'm in. Make sure your phone is on silent."

"Faster if you can, Davie."

"You want this right, or fast?"

"Buzz me when you're in. Thanks." I hung up and made sure the phone was flipped to silent.

Two hours. A hundred and twenty minutes. Seventy-two thousand seconds in the bush at night, no light, almost spitting distance from a man my fed friends thought was dead, who should be behind bars for the rest of his life.

Or dead. I really didn't care at this point. If I could call in an air strike on that house, I would.

You know those times you have insomnia the night before an important meeting, and you just can't get to sleep? Then you start feeling drowsy around 4 am, but you have to get up at 6, so you're afraid to fall asleep in case you oversleep and miss that career-changing meeting? That. It was well past my bedtime.

Despite the invisible threats of the best Australia has to offer in death critters, it was peaceful. Ninja-like. Death was sitting around me, no doubt, waiting. Lulling me into an extremely false sense of security before biting me on the neck.

I took a first aid course early in my career. Since I was part of the Federal Police, it was an extensive course. Three days of full-on training. On day two, a woman who looked like her opinion of cities mirrored my opinion of the bush came in to talk to us about snake and spider bites. Her advice was to lie down and have a nap if you were bit by any of Australia's venomous snakes or a funnel web spider. Movement helps push the venom into your system. Calmly call 0-0-0 for assistance and just lie there. And if you were any distance from your vehicle and out of mobile phone coverage, have a nap. If you woke up, you were fine. If you didn't, rest in peace.

I had mobile coverage. I'd be fine.

If Davie found me a way in electronically, it would be in my best interest to see if there were any non-electronic security systems I needed to watch out for. Did the muscle twins patrol regularly? Were there motion-detecting floodlights? Hungry dogs that wanted to dine on me?

I slowly stood and relieved myself against the base of the tree, hoping the smell didn't attract any visitors. It was worth the risk. There is nothing worse than attempting to sneak into a hostile house with a full bladder.

It took almost twenty minutes to reach the fence, moving as quietly as I could. I'm a big guy. Stealth is not my forte. I did as well as I could. No sign of new lights from the house. No sign of any lights. They seemed to be down for the night. And no muscle bursting out of the front door with flashlights attached under the barrel of a long gun.

The fence was the first hurdle. One of the meatheads had leaned on it. I heard the strand of wire strain against the staple that held it to the fence post. And if he leaned on it, he knew it wasn't hot. Unless it was switched off before they came out.

And then switched back on.

The voltage wouldn't be lethal. It couldn't be lethal. Dead animals would be stacked up below it, stinking the place up. It had to be strong enough to deter. It would be a hell of a jolt, but it wouldn't kill me.

Right?

I reached my hand out slowly toward the top strand. And *just* as I touched it, my phone buzzed in my pocket. I damned near shit myself. I pulled my hand and fell backwards, trying to escape the non-hot fence. I landed on my arse, making a hell of a lot more noise than I should have.

My heart rate topped out at over 140 bpm. It had to have.

I stayed on the ground, my phone vibrating in my pocket, eyes fixed on the house.

For a full minute, catching my breath.

The buzzing in my pocket stopped. Then, it started again.

Two minutes.

I eased the phone out of my pocket and my Bluetooth headphones from the other. Three missed calls from Davie.

And a text message. *Are you okay, mate? Wake up.*

I pushed one back. *I'm good. You find a way in?*

Can you talk?

I looked at the house. Still dark. I called.

"So you can talk?"

"I called. You got in already?"

"Super easy. Barely an inconvenience. They've got a static IP address, and the router isn't very secure. I'm walking around inside their system like I own the place."

I stood. "Are there any controls that you can see for the fence?"

"To open the gate, yes. Other than that, what are you talking about?"

"Is the fence electrified? Am I going to curl my hair if I touch it?"

Davie tapped on some keys before answering. "Not as far as I can see. But if it had manual control, I *wouldn't* be able to see it. It won't be lethal, though."

"You know where I am. I'll wait. YOU come and touch the fucking thing."

"Who would watch the cameras for you." Davie cleared his throat. "I've set it up so you should be able to walk right in the front door."

"Bullshit." I reached out and tapped the fence. No jolt. I touched it again and held it. "The fence is cold. I could go through the fence here. This side of the house is almost blind. Only one window. I could pick the lock on the back door and sneak in."

"Yeah, nah mate. There are sensors under the lawn. Based on the designators, they're on the west, north and east sides of the house. None along the driveway, obviously, because the vehicles would be triggering them continuously."

"You're smarter than you look, Davie."

"Flattery will get you everywhere. Want to hear the plan?"

I smiled and backed away from the fence. "Give it to me," I whispered.

"I've already looped all of the external cameras. Fifteen or twenty minutes each. They're blind. I can't disable the sensors, but I have control of the front gate. Get around there and let me know when, and I'll open it wide enough for you to get through."

I was already walking, heading to the road in front of the house. "Then what? I ring the doorbell and introduce myself as a Brother from the Latter Day Saints?"

Davie chuckled. "Normally, I'd suggest you pick the lock, as you do, but this one is electronic."

"And?"

"I can open it."

"Is there an alarm in the house?"

"Front and back door, all of the ground floor windows." He paused. "They're very concerned about unwanted visitors. Are you really sure you want to do this?"

"The alarm system kinda puts a dent in my efforts."

"Oh, it's off."

I slowly let out my breath. I was at the corner post on the road. A couple of hundred metres east of me was the gate. "Any interior cameras?"

"I counted seven."

"They're looped, too?"

"Not a good idea. If anyone was watching they'd find it strange if the screens weren't reflecting real-time info that they knew was happening. But there are plenty of blind spots. I can walk you through the house."

I checked the time. Coming up on 11. "You up for this?"

"You'll do it whether I help or not, and you can't do it without me. Lucy knows you're out doing this?"

I chuckled. "No. And you're not going to tell her." The fencing along the roadside of the property was vertical tongue and groove planking, about 2 metres tall. The cameras could see me, but they were out of service. "You stay on the line through all of this, okay? I'm coming up to the front gate. I hope to hell they keep it maintained."

"I'll leave it a bit open so you can fuck off back to your car if you have to."

"Make it so they can't open it all the way and chase me with a car, okay?"

"Piece of piss, mate. You there yet?"

The gate was designed to roll sideways along a track across the driveway. It was as tall as the fence walls bracketing it. "Crack it open."

A low-pitched whine preceded quiet rumbling, and the gate opened half a metre and stopped. "Come on, mate. I'm thicker than that."

"Krispy Kreme is an addiction." The gate rolled a little bit more along the track in the ground. "That good?"

"You're sure they're blind?"

"There's one guy awake in that house, and he's sitting in front of the monitors. I have no idea why there's a camera in there. Seems a bit redundant. All of his screens showing the outside of the house are looped on nothing. The rest of the house is dark. So he's sitting in the security office looking at a screen at the back of his head."

I chuckled and squeezed through the gate. The thick slabs of timber were bolted to an iron frame. It looked like it was built for a castle. It would stop a tank. Even if you could get the right angle of attack on it, there wasn't a vehicle in Australia that could smash it down.

I walked up the middle of the driveway. My thought was any underground sensors, however far away Davie thought they were, would be further away from the middle.

And floodlights, if they came on, would be trained on my bald head. Nothing is perfect.

Trust the process. "Keep the line open, mate," I whispered. "And disable the gate if you can."

"The line is open, and the gate is a useless slab of wood."

"A thick, useless slab of wood." A slight curve in the driveway ended near the side of the house. A concrete step led up to a broad porch area. A keypad on the door replaced a key lock. Its little light was red.

And there was a doorbell camera. The ring light around the camera illuminated as I stepped to the door. Shit. "You got the doorbell camera on your list?"

"What? Shit. All those cameras, and they've got a doorbell camera? Sorry, mate. Get the hell out of there. It's not on their security inventory. Take off."

"It's okay. Get me through the door."

"What?

"Now."

The red light on the keypad turned green, and I pushed the door open.

"The security room is immediately to your right. Tread lightly."

As I walked down the hallway, sticking close to the walls to avoid creaky flooring, I realised I was being a bigger idiot than I usually was. What was I supposed to do? I had an itch. I needed to scratch it.

Somebody stirred upstairs.

"You wouldn't happen to have the house layout, would you?"

"How do you think I knew where the security room was?" asked Davie. "From a fairly recent real estate listing."

"Find me a hiding place. Quickly."

"Walk-in pantry off the kitchen. At the back of the house. What's going on?"

More noise from upstairs. I double-stepped into the kitchen, blocking most of the light from my phone with my hand, and found the pantry.

"Nick? You still there?"

I eased the pantry door shut. It was cramped. "People are moving. Someone noticed the doorbell camera. Don't fucking beat yourself up about it. Why in the hell would they have a doorbell camera when the place is wired for sound?"

"You're safe?"

"I'm in the pantry. Thanks." I looked around. "They buy the same food we ordinary people do."

"What's happening?"

I listened at the door. "I think the whole house is lit up now. I'm going to burrow in the back of this hide-hole until it all blows over. Can you—" beep-beep-beep.

I looked at my phone. Instead of the carrier name on the top corner, it said 'SOS'. They had turned on a mobile phone jammer.

The SOS might come in handy at some point, but I was on my own now.

Sixteen

I switched my phone to aeroplane mode. The last thing I wanted was for them to turn off the jammer and for a flood of incoming messages alerting the occupants to my presence.

"What's going on?" The kitchen must be the gathering place. And that was Leung's voice. I'd bet my life on it. I might actually have.

"Something triggered the front doorbell." Strong Australian accent. It was probably the bald guy Leung was with. "Security is checking how someone got past them and made it to the door. Whoever it was, they're on the grounds somewhere. My lads will find him, and we'll have a chat in the stables. You're safe here."

"If they're outside, I'm safe anywhere in this house, even in my bed, no?" Leung's voice receded as he walked out of the kitchen. "I'm tired. You still have a couple of operations to show me, and we have an early start in the morning."

I heard his lighter steps disappear up the stairs and the heavier steps of his local contact head toward the front door. I listened for what seemed like an eternity. No more noise coming from the kitchen. No cutlery clattering, no kettle boiling, no chairs scraping across the floor. I was alone in the kitchen unless someone was waiting for me outside the pantry door. And these guys don't seem the subtle type. They would have dragged me out long ago if they thought I was in the pantry.

I reached for the pantry door to ease it open and stopped. I heard footsteps enter the kitchen. Someone entered, speaking in a low voice.

"No. Not yet. Almost."

I strained to hear the voice.

"I know, I know. Look, I can't go any faster. Kai'll figure something's up. Be patient."

I didn't recognise the voice. Deep and gravelly, like he lived on a diet of whiskey and cigars.

"Okay, sorry, patience isn't your strong suit. I'll call you in the morning. You really shouldn't call me. You never know when he's around. Yes, I will definitely call you." The voice receded as he left the privacy of the kitchen. "I know. It's a good idea. Tell him to ask for me when he goes back. No. Dom. Not Dominic. Some of the idiots around here don't know that name." The footsteps disappeared to nothing.

I eased the door open and peered into the kitchen. It was empty. I checked that my phone was still on silent and took it out of aeroplane mode. I waited for the phone to search for a network. No joy. Still 'SOS'.

I spotted the camera in the top corner opposite the kitchen doorway while I was looking for a decent weapon. Jesus. Davie didn't disable the interior cameras. I was fucked.

Except there was no outcry. No thudding boots running down the hall from the security room to the kitchen. None that I could hear. My heart could be drowning everything out. It was throbbing in my ears.

But Davie could see me.

I scanned the kitchen again. Big gas stove. Double-wide fridge with a notepad for groceries. There was a marker tied to it with a piece of hemp. I ripped the list of basic groceries off the top of the pad and wrote a message. It took three sheets of paper. It was a small pad. I faced the camera in the corner and held up the papers:

Davie, cell blocker

Need a

Distraction

I repeated the actions twice. The red light on the camera blinked three times. My man in the chair. I ducked back into the pantry in case shit got busy in the kitchen before Davie got his job done. I didn't have to wait long.

A siren blared from the security room. Heavy boots ran down the hall from the back of the house to the front. After a short pause, I heard the guy who had leaned on the fence yell. "Looks like three or four people coming in from the northwest. All hands."

Doors opened upstairs, and more heavy feet joined him. I assumed Leung would have stayed in his room.

I waited until the herd of muscle was well gone before peeking out of the pantry and into the kitchen.

Still empty.

I slowly closed the kitchen door behind me and was heading for the front of the house when I heard the stairs creak. I stepped into a side room and hid in the shadows. Leung walked by. Motherfucking Leung, Clear as day, no doubt, right in front of my eyes.

He poked his head into the security office, saw nobody was there, and then padded into the kitchen.

I stepped into the security office, scribbled a note on a piece of paper, and held it up to the camera.

Get a good face shot of the guy who was just in here and send it to my phone. Ta

I pulled the sheet off the pad, gave the camera a thumbs up and went out the front door.

Houses with double-brick walls block a lot of outside noise. Once I was on the drive, I could hear the ruckus in the back of the property. I turned and watched for a minute. Torch beams crisscrossed in the distance. Loud, angry yelling was getting louder and angrier—it was time to get the hell out.

I trotted down the long driveway to the gate and squeezed through. I could feel my heart rate and blood pressure stabilise.

The cell blocker range didn't extend much beyond the gate. My car was about a kilometre east of the gate—an easy walk on a moonless night. My phone vibrated with an incoming message when I was fifty metres from the gate.

It was a clear, clean, full-face picture of Leung. I called Davie.

"You made it out."

I chuckled and kept my voice low. "Thanks to you. What did you do?"

"I triggered a dozen underground sensors. Staggered them, so it looked like an army was coming in." He laughed. "I watched them scramble out of the house like a pack of dingos."

"Thanks for the picture."

"Not a problem. Look, you're clear, right?"

I looked around. A Tawny Frog-Mouth called from a nearby pine tree. Something rustled through the undergrowth. "Yeah." I looked at my watch. Close to midnight. "I'll call you tomorrow, okay? Thanks again for the help."

"Call me when you need a man in a chair. Just not before morning coffee."

He hung up, and I stowed my phone. It was a moonless night, but my eyes had adjusted to the dark. The noise from the crack security team had faded in the distance. It was cool, but the brisk walk kept me warm. I was tired but exhilarated. I found my guy. I'd call Johnson. Or Jackson, since he seemed more accommodating.

First thing in the morning.

Hell, I'd show up to their office. Shove it in their faces. Make them take me seriously and start another fucking task force.

Yeah.

By then, the exhilaration had worn off. I was getting tired—really tired. The adrenaline that kept me alert had abandoned me with every step I took.

I had to be getting closer to my car. It was dark red, the sky was moonless, and while that brought out the stars, it effectively made my car invisible.

I turned on the torch on my phone. In hindsight, a dumb idea. The light really compromised my night vision. It also reflected off my tail lights about a hundred metres in front of me. My car's tail lights. Not mine. I don't have tail lights.

Fuck I was tired.

My luck, I'd fall asleep during the hour's drive home. I inhaled a deep breath through my nose and let it out slowly.

Do you ever feel that you're being followed? It's nothing definite, just a feeling between your shoulder blades that something or someone is behind you, like an itch you just can't reach.

I turned to look over my shoulder a couple of times, but I didn't want to shine my torch back from where I came. Perhaps I should have.

More than just my taillights were reflecting my torch when I heard the footsteps behind me. I didn't look back. I ran. We talked about how much I hate running, right? It wasn't more than a hundred metres. I dug my keys out as I ran, the footsteps getting closer. I repeatedly hit the fob button until the park lights flashed orange twice.

As I reached for the car door, a hand grabbed my shoulder and spun me against my car. My phone spun out of my hand and landed screen down, the torch shining up and illuminating the bald head sitting on the tattooed neck of the man who had met with Leung.

"How the fuck did you manage to take out our security system?"

My chest was heaving. He plucked the keys from my hand and picked my phone up.

"We heading back to your place?"

He shone my torch in my face. "No. We're going to the fucking Sydney Opera House. What the fuck do you think?"

I squinted and nodded at my car. "Could we drive? I'm fucked. I sit behind a desk all day. And I don't really know what you're talking about, a security system. I was just walking down the road. Thought I saw a Tawny Frog Mouth and wanted to get some night photos."

"Horse shit. You were in the house. We got control of the system back. Your face is all over the footage. I saw the message you sent to someone about the distraction. Too clever by half."

Hard to argue against that. "I didn't take anything."

"You get the picture you wanted?"

He saw everything. I grabbed my phone from him, yelled, "Siri, Nox," and threw it into the bush. The torch turned off as it flew through the air.

He smacked me on the back of the head. "Now you don't have it either, moron. And I already know what he looks like."

Not my smartest move. We walked in silence for a few minutes. He had me by the arm, a large hand gripping me just above the elbow. It didn't hurt now, but a slight squeeze and I'd be in crippling pain.

"What are you planning on doing to me?"

He chuckled. "The anticipation is the best part. Step it up."

"Stables, right?"

He looked at me. "You heard that?"

I didn't answer. We reached the gate. It was closed. They had gained control.

He tapped a code in the keypad, and the gate trundled open. He pushed me through, held my arm, tapped the code on the inside, and closed it.

I pulled against his grip, and he squeezed. Just a bit, but enough for me to take notice. "Okay. I get it. What's your name? I like to know who's abusing me."

"You don't need to know that."

"You're the big boss. Saw you and Leung and Dom together at Bondi Junction." I was guessing the other guy was Dom. "And I *know* Leung is at the top of the pecking order."

We were walking up the drive at this point. The exterior floodlights were on. He stopped walking. "Now, why in the hell were you in Bondi Junction at the same time we were? Why were you looking for me?"

I shrugged. "Why would you assume I was looking for you?"

"Leung's been so deep in the shadows, so far underground, the mole people look down at him. As far as the world is concerned, he's dead. Been dead for years. Dom is a friendly greengrocer. Nobody would be looking at him."

I nodded. "Surprised me when I saw Leung. I thought I watched him blow up. Killed one of my close friends when he blew up." I cocked my head and looked at him. "Or didn't blow up. The Chinese government knows he's alive."

"You thought he was dead, too. So why were you looking for me?"

I shook my head. "Vanity doesn't look good on you. I had never seen you before I saw you talking to Leung. But enough about me. Tell me about yourself."

"Fuck off, mate, and keep walking. Around the right side of the house.

We were halfway up the drive. I was maybe seventy metres from the stables. There was no way I could run. It wasn't just him. His meatheads would be around somewhere. They'd devour me like rabid dogs.

And my legs were wrecked.

He stopped again. "I'm confused."

"I'm not surprised."

"Watch it, arsehole. Why were you looking for him if you thought Leung was dead?"

"Incidental contact. I was looking for someone else. I'm a PI. I was hired to find a kid who had run away. Turned out he fucked off and joined the circus. So cliche. Little shit. I was looking for him—look, it's a fucking long story, and I'm tired. So, what's your relationship with Leung? Seemed pretty chummy at the mall, and from what I overheard in your house, he's your boss."

"Who's the kid?"

"Client confidentiality prevents me from revealing that information." I smiled at him for the two seconds it took him to move his hand from my arm to my throat.

"Who. Is. The. Kid?"

I grabbed his wrist with both hands, and no amount of pulling would dislodge his hand. I sputtered as my vision blurred.

He loosened his hand a bit and pulled me closer. "Well?"

My hands were still grabbing his wrist. "Okay, okay. Some spoiled little shit named Lachlan Porter. Rich kid. His mother hired me. Why the fuck do you care?"

He pushed me away as he let go. "That was you? Jesus, what a small world." He grabbed me by the arm again, a more preferable part of my anatomy to squeeze than my throat, I guess. "You're Nick, the shit my bitch ex-wife hired to find my son. What a small fucking world." He chuckled. "Step up your pace, mate. We are going to have so much fun in the stables."

Seventeen

It was like these guys watched too many bad movies. A wooden chair sat in the middle of the central walkway down the middle of the stable, with four stalls on either side. A string of lights ran down the middle, providing bright illumination in the middle and dark shadows in the stalls.

No horses. What a bunch of fakers. It wasn't even a decent-sized stable.

Lachlan's dad shoved me toward the chair. "Have a seat."

"Are you going to tell me your name, Baldy, or do I have to keep calling you Lachie's pops?"

He shoved me again. One of his muscles stood behind the chair and patted the back of it. "Boss says sit."

"Boss have a name?"

Muscles grabbed me by the shoulders and folded me into the chair.

"What about you? Do you have a name?" His buddies held me down. Held me like my limbs were in a vice while I was cable-wrapped to the chair's arms and legs. I tested them, of course. No dice. I was strapped in for the ride.

Main muscle, whose name I still didn't know, grabbed me by the back of the neck. "You want us to loosen him up a bit, Baz?"

'Baz' glared at him.

"Bazza, Barry, how are you? Cute stables you've got here. Maybe someday you can afford real ones. And maybe some horses. You know, they say the two happiest days of a horse owner's life are the day they buy them and the day they sell them. Why are we in here, anyway? You already know everything you need to know about me."

"You ruined my night. And my guest's night. I have nerves I need to settle, and the best way I have to settle nerves is to beat the crap out of somebody."

I raised my eyebrows and cocked my head. "I find sex works."

He chuckled and pointed at the big guy behind me. "I'm not sure if Marco is up for that."

I twisted in the chair. "Marco, your mum fed you really well. Is this the best job you could get? Have you ever thought about rugby?"

"Knees." He smacked me on the head. "Face front."

The more you know.

I smiled at Barry. "So, how in the *hell* did you manage to get close enough to someone as fine as Lyla to produce a kid?"

A half smile flitted across his face. "That was years ago and none of your fucking business, Nicky."

"She's way too fine for the likes of you. A bit of vitamin K in the wine and had your way with her?"

Baz walked slowly toward me. He picked up a cricket bat leaning against one of the stalls and poked me in the chest with it. "You surprise me. You're in a no-win situation. I could take you apart all by myself, and I've got Marco and three of his friends here to help me. You're outnumbered five-to-one mathematically and at least ten-to-one physically." He jabbed me again. "I'm on a huge plot of land that backs on a National Park. I could scatter parts of you over hectares of land. Hectares. Nobody would ever find you."

"My friends know where I am. I didn't break into your security system. My colleagues did that." I looked around the stables. "If there's a camera in here, he'll record this. There's no way in hell you get away with it."

Barry leaned on the bat like it was a cane. "Is that so?" He looked past me and above my left shoulder. I bounced the chair around in small hops until I saw what he was looking at. A little camera. I smiled and nodded at it. "Say hi. You're going to let me go."

"He's locked out. My security guy locked him out."

"Did he, though?" I smiled up at him. Marco's hand squeezed a bit harder. He grabbed my shoulder when I attempted to twist away.

"My guy is good."

"My—team is better." Let him think I've got an army behind me.

"Your team? You're a one-man operation."

"You wouldn't believe my team." I shuffled my chair around so I was directly facing the camera. "If you can read my lips, mate, let these people know."

Marco spun my chair back around to face his boss. Bazza tapped one of the chair legs with the cricket bat. "Do I break your hands or your feet first?"

"I'm not sure. How's your technique? Practice on Marco—one of his hands. Wait, no. Not his hands. Go for the nose."

Marco slapped me on the head again. It was starting to hurt. He had hams for fists. I ducked down. "Okay. You've won me over. The hand. That one first."

"I'm not hitting Marco. And your alleged team has no access to my systems." He grabbed a stool and sat across from me. "So we're going to talk, and when I'm finished with you, Marco will find a place to dig. If you're lucky, he'll kill you before he buries you."

"There's nothing to talk about, Baz. I was looking for your son and ran into a guy I thought was dead, and that led me here. I don't care what you do here. I don't care what your business is." I tugged my arms against the cable ties. "So just snip these and let me go on my way."

"We'll bury the chair with you. Why did you decide to look for Leung?"

I sat back in the chair. I closed my eyes and tilted my head back. "I'm exhausted, mate. Here I was, worried about falling asleep at the wheel on the drive home and killing myself. I guess you'll save me the trouble." I sighed and tipped my head forward. I opened my eyes and yawned. "So whatever you're going to do, get on with it."

"You've got to answer the questions, champ. Why is Leung such a big deal for you?"

"Do you work for him, or does he work for you?" I shook my head. "No, he doesn't work for you. You're his local lackey." I laughed. "I'm going to get you a T-shirt that says 'Local Lackey'. What size are you? XL? 2XL?"

He slammed the end of the bat down on my left foot. "Why are you so interested in him?"'

"SON OF A BITCH." I tried curling my toes up in my shoe. "Why do people think hurting people makes them more likely to talk? I just want to spit in your face. Head butt you. Definitely not talk to you. Not answer your questions."

He held the stick above my foot again. "Maybe second time lucky."

I looked at him, then down at my foot. "The more you hit, the less I talk. And my team is recording everything you do."

He glanced at the camera again and chuckled. "The fuck he is." He tapped me gently on the same set of toes. They tried to retreat, but my shoes were too tight. "Why Leung?"

"Fine. I used to work at the AFP. Financial crimes. Did you know that?" I cleared my throat. I was attached to my toes despite how tough I tried to be. "I was a desk guy. I tracked Leung down. I had flags on his accounts. Knew all of his activities. He didn't have a clue. We knew the money he was pulling in from his drug activities and how he was cleaning it. Showed incredible restraint, not pulling the lower echelon dweebs like you so that we could grab the kingpin."

"You're boring me. That was years ago."

"Ah, so you heard about this?"

"His whole operation blew up. Of course, I heard about it. My grandmother heard about it. The Pope probably heard about it."

"The front of the AFP attack team was wiped out in the blast—a very good friend of mine. We were probationary constables together. Nothing left to bury but his feet. Small consolation that Leung and his more senior minions went with him." I took a deep breath. "Then I see the little shit driving in front of me in a pissy-arsed red Fiat convertible. And now I'm here. Trying to nail him down." I cocked my head and looked at Barry. "Tell me something."

"Why?"

"I'm curious. What do the Chinese characters tattooed on your throat say?"

He stood and kicked the stool to the side. "Enough shite outta ya. Marco, hold him while I crack some of his ribs." He swung the bat back like he was going for six, and his, Marco's, and the three Marco minions' phones started going off. He leaned the cricket bat against his leg and dug out his phone.

"Marco's minions. Gonna make you guys some T-shirts with 'I'm Marco's Minion' plastered on it."

"Maybe I just hold you hostage, and your 'team'," he used finger quotes, "gets you back when they pay up." He looked at the message.

"What do you think you could get for me?"

Barry shook his head. "Not more than a couple hundred dollars, I expect." He held his phone up and showed Marco the message.

"Bullshit, mate. I just got business insurance. You should be able to get half a mill, easy."

Barry leaned the cricket bat against the stall while he read the message on his phone. "Someone is coming in from the northeast this time. Bullshit like the last time?"

"Could be fake," I agreed. "My guys fucking with your guys again." I raised my eyebrows and awkwardly held up an index finger from the chair's wood arm. "No, you've kicked my guys out of your system, right? So it must be real. My guys have found me. Wow. You're in shit now." I was hoping it was Davie with another electronic diversion. That was the only option that would work for me.

"You stay here, Marco, and keep an eye on him. The rest of you come with me. If it is his friends, we'll bring them back here."

I sure as shit hoped Davie wasn't dumb enough to attempt a rescue in person.

A few minutes after the crowd cleared, Marco righted the stool and sat before me. "He'll kill your friend. I'm surprised you're still alive, to be honest."

I tried nodding at the camera behind me. Not easy when you're tied to a chair. "I think he's afraid my guy might actually be in the system, watching and recording." I smiled at Marco. "Smile. You want a decent shot for court, right?"

He glanced up at the camera, and a worried look flitted across his face. He exhaled a puff of air. "Hell no."

I leaned my head down and whispered. "Don't bet against my buddy, shit for brains."

"What?"

I said it even quieter. He wasn't hired for his smarts. I mean, this trick works in every bad movie I've ever seen. He stood and leaned over me.

"What the hell did you say?"

He was in almost the perfect position. Almost. It would have to do. I lunged forward, rolling to my right as I did, the wooden chair still strapped to my back. I was lucky I took him by surprise. I knocked him over and continued my roll, hitting the ground with the corner of the chair.

It cracked but didn't break, and the wind was knocked out of me. Marco was dazed. His head hit the floor when he fell backward. I had a couple of seconds at most.

I wobbled to my feet, chair high up on my back and jumped in the air, falling with my back and the chair on Marco's chest.

It broke. The chair and a couple of Marco's ribs. I pulled the cable ties off my wrists and found the cricket bat. I was breathing hard, my shirt was torn, and there was blood on my wrists from the cable ties cutting into them when I fell. But I was upright.

"The knees, hey?" Marco looked up at me, dazed, pink foam bubbling out of his mouth. I might have punctured a lung. I tapped him on his left knee with the edge of the bat. "Modern medicine can produce miracles, mate. You'll be good as new in six months. Maybe a year."

I wound up like Bazza had and took out every ligament in that knee. He'd be on crutches for months.

I looked at the camera. "You better delete that one, Davie."

The stable door faced south. They were distracted in the northeast. So I made for the drive and the gate as fast as my out-of-shape legs could carry me. The gate was partially open again. Too good to be true. I slowed and got on my stomach and peered out at ground level. I looked in both directions. It looked clear. So far, so good.

I was out, but I had no phone, and Bazza had the keys to my car.

And Davie had Leung's picture.

I walked back toward my car. I was heading east at this point, and my phone was in the bush to my right, across the road.

Somewhere.

It would be a long walk back if I didn't find it.

The noise on the other side of the fence started getting louder. Much louder. They probably found a horizontal Marco, all by himself, and no little old me.

My heart rate increased with my pace. On the upside, the adrenaline would keep me awake.

Eighteen

I did something to my back when I landed on Marco.
Turning my torso to the left hurt like I was getting stabbed.

So, I wouldn't turn it that way. Bruises, I hoped.
Nothing actually broken.

I really hoped.

I crossed the road and walked along the tree line, under any cameras planted in the branches. I walked slowly, favouring my back and attempting stealth.

I saw the first camera when I was about three metres from it. I went a little deeper into the bush and approached it from the back. Take it down or disable it? Pros and cons for both. If I took it down, they'd notice it moving (if they paid attention), but I would have another camera to add to my inventory. If I disabled it, they might not notice.

I reached up and hit the power switch.

Which made me think about how they set these up. Someone had to replace batteries on a regular basis. Maybe rechargeable? My doorbell camera lasted three to four weeks with regular traffic. Maybe they just swapped them out.

The noise on the other side of the fence was getting louder. I couldn't see exactly what was happening, but arcs of torchlights passed over trees on the east side, then nothing. Then banging on the gate and a voice that sounded like Gazza's yelling, "Open the fucking gate, you muppet!"

Yay, Davie.

There was a slight track behind the trees, no doubt worn by whoever's job it was to swap out cameras. Or batteries. I picked up the pace. They'd open the gate soon enough, and I wanted to be in my car and halfway home by then.

Three more cameras disabled, and I could see the faint glint of light off my car through the trees. Home free.

I instinctively reached for my keys in my pocket, then remembered. Bazza still had my keys. Maybe I could figure out how to hot-wire it.

Or not. A shadow passed between me and the car. How in the hell did they get ahead of me? Did they have sentries outside the wall? Shit.

I instinctively crouched. I was too tired for this crap. I was in no shape for another fight. He'd get bored by daylight. I settled down for the wait.

There was no moon, so I couldn't see any of the shadow's details as he paced around my car. He didn't look that formidable. Large, but not hard.

Maybe.

There was some kind of animal near me in the bush. Making some kind of vibrating noise. Something like I thought a rattlesnake might sound like, but they don't live in this country.

It must have been the exhaustion.

The vibrating came and went twice before it dawned on me. I was blind, but I wasn't deaf. I scrambled through the leaves—quiet scrambling—until I found it. Face down. I flipped my phone over, shielding the screen. Three missed calls from Davie.

I turned my back to the road and returned his call, whispering. "Mate, thanks for all the help."

"No problem." He was whispering back. "Where the hell are you?"

"Hiding. Why are you whispering?" It dawned on me as I asked the question. I stood and turned toward the car. "Did you bring a spare set of keys with you?" Davie's face was illuminated by his phone's screen. He held it in front of him while he talked. "And there's no point in whispering if you're shining your phone in your face."

I stepped out of the bush and onto the road.

Davie hurriedly stuffed his phone in his pocket. "Mate, you okay?" Then he took the phone back out of his pocket and used the screen's light on my face. "You got smacked around."

I pushed the phone away from my face. "Pack that away, Davie. They weren't finished with me." I opened my car door and turned off the dome light. "Please, tell me you brought my spare set of keys." I got in my car and held my hand out the door.

"Even if I knew where to look, how would I know you needed them? No. No spare keys."

Shit. Tired as fuck. Sore in more places I knew I had. "No worries, mate. Drive me back to my place."

"And we'll pick up the keys and come back." He angled toward the bush. "Hang on a sec. I'm busting." I heard him unzip and spray the base of the tree.

I groaned. "Hurry up. I am so fucking tired I can taste the colour seven. Where's your car?" I pulled myself out of mine and gently closed the door. "We really need to get out of here. They'll get that gate open soon enough."

Davie chuckled. "They'll need a wrench or two." He nodded a bit up the road. "I'm here." He thumbed his key fob, and the car unlocked. He got behind the wheel and picked his iPad off the passenger seat. "Get in." He started tapping on the screen.

I crawled into the passenger seat and reclined it. "How'd you do it?"

"Lock up their system? Their IT guy is a newbie. Has to be. Trivial firewall rules. I twisted him up so badly that he'll qualify for Cirque du Soleil before he sorts it out. Shit."

I looked up from my seat. "What?"

"They got the wrenches out. Nice work on the cameras, by the way"

He started the car. I was asleep before he pulled away from the side of the road.

"—or yours?"

I rubbed my eyes, yawned and raised the seat back up. "What was that?"

"My place or yours?"

"The keys are at my place." I looked around. "Where are we?"

"About mid-way between our places."

"The keys are at my place."

"No, mate, you're not going back to your car right now. It's 4 am. You're exhausted, and they will be through the gate by now, wondering about whether they should burn your car or just roll it into the ditch. On its roof."

I scratched the back of my head. "How about this? We stop by my place and get the keys, then head to yours, flash up those big new monitors you've got, and watch some video. I want to see what happened after I left." I wasn't being fair to my friend. He was probably as tired as I was, and I had the benefit of just having a short nap. But I had to check something.

"I'm going to need a couple of hours before I go to the office. I'm going to have to kick you out after a few minutes."

"Understood. Keep the car running. I'll be one sec." I was a bit longer than that. I'd seized up after sitting in the car for almost an hour. My back was killing me. My left knee felt like it was thirty years older than the rest of my body. And my head throbbed.

I had a spare key hidden for circumstances just like this. Or something like this. It's not like I hid a key in case I was taken by a crowd of massive jerks who wanted to bury me in the back half of their property. Just something *like* that.

I fished the key out of the flower pot on the front step and staggered into my apartment.

I caught a look at myself in the bathroom mirror. I looked like shit. Probably smelled like shit. The PI's life is glamorous. I grabbed an apple and my spare car keys and limped back down the stairs to Davie's waiting car.

His head was back on his headrest with his eyes closed. "Want me to drive?"

He angled his head to the left and opened his eyes. "You don't get to drive my car. I've seen what you do to cars." He sat up and moved the shift lever to Drive. "I'm kicking you out after you see whatever it is you want to see."

"Fair call. Let's go." I pointed at a 24-hour fast food place ahead. "Stop in there and grab a couple of coffee."

"Drive-through coffee? You're desperate."

"I don't want you falling asleep behind the wheel. It's more for you than me." I rolled down my window. A cool winter breeze cut through the brain fog. "Long black for me."

"Deal."

It tasted crappy, but it had caffeine in it. I wasn't a coffee snob. I know some people who treat coffee like vintage wines. Jesus. As long as it isn't burnt beyond recognition, who actually cares?

"Are you going to tell me what's going on?" Davie had rolled his window down, too. We had to talk above the wind.

"You saw most of it, didn't you?"

"Eh. I figured you were out for good, then the next thing I know, you're being marched in the front gate by a big unit with neck tatts."

"Yeah, that was embarrassing.

"He's really the kid's dad?"

I nodded. Coincidences don't happen in real life. "I think I got caught in the middle of a custody dispute. And she knew where the brat went." I shook my head. "Hate being used."

"So you're done?"

I looked at him. He seemed worried. And looked like shit. "Yeah. I'm done." I held up my phone. "You sent a good picture of Leung. I just need to get into the archive video for a sec to check something out."

He nodded, but didn't reply. He's smart, Davie. I don't think he believed me then.

We rolled up to his apartment at 4:30.

Davie looked at me before he opened his car door. "Tiptoe, okay? I don't want the neighbours pissed off at me again."

"Quiet as a mouse. And I'll be out in fifteen."

He looked at me like I was special. "You going to walk back to your car?"

I pushed myself out of his car. "Too tired. I could Uber."

"Two hundred bucks later. What specifically are you looking for?"

I followed him into his apartment. "The size of the team they've got, and a better picture of Baldy."

Davie fired up his system. "Why?" He headed back to the loo and closed the door halfway. I had to talk over his pissing.

"Baldy?" I didn't know. Gut feel. There was something bigger here. I shrugged. "Could be nothing."

The sink ran and he exited wiping his damp hands on his trousers. "It's never nothing. Don't get yourself killed."

"Killed? Looking at video feeds?" I checked his hands. "They're wet because you washed them, right? Right?"

Davie barked a laugh. "Believe what you want." He sat at his desk and clicked open a window. A satellite image of the house I'd been held in filled his screen. He had mapped the estimated location of the ground sensors, the cameras along the road outside the property, and the cameras surrounding the perimeter. They were all greyed out.

"Did you store the footage?"

Davie tapped a couple of keys. "No. Didn't see the need for it. Their system archives for a few weeks. I'll get back in and download everything, and then we go get your car. We can—sorry—you can trawl through it later." A login screen popped up on his monitor. His fingers flew across the keyboard, and the popup shook when he hit enter.

"What was that?"

"Huh. They've regained access to their systems. Their guy might be a bit better than I gave him credit for." He opened a terminal window and typed in an IP address. Everything after that was Greek to me. "Almost there."

A window opened with a matrix of video thumbnails, and then crashed.

"You meant that to happen?"

"Shut up." Davie hit the terminal window again, repeated some of his commands and added a couple more with a flourish. "Fuck them. That'll do it."

The window opened with the expected matrix of thumbnails. "I'll dump everything to a USB stick. You'll have more time than me today."

I dragged a chair across the floor and sat beside him. "I really appreciate this. You should join me. You spend half your time working for me. Make it full-time. The money's good."

He looked at me, my beat-up face, crusty blood on my hairline and shook his head. "Is medical insurance included? Yeah, nah. I'm good." He spun back to his monitors, slipped a USB stick into the side of his laptop and copied a week's worth of files from Bazza's network. He deleted them off their system as they copied across. Baz was going to be so pissed.

Davie pointed at one of the small windows showing live video and laughed. "I think the big guy is pissed."

He double-clicked on the video. It was from the camera in the security room. Barry was hammering on the keyboard, trying to make something, anything, happen. The file transfer window on Davie's monitor was doubled on one of the screens in the security room. Barry slapped the screen and yelled at the reedy-looking kid beside him.

Then Barry turned to the camera in the security room, pointed at it, mouthed my name and drew his thumb across his neck. The file transfer was finished, and Davie deleted the final file and disconnected from the system.

Davie laughed. "I don't think he likes you." He handed me the thumb drive. "So, how much do you like that car? That big guy is going to rip you to pieces if we show up."

I looked at Davie. He had work in less than four hours, and he was willing to take two of those hours to risk bodily harm to get my car. I didn't deserve this guy's friendship. "Let's go. Let me drive. You can grab a kip. I promise I won't hurt your car."

Nineteen

He relented. I drove.

Davie was exhausted, had been up all night, and frankly, I didn't trust him behind the wheel while I was in the car. And I knew how to get there.

I like driving at this time of night—very early morning. There is virtually no traffic, and the city lights are still on. Until I hit the suburban-rural area where the only part of the world exposed is that part the headlights illuminate.

I smacked Davie on the leg when we were about five minutes out. He wiped the drool off his mouth while raising the seat back out of the almost-prone position. "Wut?"

"My car is just ahead." The sun was about half an hour away from breaching the horizon. The early morning grey made seeing my car much easier than last night. Or early this morning. Whatever. Time's a flat thing.

I was also exhausted.

I rolled his car to a stop on the wrong side of the road in front of mine and turned off the engine. We sat there for a minute, cars nose to nose.

"Why did we come this way?"

I looked at my friend. He was barely conscious. Looked like shit. "You need some fresh air, mate. If I'd come the other way, we'd have driven in front of the house. The house you helped break into. You want me to drive in front of the house?"

He raised his eyebrows and shook his head. "Fair call." He cracked open the passenger door and looked at me. "Do you think it's safe?"

I jammed my fingers on the car's roof as I reached for the switch to turn off the dome light. "You get behind the wheel, turn your car around and get out of here. I'll be right behind you."

He didn't put up an argument. "Meet me at my place," I said.

He nodded and got out of the car, letting in a wave of cold air. He stretched and yawned. And I yawned. Why are yawns contagious? I could see his breath. It was cold out, but the day's sun would be hot.

We were near the eastern edge of Baz's property. I leaned against the tall, wood fence. Yawned again. Then Davie yawned.

"Fuck off, will you? You're making me tired." He walked to the driver's side of his car and eased himself in. "I'm going to be shit at work."

It's a good thing I was leaning against the fence. Half a kilometre to the west the gate started to roll open. I felt the vibration on my back.

I leaned down and looked in the car window. "My place, okay? Get out of here."

"Why?"

"I want to make sure you get back okay, but we need to close things off."

"Close what off? What things?"

"Just-just meet me at my place. I'll be right behind you." I needed him as far from this place as possible, as quickly as possible.

I watched him make a five-point turn on the narrow road and accelerate away. I pressed the button on my key fob, and the park lights flashed. The car was already unlocked—it was an automatic habit. The 'chunk' of the locking mechanism almost masked the sound of the car approaching. I ducked behind my car and watched the red Fiat convertible speed by with Leung behind the wheel and Big Bad Barry forcing the passenger side of the small car low to the ground.

Shit.

I really wanted to follow them to wherever they were going. If Leung disappeared, all of this would be for nothing.

But it really wasn't my problem, right? Jackson and Johnson and the rest of the fine men and women of the AFP could deal with it.

No.

I wasn't convincing myself. It took every bit of willpower to point my car back to my place. Leung killed my friend. I so badly wanted to squeeze the life out of that arsehole.

Davie's car was parked at the kerb opposite my apartment building. My relief at seeing his car was immediately negated when I also saw Lucy's car there. I was too tired for this.

She opened my apartment door as I approached. Kissed me on the cheek and stood to one side as I entered.

My apartment. My sanctum. My domain.

Who was I kidding?

Davie was adjusting the coffee machine. He glanced up as I entered and smiled. He still looked like shit. I pulled out a chair and sat at the small dining table. I rubbed my eyes with the heels of my hands and lowered my head, stretching my neck muscles. I felt exhausted. I *was* exhausted.

"How do you work this thing? I need caffeine."

Lucy pushed the basket of coffee pods toward him. "Pick the kind of coffee you want from the basket and drop the little pillowy thing in the slot on the top. Stick your cup under the spout, pull the lever and push the button." She had a tired half smile on her face. "You're the tech genius, Davie. This isn't rocket surgery."

She turned and leaned back on the counter with her arms crossed. She stared at me for an uncomfortable minute. On some days, she intimidated me. She was brilliant and, like this morning, beautiful without any effort. Her hair was tied up, with red curls sprouting from the back of her head. She wore an oversized Barbie T-shirt, cargo shorts, and ten-loop leather sandals. She was stunning, smart, and disapproving.

I stunk and had two days of growth on my face and five on my head. My clothes were dirty and torn from the fight in the stable and the stroll through the bush.

She broke the silence. "You're going to the cops now, right?"

I nodded. "Jackson and Johnson." I glanced at my watch. "I'll call one of them in a couple of hours." I let loose the yawn I was trying to stifle.

She smiled and covered her mouth as the contagion spread. "Yeah," she yawned. "They'll help." She yawned again and shook her head. "Jesus, you must be exhausted."

Davie brought a cup over to the table and placed it in front of me. "You need this more than we do."

I looked up at him as I wrapped my hands around the mug. "Thanks."

He pulled a chair out for Lucy and sat across from me. She hesitated a second, then sat to my right. The three of us, barely awake.

"Davie, thanks for all of your help." I leaned back, dug my phone out and scrolled to the screen grab he'd sent me from the house security footage. "This is one of the clearest shots of Leung that I think has ever been taken." I looked at the picture, then placed the phone face up on the table. I rubbed the stubble on the top of my head. "Weird that a runaway kid case led me to him."

"And you thought the biggest risk with the runaway was your client not paying you. There was no risk of that at all." Lucy took a sip of her coffee and winced. "Davie, how do you fuck up pod coffee?"

I gently took the mug from her and placed it on the table. "Why wasn't it a risk, Luce?"

She took the mug back. "It might be shit, Nick, but it's caffeine. And god knows I need caffeine. It wasn't much of a risk because of this." She showed me a document on her phone. "Your first real client has an increasing network of offshore accounts."

I scrolled through the document, picking up the salient points. "Six accounts in six countries. All of them started up within the past month. The most recent, three days ago." I nodded and slid the phone across the table back to her. "No balances?"

She shook her head. "I don't know yet. These are on the edge of that big money laundering thing I'm looking at. Tangential, at best. I couldn't dig much deeper without violating the compliance requirements I put in place myself." She locked her phone. "But there's more to her than I think you realise."

"That case is closed, Luce." I nodded at her phone. "That's a problem for someone else."

Davie choked on his coffee and pushed himself back from the table. "Nick? Turning away an intellectual mystery?"

"Nothing intellectual about it, Davie. She's as crooked as her ex-husband." I stopped my mug halfway to my mouth. "Wait."

"What?" Lucy flipped over her phone and looked at the document she had just shown me. "Did I miss something?"

I put my mug down. "I think *I* might have."

"Oh, no." Lucy put down her mug and took my hand. "You've got another case, right? That business intelligence thing at the office. The background check."

I nodded and patted her hand, "Definitely." I rechecked the time. "You two should go. You've got real jobs that start very soon."

"What about that whole 'closing things off' you talked about?"

"We're closed off, Davie. The case is closed." I looked at Lucy. "Right?"

"He's right, Davie. I've got meetings this morning. The case is closed, and Nicky looks like he needs a shower and some sleep before he meets his next client."

She stood and pocketed her phone. She leaned down and gave me a kiss on my cheek, but then she wrinkled her nose. "Oh, Nicky, you *really* need a shower."

"Love you too, Luce." I laughed as I stood and nodded for Davie to get up, too. "I would prefer a long, hot soaking bath, but this place doesn't have a tub. I'll catch up with the two of you tonight, okay?"

I followed them to the door and attempted a kiss with Lucy, but she held up a finger and shook her head. "Later, when you smell better."

I laughed outwardly and closed the door behind them. I peeled my clothes off as I headed to the shower. I would probably end up burning them.

Hot needles pummelled my neck and back as I stood under the spray, thinking.

Was Lyla in business with Bazza but better at hiding her money? If so, had *she* met Leung? Was she working for him? What was behind her kid allegedly running away to the circus?

I towelled off and padded naked into my little office away from the office. Dropped the towel on my chair and sat. I'm not a complete animal.

Back to the beginning. The circus. I hadn't given it much thought, but the signage didn't look like any circus I remember going to as a kid. I opened a search engine, closed my eyes and tried to drag the name in front of the main tent from my exhausted memories. There were a few that toured Australia, hitting country fairs. The Moscow Circus. Hudsons. Ashton's. It wasn't any of them. The name teased at the corner of my brain, peeking out but not enough to grab it.

I sighed. I typed 'Circus+Warriewood'.

Bingo.

Bonza's Circus. I had never heard of them before. I searched for that name and still couldn't find a website. They had a couple of social media pages with a very low profile. In both cases, follower numbers in the low hundreds.

There was no advertising. Visitors tagged them in some pictures from past shows, and the reviews were only fair.

A couple of options came to mind. Maybe they were a new operation trying to go head-to-head against the established organisations. If so, they were doing a piss-poor job of it. It cost a shit-tonne of money to mount a circus and move it between towns. They wouldn't last a couple of months. Yet they were tagged in social media messages over a year ago.

So maybe, more likely, they were a piece of a money laundering operation.

I'd seen things like this before. A cash-heavy front business filtering illegal cash in with the real receipts to clean it. There had to be more, though. The circus wasn't big enough to hide real numbers.

My next leap, logical or not, was that either Lyla, or Bazza, or possibly both, were using it to clean the cash they got from whatever businesses they were in.

Why in the hell would her son allegedly run away to join a circus where his mother was laundering money, though?

Clearly, he didn't know what she was doing.

Except now I was making a leap that she was laundering through the circus. Maybe it was just Bazza. Maybe neither one of them.

Sorting through problems on almost no sleep in the previous 48 hours was monumentally stupid. Making decisions based on poorly formed assumptions was just as stupid.

I needed more information.

The cops would have to wait. I had to talk to Lyla and get more information about her ex. Something smelled off, and it wasn't just my clothes.

Twenty

It was still pretty early—too early to rock up to a former client's front door and demand answers. I poured the remaining coffee into a travel mug and got dressed. I needed food. Drive-thru grease and carbs would have to do. I could eat a horse, and the odds were better than even that horse is what these guys put between their burger buns.

Time had progressed enough. If Lyla was still asleep, I'd wake her.

I pulled to the kerb in front of her house in Vaucluse. Her car was in the driveway. It wasn't the largest house on the street by any stretch of the imagination, but it was nice. Lace curtains were drawn on all the windows, but those near the front of the house fluttered as someone walked by the window.

The front door opened a minute later, and Lachlan exited, his school bag over his shoulder. A Range Rover was pulled halfway into the driveway, and Lachie hopped in the front seat. It backed out, the exhaust billowing a cloud in the cool morning temperatures. I couldn't see the driver, but made a note of the registration—occupational habit.

I waited another minute before getting out of my car. I stretched. I was still exhausted physically but just about on my game mentally.

The yard was well maintained. A slab rock, waist-high retaining wall was split by five steps up to the walkway. A well-edged and recently mown lawn led to a flower bed along the front of the house. Flowers and low shrubs.

The front door was almost entirely glass, with lace curtains providing privacy against those looking in and light for those inside. I raised my hand to knock, and the door opened. Lyla stood in front of me, one arm across her middle, holding a bathrobe closed, the other holding up the door frame.

"I've paid you, right?"

"Good morning to you, too, Miss Porter."

She stood to one side. "The neighbours will start talking if you stay out on the step. Come on in. You're letting the heat out. Coffee? Tea?"

She cinched the belt on her robe and led me into the entry hall. There were double doors on the left opening to an opulent formal dining area. I caught a glance at a highly polished cherrywood table with six matching chairs in the centre of the room. I followed her through the end of the entry hall, then right to a kitchen that bled into a large family room. She pointed to a barstool at the counter in the kitchen. "How do you take your coffee? Black, right?"

The house was very well furnished. She didn't live like she was broke. I turned on my stool and leaned back, elbows on the counter, looking out through the wide-open folding wooden accordion doors onto the terrace. A glass-topped patio table with eight chairs around it sat at the end of the patio near an open-air fire pit. There were more goddamned places to eat in this house than a small cafe.

I turned back on the stool.

"Black coffee is fine, Miss Porter."

"Lyla."

I nodded in deference. "Lyla. Black is fine, but I don't know how long I'll be here. I think you'll throw me out before the coffee is ready."

That stopped her halfway to her fancy coffee machine. "Why would I want to kick you out? You brought my son back to me. And for that, I'm eternally grateful."

"Nothing to do with your son. I want you to tell me everything you know about Barry Williams' organisation and if he uses the circus your son was at to launder his dirty cash." May as well get to the point early.

She thought for a second, then continued to the machine. She did some noisy stuff with some noisy things and fiddled with some knobs, and the smell of exquisite coffee filled the room. She returned with the steaming cup of black heaven and sat across from me. I leaned down, took a deep sniff and sighed.

She smiled. "First cup?"

"Third. But this one smells a lot better than the other two." I sat back and let it cool. "So, are you going to kick me out, or are you going to tell me some juicy details about your ex-husband's drug business?"

"You're direct." She seemed to compose herself, sliding the robe's sleeves up her arms. Her very muscular arms. How had I missed that before? Sinewy, not at all bulky. She wouldn't be a pushover in a fight.

I said nothing. Interrogation trick. You've probably seen it used in movies and some of the better television programs. Just sit there, let the silence envelope the person you're questioning, and eventually, they will blurt something out to break the silence. The longest I've ever waited was twenty-three minutes.

Seventeen seconds, this time. As long as it took you to read that.

"If you're hoping to wait me out, I've seen the same movies you have. I've got nothing to hide," she said. "Barry hasn't been part of my life since he left almost fifteen years ago." She shrugged. "I have no idea what he does now, and money laundering through a circus? I wouldn't have a clue about that."

She was a pretty good liar. It's not the best I've seen during my career in law enforcement, but she was in the top ten.

"You don't believe me, and that's fine. It's on you, not me."

I nodded. "This is a beautiful home. It must be worth, what, six or seven mill?"

"It was four-four when I...bought it fifteen years ago. I could probably get ten for it now." She sighed and looked around. "Not that I'm planning on selling. This is home."

"Pretty big for just the two of you."

She narrowed her eyes. "What are you getting at, Nick?"

I sipped the coffee. Perfection. I tried keeping the conversation light. "Nothing at all, Lyla. I was just commenting on this beautiful, very expensive house."

"And my obvious non-job, just sitting around in the morning in my bathrobe, tonnes of time for coffee with an obnoxious PI." She sipped her coffee with a small smile.

"I'm not obnoxious. I *am* curious."

"Maybe I'm a successful author writing under a pen name. A whole series of romance novels under my belt with movie options." She sat up, the realisation of a new fact on her face. "Wait a sec. You were the credit enquiry I was flagged on. Why?"

"I want to make sure my client can pay before I take a case." I placed my cup on the counter. "And for my very first case out of my new office, I broke the rules. Your credit report was horrible."

"And *that* was the reason for the retainer." She nodded. "Makes sense."

I waved my hand around, encompassing the house. "I'm curious. This isn't listed as an asset on your credit report. There are no records of mortgage payments. Your personal credit score is 573. Five. Seven. Three."

"I don't see how that's any business of yours, Nick."

"Maybe not. Something's weird about this, though. While looking for your son, I found out someone I thought was dead is actually alive, affiliated with your ex-husband, and one of your ex-husband's associates works at the circus where I tracked your son. And that circus isn't one of the usual ones you see terrorising kids around the country. Some janky organisation that probably violates all kinds of safety regulations. I don't believe in coincidences. Ever." I sipped more coffee. "So you can see why I'm curious. Does your ex- own this place?"

Lyla choked on her mouthful of coffee. She wiped her mouth on her bathrobe sleeve. "No, this is mine. Under a company name. My credit score may be crap, but my business score is just fine."

I nodded. A good surface layer response. "What's your business? And why didn't you engage me through it?"

She shrugged. "My business wasn't missing a son."

It was stupid of me to ask two questions at the same time. Gives the subject of an interrogation a chance to ignore the first question. "Fair call. What's the business?"

"What business is it of yours?"

Well, she had me there. "Curious is all. Like I said, I don't like—don't believe in coincidences." I had some more of the exquisite coffee. "Somehow, something links you and your ex-husband. More than just your son. The man I thought dead? I'll be tracking him down. Huang Leung." I watched her face. "Would you know him?"

There was a slight glimmer of something. But I'm not sure what. She slowly shook her head. "Asian, I assume. No. I don't know anybody by that name." She took my cup and hers and placed them in the sink. I wasn't even close to being finished. "You should leave now, Nick. I could physically throw you out, but I wouldn't want to embarrass you."

I chuckled, but my heart wasn't in it. I don't like fighting, and I especially don't like fighting women. Particularly those who look like they could take me.

I stood and stretched my aching muscles. "No problem. I'll get out of your hair and let you return to your romance novel writing or whatever the hell it is that you do."

She followed me to the door without saying a word, held it for me and latched it when I left. Threw the bolt, too, by the sounds of it.

I made a mental note to check businesses where Lyla was owner or director. Something about the ownership of the house, too. Then, I took out my phone and added a tangible reminder. One that would vibrate in my pocket later if I forgot it. Which I most assuredly would.

I was at that proverbial fork in the road.

Down the fork I *should* take were the CBD offices of the Australian Federal Police. Wrangle Jackson and/or Johnson, show them all of the pictures I'd gathered of Huang Leung, drug kingpin, from all of the possible angles photos could be taken, convince them to join the hunt and wash my hands of the whole fucking mess.

Down the road less travelled, the road I should avoid but never seem to, was the battering and bruising I always seem to attract. That's the downside. On the upside, I get results a lot faster.

I leaned on my car and scrolled through my recent destinations. The circus would be my best bet. Leung said he had one more stop north of the house in the Hills District. Gosford fit that description. Of course, so did all of Queensland and The Northern Territory.

But it was a start.

It was just after 9:00 am. I'd be there by ten at the latest. I'd have this wrapped up by noon.

My phone rang as I got in the car. I didn't recognise the number. "Harding. What can I do for you?"

"Mr Nick Harding?" She sounded like an Australian Kathleen Turner.

"It is." My phone connected to the car's Bluetooth, and I dropped the phone in the centre console. "And who might this be?"

"My name is Harriet Gosling. I'm hoping John has already reached out to you. John Ravenhill. I run a small consulting company and was hoping for some discrete potential-client background checks."

I nodded, paying more attention to the narrow roads out of Vaucluse than the conversation. "He did, Miss Gosling."

"Excellent. And call me Harriet. Or Harry. It sounds like you're on the road. Is this a good time to talk?"

I was out of the twisty bits of Vaucluse and onto one of the main roads in and out of the exclusive suburb. "It is. John mentioned something about a client of yours, or potential client, out of PNG and a background check you'd like me to do. For insurance purposes, I expect?"

"He briefed you well. I'd love to face-to-face with you to give you some background. Do you plan to be in the office this afternoon?"

"I wasn't expecting to hear from you until Wednesday."

There was a lengthy silence. Then she cleared her throat and spoke like she was talking to a simpleton. "It is Wednesday, Mr Harding. I just arrived back home. I'll be in the office from noon."

Shit. "Right. Apologies. It's been a wild week so far."

"I get it. I've had some of those myself. *Are* you available this afternoon?"

I was still on schedule. Circus in less than an hour, call in the cavalry from there, back for lunch. I nodded to myself. "Absolutely. Pencil in 2 pm? I'll buy you coffee."

"2:30 is better for me if that's okay with you. I've got to debrief the team. See what they've done in my absence that

I may have to answer for." She laughed. "Herding cats, Nick. So, 2:30?"

"Sounds good. Thanks for the call. I look forward to meeting you."

She signed off, and I went into mental cruise control. Hers was a problem for later. Right now, I needed to infiltrate a circus, figure out Leung's connection and close this one out.

And remember which day of the week it was.

Twenty-One

I was putting too many non-billable miles on my car. This wasn't technically a case, but here I was, hoofing it north to Gosford again. North on the M1, through granite cut-outs behind painfully slow trucks. The hills are steep enough that more than one older truck has overheated to the point of combustion.

Not today, though.

I've mentioned that Gosford is a slow place, right? The locals would disagree, but other than tourism, not a hell of a lot happens there. I've been up to watch The Central Coast Mariners, who aren't that bad, but the stadium capacity is less than 50,000. The few matches I went to, back when I had time to go to games, the atmosphere was pretty good, but still small-town shit.

So the circus would be a big deal. Enough civilians around keeping staff busy so I could sneak in and get the pictures and physical evidence of Leung to satisfy the Feds.

I had to get there first.

Gosford is just off the main north-south motorway on Australia's east coast, the M1. A hilly, twisty road off the M1 called the Central Coast Highway led east, generally, to Gosford through the small village called Kariong. Kariong is so small I don't even consider it a separate place. The twisty bit started after Kariong. Once it straightened out and crossed a small river, I'd be in Gosford proper, and the circus would be about a kilometre to my left.

Davie called me just as I exited the M1. I had maybe three minutes before I needed all of my attention on the windy bit of the road. "What's up, mate? It's gotta be quick. About to hit bad road."

"So you didn't go to the feds."

It wasn't a question. Davie could be really astute some days. "Had to make one quick stop first."

"You're back in Gosford, aren't you?"

See? Astute. "Almost. Just got off the M1. What's the purpose of your call, sir?"

He chuckled. "Lucy got me access. Don't tell anyone. I did a bit more digging. Lyla's accounts are empty. And all set up within the past two weeks. She's preparing for something. Something big, by the looks of it. Half a dozen accounts in half a dozen countries."

"Thanks. Thank Lucy for me, too. Can you do some digging and see what businesses Lyla is a Director of? Tonight is fine—no rush at this point. Something smells off with her."

"You coming by?"

I chewed the inside of my cheek for a second. "No. I've got to catch up with Luce and make sure everything is still cool with us."

He grunted. "Cool, cool, cool. I'll ping you if I find something."

"Thanks, mate. I've got to—" The arse end of my car skidded to the right as someone tapped my left rear quarter panel. "Shit."

"What was that?"

"Somebody just tried to PIT me. Gotta go." I jabbed the Disconnect button on the steering wheel with my thumb as I corrected for the drifting. I was less than a hundred metres from the first corner down through the hills to Gosford. It was a tight left-hand curve, a guardrail separating me from oncoming traffic on the right and bush down a drop-off to the left. I straightened myself out and accelerated, keeping an eye on the rearview mirror. A white truck with two overly large men in the front was gaining on me. Karl was driving, and Mika was riding shotgun. If I hadn't been so tired, I would have noticed when the truck started following me. They must have picked me up once I came off the M1.

I was sure my car could navigate the upcoming corners better than the truck could.

Positive.

Had no doubt whatsoever.

So imagine my surprise—no, dismay, when they caught me just as I came out of the corner. They hit me in the rear, square on with the bumper. My head snapped back against the headrest. I fought the urge to slam on the brakes.

My phone started ringing. I glanced at the display on my dash. Lucy. Not now. A little busy.

My tyres squealed as I took the corners down the hill into Gosford. My car had slightly better handling than their truck. A quick glance at the rear-view mirror showed me that they were falling behind.

I couldn't count on that happening or that they wouldn't call ahead and head me off. I got across the small bridge over the river and pulled a hard left into the back streets. Small shops quickly transformed into small homes. I made quick random turns until I was on a street where the homes backed on bushland. The circus was less than a kilometre away. If I walked through the bush, I could approach from the back, getting access without running into any faces that wanted to bend *my* face.

I was tired of getting pummelled.

Goes with the job, I guess.

I parked, got out and locked the car. I stood quietly for a second, facing the tree line, listening for carnival noises. Through the bush, and by the sounds of it, closer than I thought. A quick drop-in, confront Leung, get some DNA from an abandoned drink, or something. Take it back to

J&J and drop this horseshit. Same plan I'd been trying for a couple of days. Maybe this time I'd succeed.

"Hey, buddy."

Shit. The accent was unmistakeable. I didn't turn. I looked up at the sky.

"Boofheads. I thought I lost you. What do you want, Mika?"

"You been bothering the boss. We're going to have a chat with him."

"After we rough you up a bit." And Karl actually speaks.

I turned slowly, hands up by my waist. They were a couple of metres away. Mika was on my left, and Karl, the bigger brother, was on my right. A good distance apart, maybe three metres. I couldn't take them singly. No way in hell could I take them together. I wasn't even going to try.

But I wasn't going to surrender. My options were limited. I wasn't very fast, but faster than these two, I bet. They had fifty kilos each on me. But they were soft heavy. They could move heavy things around, but not quickly. "Look, guys," I took a step back with my hands up. "I don't want to fight you two. You'd kick my arse."

They split to flank me, which is what I'd hoped they'd do. The instant they started moving apart I sprinted forward, splitting them. Their inertia worked against them. Mostly.

I got between them, but Karl managed to grab my arm as I passed. It knocked me down, and I tumbled across dirt as they rounded on me. I scrambled back to my feet and started running away from them and, unfortunately, away from the circus. My hip hurt. I landed a bit rough, but I was still faster than them.

Not much, but faster enough.

Thank god that little fuck Kai wasn't with them. He's fast. You can tell by looking. And nasty.

Their lumbering-through-the-bush noise faded in the distance. The swearing was all in Finnish. I think.

I doubled back to my car. Or I tried to double back. They were apparently smarter than I gave them credit for.

Karl was near the front of my car and Mika was at the back. A drop of luck flowed my way—they were both looking away from me when I rounded the corner.

I pulled a muscle in my back when I changed course and dropped behind a caravan. Fuck this job some days.

If Lucy could see me now. I sat with my back against the caravan and sent her a message. *Hey, Luce. Thanks for helping Davie. If he hasn't mentioned it, I'm in Gosford. I know. I need to close out the Leung thing. He's here at the circus. I'll get some DNA from something and take it to Jackson. Or Johnson. And then I'll be done with it.*

I'd travelled too far east in my efforts to free myself from the massive Finns. The circus was well behind me, and between me and the Big Top were those who wished to bend me into a pretzel and toss me into the harbour.

So I continued east. Jogging, though I really wasn't in good enough shape. You know what they say, you don't have to outrun the bear, just your slower friend. Except I had no friends. The Finnish bears had only me as a target.

The park on my left eventually ended, and I turned left and headed north to the top end of the park. It was a long, straight street. I'd be in the open, but there was nowhere for the Finns to hide if they were following me. And nowhere for me to hide of the Finns were following me.

My phone warbled on the trek west back to the circus. It was Lucy. "Hey, Luce. I'll be finished up here in about an hour. I'll grab a cup or a napkin the old man has touched and I'll be out of here."

"I'm at the A&E with Davie."

I stopped walking. "What the hell? What happened?"

"I don't know," she said. "He just collapsed."

I looked back from where I'd just come. "I'll be an hour. Fifteen minutes to get back to my car and forty-five back to Sydney."

"No, no, Nick. Finish what you're doing. He's back with the doctors. No telling how long it'll be. Finish what you're doing and then get back here. I'll keep you up to date. Seriously. There's nothing you can do here."

"It's my fucking fault. I've been driving him too hard. Fucking hell."

"You've been going harder than he has, and you're still upright. Don't blame yourself."

If that was meant to mollify me, it wasn't helping. "Are *you* okay?"

I heard her exhale a long, slow breath. "I am now. He was touch and go. Looks like he'll be in Vinnie's overnight. Finish off what you're doing. I'll meet you at your place. Good luck. Be careful."

She hung up. No chance to discuss options.

This was a lot to process.

Twenty-Two

She wasn't wrong. Nothing I could do here, and she'd let me know if things got worse. I could either abandon my efforts and dash back to St Vincent's Hospital, where I would sit around for hours waiting for information, or I finish things with Leung and put it behind me.

Not a difficult decision, if I'm honest.

The Fiat was parked in the circus lot. His Fiat. I was assuming it was his Fiat. Not that many of them around. Unlikely there'd be a different one here when I was expecting to find Leung's. He parked it near the front, by the line of people queueing to buy tickets to get into the half-rate circus.

In the middle of the goddamned day. Jesus. Does *nobody* have a job? It must be nice.

I walked between the cars toward the admission gates. Kai was manning the entrance. I wasn't going to get in that way.

But it was a fucking circus. Mostly outdoors, and a bit of it in tents. If I couldn't find a way in, I should hand in my PI credentials and find another job.

I veered right and circled the mess of tents to the far side. I found the kitchen, of sorts. Sausages, popcorn, reheated pretzels and drinks. It was actually more of a staging area than a kitchen. The food came in past a thick-looking guard, was cooked in bulk , and then moved out to the various people selling from carts. Not a health inspection sticker in sight.

But boxes on a truck need shifting, so I picked one up, put it on my shoulder and lugged it in. It smelled of sausage. A little off. The guard didn't take a second look at me. I dropped the box of almost rancid meat in a prep area of some sort and left the kitchen tent.

It was getting warm, and I was enveloped in an overpowering smell of slightly burnt popcorn. The number of people behind the scenes was surprisingly small. And I couldn't figure out where Leung would be. No office area to conduct business. No quiet corner to discuss illegal activities with drugs and bales of cash.

"Hey, mate. Who are you?"

Shit. I turned, expecting to see someone who I'd already met and who would enjoyed beating the crap out of me. I was pleasantly surprised to see a face I didn't recognise. "Catering. Thought I'd look around and check the place out. Never been in a circus before. You the big boss?" He wasn't. He was dressed like he shovelled elephant shit. Torn-up steel-capped boots with muddy snake gaiters. Too short shorts. Filthy singlet stretched over bulging muscles. A mishmash of unmatched tattoos up both arms, like the kind you get when you've got a spare $50 in your wallet and no impulse control.

"There's no snooping around." He pointed back from whence I came. "Out."

"No problem, mate. Somewhere I can piss first? It was a long drive here. And a long drive back." I tugged the shirt from my chest. Oppressively warm.

He stared at me, malevolent, like he was daring me to start something so he could bleed off pent-up bile. "Go left on the way out. Row of dunnies." He took a step toward me. "I see you poking around again, and I'll break something."

"Sure thing, pal." I had no doubt he could. With one hand tied behind his back. I was making all kinds of circus friends.

He watched closely as I exited the tent. I turned left. There were two portable outhouses—not a row, if I'm honest—just for circus staff. And unless Leung was pissing in one of them, I was wasting my time.

And Lucy was wrong. I needed to get back and check on Davie. Leung could wait.

Someone once said, "The best-laid plans of mice and men", something or other. Leung's recognisable voice drifted across the open field between the dunnies and the far tent, the one they did the dog tricks in. I did a quick check to make sure the shit shoveler wasn't watching me and trotted through the field to the outside of the tent.

It was definitely Leung's voice. He was pissed off at someone.

"Should I be concerned about your security measures?" He bit his words off like a snapping turtle. "What was that bullshit at the house?"

"It was handled." That was Baz.

"Was it? Where is the intruder? Have you taken care of him?"

I would have killed to see the look on Baz's face as he stood silently in front of his boss. The intruder was definitely not taken care of.

"I thought not. Find him and bring him to me."

"That's going to divert resources from—"

"Like I give a fuck."

Getting Leung's DNA was going to be more of a challenge than I thought it would be. I ducked into the tent and stayed behind the stand of bleachers. I walked along the back until I could hear Leung's voice. He was still giving Baz shit about his shit performance.

I peered around the end of the seats, past the ass-crack of an overweight spectator. An army of poodles was performing a choreographed—poorly choreographed— dance in the middle of the tent. To the right, near the back of the tent, Leung faced down Baz. Both had a couple of lackeys with them.

It was a lost cause. Leung had a finger pointed at Baz's face. I couldn't hear what he was saying over the yapping dogs. But it didn't look like I'd be getting anything that would further prove his existence to my AFP pals.

"Hey." A hand clamped on my shoulder. I looked at it and turned. Kai looked up at me and shook his head. "How many times do we need to kick you out of this place?"

"Hey yourself, Kai. Surprised you folks make money off this shithouse of a circus."

He narrowed his eyes. "Lachie stays here. Tell mumsy to piss off."

I held my hands up, surrendering. "Not here for the kid this time. I've already been paid to collect him. Not doing it for free." I nodded toward the dogs. "Does PETA know about this?"

"Leung should talk with you." He nodded, landing on a course of action. "Yeah." He grabbed me by the arm. "Come with."

The little guy had a surprisingly strong grip. I had about six steps to decide whether to front up to Leung now or push it to another day.

Ideally, I should end this today. Ideally, I should be picking thrown-away gum or discarded tissue, or possibly a used take-away coffee cup. He had nothing like that with him. The best I could hope for would be him spitting on me. Or bleeding on me.

I wrenched my arm free. "I'm good, thanks. I'll see myself out."

A couple of seconds head start. That's all I had. He was fast.

I heard "Mika! Luka!" behind me as I ran. Dammit.

Twenty-Three

What was that movie where the guy keeps saying, "I'm getting too old for this shit"? I get him. I'm for sure going to need my left knee looked at after today.

I scrambled through the gravel parking lot tripping a couple of car alarms as I bounced off them. I didn't have a lot of time to get clear.

A hard right, and I was into the bush. It was about a two hundred and fifty-metre wide stand of trees, almost a kilometre long. If necessary, I'd hide.

It was necessary.

I heard the big guys hit the scrub less than a minute after I did. I dropped behind the trunk of a large gum tree and sat with my back against it, struggling to calm my breath, ears open for the sound of two elephants crashing through the trees. The Finns were not subtle.

They came close. If I were a more timid person, I would have bolted and squashed like a bug.

I was just the right amount of timid.

I sidled around the base of the tree, keeping the noise on the far side. I ended up facing the way I came in. A bit disconcerting, if I'm honest. I could see the rides through the trees. I could see the tents. I swear I could smell the popcorn.

Big unanswered question when in a situation like this: How long do I wait? When is it safe to venture out? The noise had diminished to the point I wasn't sure if it was gone or if I'd normalised it into the usual bush noise.

But my arse was hurting and I had things to do.

I turned my back on the circus and pushed through the bush. My car was on the other side. There was a distinct possibility that it would have been faster to head back the way I came from and take the road around. But that would mean re-tracing my steps, and I'm not a huge fan of re-tracing steps.

So I pushed through, taking my time and making as little ruckus as possible. Still had a heap of scratches across my arms and face. I'm repeating myself, but I hate the outdoors.

I got to the far side of the bush and stopped alongside a tree. My car was off to my right, about half a block away.

Alone. Nobody paying it any interest. A couple of older blokes mowing their respective lawns. A Postie on his electric cart delivering mail.

Boring suburbia.

I crossed the street and relaxed. I'd get Leung another day. Maybe not. Maybe I'd just let the AFP do their job. Now I could get back to Davie and see what the hell was going on with him.

Happy thoughts for about twenty metres.

Two black Haval SUVs pulled alongside. Kai was driving one of them. Someone was driving the other with Karl in the passenger seat and Mika in the back. He jumped out and pushed me toward the open door.

"Get in."

Karl jumped out of the front seat and stood behind me.

I hesitated; Mika raised his hand, and I complied. I hurt enough already.

He pushed me across to the other side of the backseat. I reached for the far door, but Karl beat me to it. He pushed me back toward the middle of the back seat. The Haval was big, but it wasn't that big.

I was jammed between the two of them. I wasn't a small guy, I may have mentioned, and I was the peewee in the middle of two mountains.

"Hey, guys, there's room in the front. Mind if I take that, and you two hang out back here?"

Mika elbowed me in the ribs. Not a hard blow. He didn't have enough room to put any effort into it. Still hurt. "Shut the fuck up."

"Sure," I said. "In a minute. Where are we going?"

"Leung would like to have a word with you. He thinks he remembers you."

I'd be surprised if he did. I was a behind-the-scenes guy.

I shook my head. "I really don't think so."

"Oh, he's heard of you. Set his operations—our operations—back a few years."

I smiled. "My reputation precedes me. I'm flattered. Sorry it couldn't have kneecapped him for longer." I stretched in the seat, unsuccessfully attempting to look out the side window. "Where in the hell are we going?"

Mika shoved me back in the seat. "You'll find out soon enough."

"But what if I want *soon enough* to be now? I'm not a patient man."

Karl elbowed me this time. Considerate of him to ensure my bruised body was symmetrical. I groaned and arched my back. The muscles were spasming. They started cramping. The Finns didn't care. Both of them shoved me back against the seat.

We were heading north. We'd left Gosford and were heading north on the M1. Away from where I wanted to be. Away from whatever Lucy and Davie were dealing with.

I leaned back and fished my phone out of my pocket. My plans to send a message to Lucy were aborted by Mika's fist. He grabbed the phone and held it near the window.

"I'm hanging on to this. Make a fuss, and I'll toss it out at speed."

"Okay, okay. You've already broken one of my phones. That one belongs to a friend of mine. The boss and I are just going to talk, right?"

Karl laughed, and Mika shushed him.

"Yeah," said Mika. "Just talk."

Karl laughed again. It wasn't going to be just a talk.

Twenty-Four

I didn't get much of a chance to check out my surroundings. Tall hedges lined the wide curving drive to the house, so I couldn't see the yard. Being stuck in the middle of the back seat, between two large, smelly oafs, didn't make the sight-seeing any easier.

Giant pine trees dotted the yard around the house. The drive led to a circular entryway. The truck stopped at the door, and Karl turned to me.

"I'm going to get out, and you will slide out behind me. If you try running, I'll break both of your legs."

"Mate, that's the most you've said to me since we first met. You get out, I'll follow, and you can introduce me to whoever is in charge of this shit show, and I'll finally be able to tell them they've made a horrible fucking mistake."

If you've been following closely, this was naked, bullshit, performative art. Self-bravado, for the most part.

Karl grunted and got out of the back of the truck. I followed like he said I should, and by the time my feet were on the ground beside him, Mika was on my other side.

Even if my knees were good I wouldn't be able to run from these meatheads without a head start. And my knees were getting progrcssively less good as the day wore on. No point in even thinking about it.

The house was nice—lots of money behind this operation. It was built on the side of a hill looking over a golf course somewhere north of Gosford, but not as far as Newcastle. I walked to the front door without waiting for them. "Let's go, dickheads. Take me to your leader. He wants to talk? I'd love to talk, too."

The door opened just as I reached it.

"Hey, Baz. Fancy seeing you here." One of the Finns shoved me across the threshold into the expansive marble foyer.

"You just keep pissing me off, Harding." He nodded at my escorts. "Take him downstairs."

They clamped my arms just above the elbows. I'd have nice bruises, but again, at least they were symmetrical. My feet barely touched the floor as they navigated through a white and chrome living area to a set of stairs leading down to what I could only imagine would be a really great time.

The stairwell wasn't wide enough for us to head down three abreast. It was barely wide enough for one of the Finns.

Mika grabbed my shirt by the back of the neck and gathered the material in his fist.

I popped open another shirt button to give myself some breathing room. "I get it. I'm going downstairs. Don't be a dick about it."

At the bottom of the stairs, we turned left. A door opened to a small office and beside it, a half-bath. Beside that was a short hallway to a back door. A possible escape route? Time would tell.

No time to check that out, though, because I was the meat in a Finn sandwich again as they escorted me into a rumpus room. The wall on the right comprised floor-to-ceiling windows and sliding doors. On the left was a wet bar. Mika dropped my phone on it.

"Whiskey on ice, if that's okay. I prefer Jameson."

Mika held my arms while Karl patted me down. My wallet and watch joined my phone on the bar.

"That whiskey and ice? Any time, mate." Worth a try, right?

That got me shoved to the middle of the room. A solid wooden chair with armrests sat on top of one of those blue tarps they use when there's a hole in your roof, and it's still raining. I was muscled into the chair, and my arms and legs were secured with Velcro straps.

I was facing the windows. A fence blocked the view of the golf course. Between me and the window was another chair, just on the edge of the tarp.

"Guys, how am I going to drink my whiskey if my hands are Velcroed to the chair? And I don't do paper straws. They get all mushy."

Karl backhanded me across the face. Definitely didn't put everything he had into it because it didn't kill me. Fuck, it hurt, though.

Mika gripped my arms and the chair arms tightly and leaned down close to my face. His breath stunk of cigarette and sausage. "Shut up, or we will shut you up." He glanced down at the tarp. "As many times as we like."

I heard footsteps on the stairs. I craned my neck to see who was coming. I was surprised but not pleasantly. I was expecting Baz, but Leung shuffled in, sipping a can of soda through a straw in one hand and holding a sandwich in the other. I tracked him into the room, wrecking my neck until he wandered in front of me. He sat in the chair across from me, suppressed a belch, and looked around before placing his can of soda on the floor beside him. It felt good, knowing I wasn't going crazy. Up close like this, not at a distance like at the circus or in a blurry photo, I was more than 100% convinced he *was* alive.

He stared at me for a long minute. Cleared his throat. "Who the fuck are you? Why the fuck do you keep showing up like flies on shit?"

"So if I'm the fly, then you must be the shit, right?" I nodded. "Makes sense, when you put it like that." I cocked my head. "The big boys told me that you knew me, which I find surprising."

He finished his sandwich and wiped his hands on his shirt. "I know you as the little shit who keeps pissing in my pool. Who the fuck are you, and why do you keep poking around my business?" He stood and slowly walked toward me, stopping about a metre away. "Do I know you from somewhere?"

"Look, Leung, why don't you take these straps off me so we can share a drink and talk like reasonable people?" I grimace. "Sorry, I forgot. You're not a reasonable person. But you don't need to use the Finns to extract info from me. I'll volunteer it. I used to work for the federal police. When you blew up your warehouse a decade ago, one of my good friends was vaporised, and we thought you'd died." I nodded at him. "Cool trick, by the way. Maybe over dinner and drinks, you'll have to tell me how you did it. Someday."

He stared at me, his blood pressure rising if the colour of his face was any indication. He raised his eyebrows. "You were part of that?" He clenched his jaw. "I lost two sons and millions in product."

"Bet the product hurt more."

He stepped forward and kicked the front edge of the seat of my chair, knocking me onto my back. I tucked my chin to my chest so the back of my head wouldn't hit the tiled floor. It still knocked the wind out of me.

I took a deep breath and looked up at him. "You seem to have gotten back on your feet. You're laundering your money through more than just that shitty circus though, right? And how is Lyla involved in this?"

His face flashed with confusion for a fraction of a second. He kicked the bottom of the chair, and even though it was a secondary hit, it transferred through the wood, and I felt it in my balls. Not as bad as a direct hit, but not fun.

He waved the Finns over. "Play with him as much as you'd like, then clean the place up and dump his body somewhere." He left the rumpus room, and the two Finns righted my chair.

Mika open hand slapped me while Karl laughed. Encourage, Mika bunched his fist and drove it into my stomach. Below the solar plexus, fortunately, or I would have been starved for air for months. It still hurt.

He stepped out of the way and his brother punched me in the ribs. He seemed dissatisfied with the effort. My ribs didn't think so.

"This is too hard, bending over all the time, Mika." He looked up at the ceiling. I followed his gaze. An industrial-sized hook was anchored about three metres above me.

Mika looked up also. "I'll get some rope. You get us some food. We'll make an afternoon of it." He smiled. "I will enjoy this."

Karl laughed along with him. A couple of big idiots looking forward to playing with a chew toy.

I waited until they reached the top of the stairs.

Leung had fucked up. Knocking the chair over loosened its left arm. It wasn't my strong side, but adrenaline is a wonderous thing. I worked the chair's arm side-to-side until I wrenched it free. I stuck part of the arm between my legs to hold it and slid the Velcro strap off the end. From there, it was a piece of cake.

The Velcro was unbelievably loud. Nothing I could do about that. I collected my stuff off the bar and grabbed the straw out of the can of soda Leung had left behind. Tried one of the sliding doors. It was locked. I ran to the back door and unbolted it. I was spared having to jump the fence. There was a gate on the far left end that opened onto the golf course. Unlocked. Leung was sloppy. But I guess Leung wasn't expecting someone to show up.

I heard them just as the gate closed behind me. Time to run.

Again. For fucks sake.

I headed straight across the fairway. A stand of trees blocked errant golf balls from hitting the retirement village across the road on the far side. A litigious bunch in those communities. Nothing else to do all day but cause trouble.

They ploughed through the bush behind me like rhinos chasing a poacher. Curious octogenarian eyes watched me run past. None of them showed more than passing interest until they saw the big guys chasing me. *Now* they had a show.

The rest of it played out as I described at the beginning of this tale.

The drunk behind the bottle shop slowed them down a bit. I still owed him a bottle. I made it through the nursery unscathed, ran my arse off to catch the train, only to be pinned between Mika and Karl, with Baz sitting across from me.

Trains in NSW are double-decker. You enter a door at either end of the carriage. There is wheelchair-accessible seating on that level, with room for maybe four on either side of the aisle. To get to the body of the carriage, you go either up or down six stairs. I had gone down. I'll always second-guess whether it would have been smarter to go up. You're less visible if you go up. Less likely to be found.

The windows in the newer trains only open in case of emergency. And while I may have thought that this situation qualified, the rail company didn't. The cloud of sweat-stench from the Finn brothers choked me.

"Now what, guys? You going to beat me up in front of all of these people?" They looked around the carriage. It was almost full to capacity, with fans of the Newcastle Jets heading to Gosford for one of the biggest rivalries in Australian round ball. That sport Americans call soccer.

Baz snapped his fingers. "Hey. Look at me. You're pissing me off. We're getting off at the next stop." He sat forward and lowered his voice. "We'll thrash you up then.

And it will be permanent. I don't know what the fuck you're up to, but it ends now."

"How do you plan on getting me off the train without a tussle? If you're going to kill me, I've got nothing to lose. I'm going to make as big of a scene as I can."

Baz checked out the other passengers again. He shook his head. "They're all pissed. In the bag. They won't notice or care." He smiled at me. "Make a scene, and we add time to the beating. You'll *wish* you were dead."

I love it when someone gives me an idea that will hurt them in the long run. Or, in this case, the short run. "They're drunk, but they'll pay attention. You fucked up, boys." I checked the status screen above the inter-carriage door. Five minutes to the next stop. "Before it gets ugly, tell me how Lyla is involved in all this. That question's for you, Baz. The meat slabs wouldn't have a clue."

Baz looked as confused as Leung did. "My ex? What the fuck are you talking about? She has nothing to do with any of this. Don't change the subject. Get up and head to the door."

"We're still more than four minutes from the stop. You're going to draw unwanted attention. Do you want to draw unwanted attention?"

He didn't, but I did.

As Baz settled back into his seat, I stood. I pointed at the biggest of the travelling fans, who were wearing a Newcastle Jets jersey, and yelled. "Oi, mate! These arseholes think the Jets are shite, and the Mariners are going to shit on your graves. Wooden spoon for the Jets."

Mika grabbed my arm and pulled me back in the seat, but it was too late. The big lad and half a dozen of his friends stood, half in the bag and ready for a fight.

Twenty-Five

The big guy, who I later learned went by Bulldog to his friends and Robert by the police, stormed up the aisle with his lads falling in behind him.

"Fuck," said Baz. He glared at me and stood, his hands up in surrender. "Hey, big guy, just kidding."

Bulldog connected with a hard right jab that caught Baz on the cheek. Mika pushed me out of the way, and Karl followed his brother into the fray.

I backed up the stairs into the carriage's vestibule to keep from getting squashed. There were more Jets fans there, standing, hanging on to the loops and peering down at the fracas. A few pushed me to one side and descended into the fray.

Baz was backed into a corner and holding his own, mainly because the fans had to line up one at a time to get to him. Mika was facing the back of the carriage, fending off three at a time back-to-back with Karl, who was facing the front, doing pretty much the same.

Two minutes to the next stop.

A voice came over the internal speakers. "Transit police have been notified of the disturbance in the first carriage and will be at the next stop. Video is being collected."

There are doors between carriages. I could conceivably walk upstairs, make my way to the fourth carriage, and duck out when the cops arrived. The upper deck appeared to be far less volatile.

Except they'd be expecting that.

I picked up a discarded newspaper and tucked it under my arm. Leaned against the wall near the door and took out my transit card.

The train slowed to a stop at Warnervale. The doors slid open, and a squad of NSW Police boarded. I held up my transit card for them to read, an innocent look plastered on my face. They shook their heads and walked past and down to the lower carriage. As much as I would have loved to hang around and watch the fun, discretion was the better part of valour, and I had things to do. Getting wrapped up by the police was a delay I couldn't have.

I tapped off and checked my phone for the nearest News Agent. Bought a pack of envelopes and sealed the straw Leung had sucked on in one of them. Wrote Jackson's name on the front of it and flagged down a taxi.

"Where to?"

I leaned in the window and handed him the envelope. "I need you to take this to the AFP office on Goulburn in

Sydney." I gave him the address and watched while he tapped it into his GPS.

"Fuck, man. That's going to be $250. Maybe $300 if there's traffic." He pushed the envelope back out through the window. "Just drop it in the mail."

I handed him my credit card. "Make it $400 and as fast as you can. They're waiting for this. Give it to the front desk. Tell them it's for Inspector Jackson." Johnson would bin it and pretend it didn't arrive.

He trapped my card between his thumb and the envelope. "$400?"

I looked at my watch. "Yeah. Time-sensitive."

"AFP. Got it." He ran my card and held the terminal through the window for my authorisation PIN. I had no case to expense this against. My accountant was going to kill me. And by accountant, I meant Lucy.

He took the envelope back and slid it onto the dash, saluted me with two fingers and took off.

Jackson answered after three rings. "What now, Harding?"

I looked at my watch. "There'll be a package—an envelope—waiting for you at the front desk in about 2 hours."

"Should I get the bomb dogs involved?"

"It's a straw that was recently in Leung's mouth. You'll have the DNA that proves I'm not as deluded as you think I am."

"Come on, Nick. You know better than that. No chain of custody. Can't be used as evidence."

"*Come on*, Jackson. Are you that thick? I am a credible source. Former AFP. Providing compelling information that should kick things up a notch. Start an investigation. Finally, get this motherfucker."

I let him stew on that for a few seconds. "I'll look at it. We'll run it through the lab. I'll let you know what we find."

And that will take weeks. Jesus. "Give it a bit of a shove, okay? He's leaving the country soon. Never know when you'll get another chance."

"I'll let you know what we find," he repeated, then hung up.

Great.

I had to make another call.

"Nicky, where are you?"

"Hey, Luce. Warnervale. Long story. How's our guy doing?"

"Want to talk to him? Hang on a sec." There was the background noise of a phone changing hands.

"Nicky, what have you gotten yourself into? Warnervale? That's hell and gone from here."

I shook my head and stepped into a coffee shop across from the station. "Hang on." I held the phone to my chest and talked to the barista. "Large flat white and one of those sticky buns, thanks."

I leaned against the counter and returned to the call. "Forget about me, are you okay? Did I do this to you?"

Davie laughed. "You're not going to believe this. Turns out O'Shea and I have something in common."

Terry O'Shea was a money launderer who strong-armed into finding his daughter and the ten million she stole. He was arrogant, ignorant and grossly obese. "I can't possibly imagine."

"Turns out I'm diabetic. Damnedest thing."

"Jesus, mate. How did you find out? What happened?"

"Thank your girlfriend. Hey, gotta run. Doc is going to tell me all about how my life has changed before I'm discharged. Here's Lucy."

I could hear the conversation in the background before Lucy got on the phone.

"I'm back."

"Where are you guys?"

"Still at the hospital. Davie's 100% better than he was."

I took my coffee and bun and walked across the road to the train station. "I have so many questions. What triggered this?"

"A failing pancreas, I assume. He got wobbly and wasn't keeping anything down. I drove him to the hospital, and they did extensive blood work and glucose testing. Prescribed insulin, and he's good to go. Almost. He has to pick up some vials at the chemist, and I'll drop him off at his place. What are you up to? You're missing all the fun."

"First, how is he, really? He'll bullshit me."

Her voice lowered, and I assume she walked a bit of a distance away from him because it took a few seconds before she replied. "I was really worried about him. He could barely stand. He seems fine now. His blood levels are good. The doctor showed him how to check his levels and how to calculate how much insulin he needs. You know him. He'll have a program automating it within a week." She cleared her throat. "Why are you in Warnervale? What's going on?"

Where to start? "I've sent confirmational info about Leung to Jackson. A straw he sucked on that will conclusively prove I'm not a lunatic. Evaded some big guys who wanted to dismember me by hand. Now I'm sipping coffee and talking to my lady friend while I wait for a regional train that will be here in roughly fifteen minutes to take me to Gosford, where I involuntarily left my car. Ah, shit."

"Shit? What? What's happening?"

"I sent the straw to Jackson by cab. For the amount I'm paying the cabbie, he could have dropped me off at my car."

Bless her, she laughed. "You'll have to tell me about the averted dismemberment when you get back. But Davie has his vials and needles and needs a lift home. Unless you want to foot the cab for him?"

"I've spent enough money today. I'll catch up with you when I get back."

It was warm. Like all regional platforms I've ever been on, it was open to the elements, and the elements were hot and sunny. Spring had arrived.

I found a bit of shade and checked my emails. Felt like I was being pulled back into some form of normality. Emails can't give you a black eye or broken ribs.

Too much spam, though. Time to adjust the junk rules. Among the crap was an email from Harry. I'd completely forgotten about her case. She had sent a meeting request for, I checked my watch, about thirty minutes from now.

That wasn't going to happen. Not in person, anyway. Her office and mobile numbers were in her email signature. The mobile went to voicemail after three rings.

The office line was picked up by Maria.

"Hi there, CommTech. Maria speaking. How may I help you?"

"Good afternoon, Maria. Nick Harding calling for Harry. Harriet."

"Sorry, but she's in a meeting right now. She's free in about an hour and a half if you want to call back."

"She's expecting me in a meeting in about thirty minutes. I'm not going to make it. I'm a couple of hours out of town on another case. I can do it by phone, but I'll be on a train or in my car."

"Hang on a second, and I'll see if she can step out."

The local Smooth Jazz radio station played until Harry picked up the phone. "Mr Harding, thanks for calling. Maria tells me you won't be able to make the meeting."

"Unless I can do it by phone. Up to you. I should be in the office tomorrow. Another case has taken me to the mid-North Coast."

"Then let's do it tomorrow. Mobile coverage on the way back into the city is dreadful. Does tomorrow morning, say 9:30, work for you?"

"Thanks. I'll see you then." I hung up. I had one more chance with her. I had a feeling she'd find someone else if I didn't make it to tomorrow's meeting.

The next train wasn't much quieter. Tonnes of Jets fans turned up looking for a win in Gosford. The Central Coast Mariners were on a run. It'd be a good game.

I didn't see Bulldog in the crowd. Too bad. I would have loved to have a quiet word with him. I guess he was still tied up with the coppers.

The train emptied when it reached Gosford, and I went with the flow. I oriented myself and walked back to my car. Once I got out of the throng that were headed to the bars around the stadium, foot travel was a lot easier. My car was parked about a kilometre away, almost due west of the station. I used the walk to loosen up the tight muscles the Finn brothers gave me.

I should have walked slower. Avoided the disappointment.

My car was a mess.

The brothers had kicked the shit out of it. Dents on every panel. The windows held firm, except for the back passenger. Spider cracks seemed to indicate one of them hurt his fist on it. This was turning out to be an expensive case. Definitely not making money on this one, and I wasn't finished yet. I'd find out how good my car insurance was.

Lyla was tied up in this somehow. Yes, I know what you're thinking. She hired me to find her wayward son, and I found him. But that just scratched the surface. There was other shit she was into, and it was making my Spidey-sense tingle.

I was out of Gosford and on the highway in my badly damaged car heading south to Sydney when my phone rang. My mate was reaching out.

"Davie! Mate, what the fuck? You okay?"

"Good afternoon, Nicky. Lucy tells me someone tried to dismember you. Are *you* okay?"

"Yeah, yeah, yeah, this isn't about me. What the hell are *you* up to? Diabetes? Can stress cause it?"

"Fuck no. It's my genetics. It runs through my ancestors like shit through a goose. It was only a matter of time. Fortunately, Lucy and I were having coffee when things went pear-shaped, and she got me to the hospital on time."

"So you're good now?"

He grunted. "Good? I've got to jab myself on the regular, take anything sweet out of my diet, reduce carbs and start eating healthy. They say exercise is good, too. Yeah. I'm great. I get to get rid of all the fun stuff."

"You're at your place?"

"Just got in. Had to buy a bunch of groceries that are now considered 'acceptable'. Where are you?"

I checked the GPS. "About half an hour from home."

"I'm going to rest up a bit. I really owe Lucy. All of that tiredness, pissing all the time, not keeping food down the past few days was my pancreas fucking with me."

"Wow." I shook my head. "I had no idea."

"Either did I, mate. Though I should have expected it. Half a dozen relatives on both sides of the family are diabetic."

I smiled as I thought about Davie's dietary habits. "Well, mate..."

"Okay, I probably contributed to it. I'll admit that. Fuck me. No more pizza nights."

"So you're making your problem *my* problem now?" I laughed. "Wings and salad."

"We'll make it work. I'm back on board, though. Reach out if you need anything. I'm taking sickies for the rest of the week."

"Because you're fucking sick, mate. Take it easy. I'll catch up with you tonight."

I hung up just as Lucy called.

"Hey, Davie says he owes you." I eased onto the offramp in Hornsby and hit the Pacific Highway south. Not a highway by anybody's stretch of the imagination. Traffic lights every other block, almost.

"He does. When are you home?"

"Fifteen minutes. I'm going to need a shower first."

She laughed. "Down, boy. This is work-related. It looks like Lyla's house is on the market. And has been for a couple of weeks."

Twenty-Six

"Really? She swore it wasn't. I'm going to make some calls. See what I can find out. Are you still in the office?"

"Had to. I'm a new employee. Technically still in my probationary period. I have to keep my nose clean. Which means I should get back to it. Let me know what you find out. We should check in on Davie tonight. Make sure he's okay."

"We will. Thanks for the call. I've got to track down the house sale. Love you."

She signed off as I pulled to the curb. I retrieved Fiona Parker's business card from my wallet and tapped her number into my phone and resumed driving.

"Hi, this is Fiona. How may I help you?"

"Nick Harding speaking. We met at Huang Leung's house a day or so ago. You were setting up for an open house, and I was wearing a horrible disguise."

She laughed. "Nick Harding. I do remember. How can I help you?"

"There's a house in Vaucluse for sale. I was wondering if you could get some info for me."

She sucked air in between her teeth. "Way out of my geography. And, no disrespect intended, way out of your budget I think. I'm assuming this is more like info for a case and not an actual buying opportunity."

"I can't afford lawn care in Vaucluse." I gave her the address. "I've been told it's on the market. Can you check?"

She tapped keys on her keyboard. "I can." She made a couple more taps, then paused. "What's in it for me?"

I was being bled dry. "The excitement of being involved in a wide-ranging case of mystery and intrigue?"

Fiona laughed again. "I'm doing this because that ridiculous outfit you were wearing when we first met was the first laugh I'd had in days. We should get together for a drink sometime."

"Flattered, really, but—"

"But you've got a girlfriend. Boyfriend?"

"Girlfriend. Again, flattered. But I do have a single friend."

"Now I'm sounding desperate. The house has been on the market for a week."

"Davie's a nice guy. Funny, too. How much are they asking? And is it at auction?"

"No," she said. "This is strange. It's assessed at between $11 million and $12.5 million, but there's an offer in for $20. Quick settlement."

"Real estate is your game, not mine. Money laundering is mine. Or it used to be. This smells. I may have mentioned I used to be at the AFP. I had tools there I don't have now. Can you find out when Lyla bought it and for how much?"

She sighed. "And again, what's in it for me?" But she was still typing. "This is getting stranger. Fifteen years ago?"

"Roughly. Say fourteen to sixteen, based on conversations I've had with her."

"The last recorded sale was in the last millennia. Late nineties. Almost thirty years ago. Is that another laundering red flag?"

"Not typically. It's in Layla's name now?"

"It is."

"And whose name was it before, in the 90s?"

"Okay, that's way out of my capabilities."

"Thank you, Fiona. You've been very helpful. When business picks up, and I can afford to buy a house, you'll be the first one I call."

"I'll hold you to that, Mr Harding. It's been a pleasure."

I smiled and tapped the button on my steering wheel to hang up. I thought for a second, then scrolled through my contacts until I found Jackson's number.

He answered on the fourth ring, just when I expected it to drop to voice mail. "Yeah, we got your gift. Tell me where *you* got it."

I pulled to the kerb. "Thanks for taking the call, Jackson. Are you going to do anything with it?"

"Contemplating binning it and getting a tetanus shot or something. This has someone's dried spit on it."

"Are you going to send it to forensics for DNA work, mate? Or did I waste my time facing off against Leung and the muscle-bound fuckwits he keeps company with? Looked in that motherfuckers face, Jackson. It's Leung. Ten years older, ten times as smarmy. He's heading out of town in a day or so. I'd *really* like you to get on that."

"Where, Harding?"

"A house somewhere near Wyee on a hill near a golf course. I was strapped to a chair, sitting on a blue tarp in their rumpus. Leung was eating a sandwich and drinking a soda with that straw. Some of his henchmen stepped out for a bite before their scheduled beating on me, and I ducked out. Grabbed the straw on the way."

"Can you send me the location?"

I scrubbed my scalp with my fingertips. "Yeah, it's probably on my phone somewhere. It saves all the locations I've been to, right? But they're not going to be there now."

"You're probably right, but there'll be something useful for the forensics team."

I put the car in gear and pulled from the kerb. "At least it sounds like you're taking it seriously. I'm heading home. Let me know if you need anything from me."

"There's still that trial prep. You good tomorrow?"

Ah, shit. I forgot about that. "I've got a 9:30 with a new client I can't miss. I'm losing money on this case. I've got to make a buck on the next one."

"Call me from the front desk. No later than 11."

"Sure." I poked the key on the steering wheel and dropped the call.

I made it through the motorway spaghetti and across the bridge to Bondi Junction and my apartment. I eased myself out of my car and stretched, wincing at the numerous pains visited upon me by a couple of Finns. So unlike the Finnish people I know. Usually kind, always smiling and could drink me under the table and still pass a roadside sobriety test.

I slid the key into the door, and it opened on me, pulling me off balance.

"Hey, Nicky. Thought I'd stop by." Lucy wrinkled her nose. A very cute nose. "You need a shower."

"I'm not arguing with you." I kissed her, but not as long as I would have liked. She kept as much distance from me as she could and still kiss me. "Point taken."

She followed me into the bathroom as I peeled off my clothes. She turned on the shower and tested the water. "I'm joining you.'

"I'm definitely not arguing." Despite living her entire thirty-plus years in Australia, her skin was still alabaster. She put her hair up in a bun, a single strand of red hair dangling onto her shoulder.

She stepped into the stall, pulling me with her. "Wash my back."

Well, we didn't completely run out of hot water. But it was starting to cool off by the time we got out and towelled off.

"There are some big bruises on your back, Nicky. Are you okay?"

I nodded. "Better than my car. But that's a problem for tomorrow." I hung my towel on the rack and pulled on a pair of shorts.

"I still think Davie should be over tonight. Are you okay with that?"

I watched her pull on one of my larger T-shirts. It reached comfortably to her mid-thigh. I really didn't want Davie over. I leaned in and kissed her. She didn't pull away this time.

"I had other plans for tonight, but you make a good point. The diabetes knocked him for a loop, huh?

She nodded. "Brave face, but it's a major lifestyle change. No more pizza and beers."

"None?"

She shrugged. "I'm not a medical professional, but that's the gist of it. Lots of careful lifestyle management."

I nodded. "I'll give him a call." I pulled a polo shirt over my still-damp torso. I fought to get it down my back while Lucy silently judged me with a laugh in her eyes. "Don't have anything to feed him, though."

"I brought stuff with me." She walked into the kitchen. "You like chicken Caesar salad?"

"Pre-meditated. I'm shocked." Her laugh pealed from the kitchen among the clatter of pans. "I get no respect." I called Davie's number.

"Hey, Nick. How are you?"

"Better than you, by the sounds of it. Come over tonight."

"Are you sure?"

"Absolutely. We need to catch up. Lucy's making Caesar salad." I could smell bacon cooking. "She's a decent cook."

"Sounds good."

"Okay. See you in—" There was a knock on the door. "A couple of seconds?" I opened the door to see Davie sliding his phone into his pocket. He had a small backpack on his shoulder. He looked a million times better than the last time I saw him.

He fist-bumped me. "Good to see you, mate. What the fuck happened to your car?"

"Did you guys plan this?"

"What's that now?" Davie was the picture of innocence.

"Lucy was here before me. Brought the ingredients for the salad. You show up just as she's preparing it. Awfully coincidental."

He placed the backpack on the sofa and sat beside it. "That's all it is. Coincidence."

I heard the fridge open and then close. "Nicky, you don't have eggs?"

Davie got himself off the sofa and walked into the kitchen behind me. Spotted Lucy in my T-shirt and pulled up. "I'm not interrupting anything, am I?"

"No." She pointed at the Cos lettuce on the counter. "Cut that up for me, will you? Wash it first."

I opened the small pantry in the corner and extracted a carton of eggs. "Want me to hard boil these?"

She looked at the pantry door, then at the eggs. "You don't keep them in the fridge?"

I shook my head. "They don't last long enough to worry about. If the grocery store doesn't refrigerate them, no reason I should." I filled a saucepan with water and placed it on the stove. "Two should be good."

We were chattering with each other, pulling the salad together, when there was another knock on the door. It was comical how we all stopped and looked at each other, like, "Who else could it be?"

"Wait here," I said. "And remind me tomorrow to get a doorbell camera."

I peered through the peephole, then pulled the door open. "Fiona? What's going on?" The real estate agent looked like she was still dressed for work, in a skirt and blazer, hair up and a bag over her shoulder.

"I've got info about that house in Vaucluse." She had a big 'mission accomplished' smile on her face.

"I appreciate that, but you've got my number. You could have just called me."

"I thought I'd give it the personal touch." Her smile faltered as she glanced over my shoulder. "Am I interrupting something?"

Lucy leaned against me with her hand on my shoulder. "Nicky, who's your friend?"

"Lucy, this is Fiona. I ran into her while I was trying to track down Leung. Fiona, this is my girlfriend, Lucy. We're just making dinner. Have you eaten yet?"

"No," she demurred. "I couldn't impose."

"Don't be ridiculous," said Lucy. "I'm making too much. Nicky here will put the leftovers in the fridge, then throw them out in a couple of weeks."

"At least. Maybe longer." Davie had entered the chat. "You have info? Come on in. We live for info."

Fiona looked at me, questions on her face. I nodded. "That's Davie. You're more than welcome. Excuse the informality." I stepped to one side and let her into my apartment. It was starting to get cosy.

"Thanks." She sniffed the air. "What's on the menu?"

"Chicken Caesar salad, and I think I'm burning the chicken." Lucy ducked back into the kitchen.

Fiona placed her bag on the sofa beside Davie's. "This is a nice place. Renting?"

"For now. Nice walk to the beach, but far enough away to avoid the tourists looking for free street parking." I pointed to the sofa. "Have a seat. Tell me what information you've got for me."

She settled on the sofa. Davie took the chair at my desk, and I sat in the chair next to the sofa. "You were wondering about how the house came to Lyla, right?"

I nodded. "Davie, to get you up to speed, since you were lying around doing fuck all, near as I can tell, all day, Lyla's house is on the ghost market. No listing, and under contract for almost double its appraised value. Lyla told me she'd bought it just after her son was born, so about fifteen years ago. Fiona informed me this afternoon that the last registered sale was in the last century, almost thirty years ago."

"Does it matter? You found her son, and you've got your AFP pals on the scent of Leung. Cases are closed, as far as I can tell."

I shook my head. "Something smells. There's something lurking underneath the shadows."

Fiona laughed, then stopped when she noticed neither Davie nor I joined her. "Seriously? You actually talk like that?"

I liked her a tiny bit less after that.

Lucy stood behind me and put her hands on my shoulders. "Yeah, these guys seem to find the most twisted roots of any tree. You all want to eat?"

"She hasn't told us the info," Davie said. "She's got to tell us the info."

"I'm starving, and the info is that the house title was transferred directly to her fifteen years ago. Not on the market, no actual sale, just a deed transfer."

Twenty-Seven

"Happy now? Serve yourselves food. It's in the kitchen." Lucy patted me on the shoulders. "Time to turn it off."

Fiona chuckled at that. "You really don't need to feed me. I should get going." She stood and threw her bag over her shoulder.

Davie grabbed his backpack from the sofa. "Bullshit. I chopped up enough lettuce to feed a dozen of us." He unzipped the front zip on his backpack, pulled out some smaller bags and put them on the table. Then looked in the backpack, turned it upside down, shook it, and swore. "Son of a bitch." He sighed and returned the smaller bags to his backpack. "Sorry, Nick, Lucy. I've got to head back home."

"Bullshit, mate. There's plenty."

Davie glanced at Fiona and shook his head. "It's this diabetes thing."

"We can talk about it after we eat."

"That's just it. I can't eat. I've got to check my glucose."

Fiona leaned forward. "You're not feeling well?"

"I don't know. I guess so, but I'm new to this. I think I need to test just to be sure. Sorry, folks, I need to run."

Fiona lifted the sleeve on her right arm and showed him a white disk stuck to the side of her upper arm. "You should get one of these. Constant measurements and an app on your phone records it." She dug a small black wallet out of her bag. "But I carry these just in case." She handed it to Davie. "Check your levels. The food smells great."

She watched while Davie pricked his finger with the disposable needle and read the levels on the glucose monitor. He smiled and returned the kit to Fiona. "Many thanks."

"A new Type 2, right?"

"Yeah. You?"

I watched Fiona stow the kit. "Type 1," she said. "Living with it my whole life. Where's this food? I feel like I've earned it now."

Davie watched her follow Lucy into the kitchen and sidled over to me. "Who is she again?"

"Real estate agent I met at Leung's house. She was getting it ready for an open house."

Davie nodded. "I like her."

"She saved your life. Relax, champ."

He shook his head. "My numbers are fine. Well inside the range that I need to keep them. Saved my sanity, maybe." He nodded toward the kitchen. "I'm starving."

I followed him into the kitchen. He really was in the best mental shape I've seen him in in months. I stopped at the door and pulled out my phone. I called Layla. Better to address this now while I remembered.

She answered with a curt, "What?"

"Layla, this is—"

"Nick. I know. Why are you calling? The thing I engaged your services for has been resolved. Fat lot of good you were. Lachie is back at the circus. Are you looking for more money?"

"Nice talking to you, too, Layla. No, I'm looking into something else. You seem to be connected in some way. I noticed that your house is under contract for twenty million. It can't be worth more than eleven or twelve. Care to explain that?"

She replied with one of the most Australian phrases in the books. "Get fucked."

Then she hung up.

I laughed as I joined the others in the kitchen. They all had bowls of salad and were looking at me.

"What?"

"What were you laughing about?" Asked Lucy.

"I called Layla. Asked her about the offer on her house that she absolutely wasn't even thinking about selling a couple of days ago. She told me to get fucked." I smiled. "But then she hung up before I could negotiate."

"You're not turning it off, are you?" Lucy handed me a salad bowl. "Eat up. Get your energy. I have a feeling it's going to be a long night."

"Maybe later," I said. "Can you have a beer Davie?" I looked at Fiona. "Can he have a beer?"

"One or two won't be a problem. Just keep an eye on the numbers for a couple of days."

I pulled open the fridge and handed out beers. "To the living room."

"This has been lovely, and it's been great meeting all of you, but I have a viewing in the morning," Fiona said as she slung her bag over her shoulder and pecked Davie on the cheek. "Your numbers are still good. Check them again in the morning. It's a lifestyle change, not a handicap. Remember that."

Davie closed the door behind her, mouth agape. He turned to me. "I'm going to need her number." He followed me into the kitchen and helped me clean up. "You've got her number, right?"

Lucy leaned against the door with her arms crossed. "You didn't ask her? She would have given it to you."

"You think?" Davey seemed pleased with that.

"She's a real mothering type. You're a diabetes baby. She wants to take care of you. Don't fight it."

"I won't. Believe me."

The pans were cleaned, and the dishes were on the drying rack. I had held off as long as I could. "Sorry, Luce, but this has been driving me crazy. I'd love to keep the beer going or open up that bottle of red you brought with you, but I'm switching to coffee."

"Layla?" Davie asked.

"Tangentially, but yes." I scratched the back of my head. "I have a lot of catching up to do with both of you."

I told them about the interaction with Baz, the Finns, and then the Finns and Leung. I told them how I sent the straw to the AFP and how Leung was planning to leave the country soon.

Lucy leaned back on the sofa and sipped her beer. "Doesn't explain the bruises all over your sides and back."

"Or the bruises on your car," said Davie. "Or Layla.

"He mentioned something about that. What happened to his car, Davie?"

He chuckled. "It looks like an elephant fought with it. And won."

I placed my cup on the coffee table and sat beside Lucy. "Two elephants. You saw them at the circus. Thanks for reminding me. I've got to talk my insurance company tomorrow." I sighed. "Same elephants who beat on me. Mika and Karl, with a K."

Davie nursed a glass of tonic water and lemon juice. "So, were they beating on you because you were getting too close to something or because you'd annoyed them more than they could bear and just wanted to get rid of you?"

"The first. I broke out of their place up in Wyee after a few of these punches. They chased me to the train. Thank god for that FFA Cup match in Gosford. A bunch of Newcastle fans distracted them enough for me to give them the slip."

"So they're still looking for you? Do they know where you live?" Lucy had put her beer down and looked concerned.

"I have no idea. They haven't shown up around here, so I think I'm good."

"What's the thread you still haven't pulled, Nick? What's Layla got to do with it?" Davie was on the edge of the sofa now, his interest piqued. This was the Davie I knew from six months ago.

I raised my eyebrows and looked at Lucy. She was showing signs of interest, also. Arms on her knees, leaning forward, ready to listen. "You in?"

She shrugged. "Why not?"

Okay. I got up and sat across from them. "This is what I know. If Leung is in contact with Dom and Baz, both from the circus, then he's using it to launder money. It's not a big enough operation to launder a lot of money, so he's probably got some other channels going. But I don't really care about that. The AFP will take that and run with it once they've convinced themselves that I'm not an idiot."

"How long do you give them?" Davie's face was the picture of innocence. I pretended to ignore him.

"I *know* Layla is involved somehow, but I can't figure it out. She claims she hasn't seen Baz since her kid was an infant. She seemed really pissed that Lachlan took off to join Baz's circus. Was that an innocent coincidence, or has Baz been contacting him? I don't know. But he's back there again, and she doesn't seem as upset. The inflated price she's getting for the house she didn't seem to buy is even more suspicious." I shook my head. "Maybe I've been beat around too much."

"Maybe she's working for Leung?"

"Nah." I rubbed my hand over the softening stubble on my scalp and winced. A lump on the side of my head. Another trophy from the Finns. "I mentioned her name, but he showed no sign of recognition. And he's not a good actor. Flash temper. He'd show something if he knew her, and he knew *I* knew her."

Lucy held up a finger. "Her ex? The son is back at the circus."

"I don't know. Worth checking, I guess. It seemed like she wanted nothing to do with him. And the ex was adamant she had no involvement." I nodded at Davie. "Too late to do some digital searching?"

He grinned. "Never too late." He grabbed his coffee and sat in my seat in front of my computer.

"Sorry, mate. I don't have your whiz-bang spy software on my computer."

"I have it on mine. I'm connected to the web. You're connected to the web. There is a path. There is always a path."

Lucy muttered something about the total lack of privacy in the world, and Davie chuckled. "This is a secure path. I'm remotely VPN-ing into my machine." His phone chimed. He looked at the message and typed an 8-digit number into the popup on my monitor. "And it has two-factor authentication, so even if someone found the path—1 in a billion chance of that—they still couldn't get in. 1 in a 100 million of guessing the correct code. Effectively 1 in way too many to count "

"Thanks for the tech talk. I feel slightly reassured. I want you to look at my set-up later, okay?" Lucy tapped him on the shoulder. "You listening?"

Davie looked up at me and rolled his eyes. The tap on the shoulder transitioned smoothly to a smack on the back of his head.

"Okay, okay. What am I looking for, Nick?" He tapped a couple of keys, and his security camera program was displayed on my television. The map displayed all of Greater Sydney, tiny dots representing locations of home and business security cameras he had mapped to date. Almost half were grey, inaccessible. The remaining were either red or green, indicating their off or online status.

"Let's see if we can find any pictures of Layla and her ex together."

"I need a picture. Or two. One of each of them, if possible. Much faster if I've got both."

I don't normally take pictures of my clients. That'd be kinda weird, right? I paced back and forth behind for a few seconds. "Can you work backward? I've got a picture of her son. It's on the computer desktop. See if you can find them together. Then you'll have a picture of her. You should have Baz from the house you helped me escape from."

He dragged the photo from my desktop to his program and started searching. Lucy made herself comfortable on the sofa and watched the story unfold on the TV.

A progress bar inched across a panel in the top left corner of the screen. "Okay. That's the kid. Let's see if I can find a good shot of the ex." A pop-up window started playing the captured footage from the house in the Hills District at 5x speed. He maximised the window and leaned forward, intently watching the display, his hand hovering over the space bar. He blurted out a "Ha!" and tapped it.

The image on the screen was a three-quarter shot of Barry Williams from behind, caught as he was turning away from the camera. Davie backed up the footage half a dozen frames until Baz's face was full-frame. "That's the guy, right?"

"Yeah. A face for podcasts. Any luck with Lyla?"

Davie took a screen grab of Baz's picture and minimised that window. The progress bar has stopped, and half a dozen cameras were highlighted around Lyla's house. He quickly flipped through the footage until he found a good side-by-side shot of Layla and her son. He had just exited the back of an SUV and was standing beside his mother."

Lucy leaned forward and sighed. "They look so happy there."

I sat beside her. They did. Unreasonably happy. "When is this from, Davie?"

He checked the file name. "Yesterday."

"She doesn't seem to be too upset," said Lucy. "Considering her kid has taken off to the circus again."

Huh. More threads. The last thing I needed when I was trying to tie things up. "Can you get the plate on the SUV?"

"It's the same one you sent before. Still running it down." Davie plugged Layla's and Baz's photos into his program and set it running. "This could take a while." He picked up his coffee and sat across from Lucy and me.

"Have you patented this yet, Davie?" Lucy pointed at the TV with the neck of her beer bottle. "This is powerful stuff."

His phone chimed before he had a chance to answer. Pity. I was curious. It *was* a powerful tool.

"Do you know a Dominic Stephenson? The SUV belongs to him."

Twenty-Eight

"Dom has been shuttling the kid back and forth to school? What the hell?"

"Who is this Dom guy?" Lucy was on the edge of the sofa, elbows on her knees, fully invested.

"A pony-tailed former hippy who works at the circus. Looks as hard as nails. Lyla told me he and Baz have been friends since childhood. I've bumped into him a couple of times and really didn't rate him. Davie, can you look for photos of Layla with *any* random person?"

"Sorta like a physical wild card?" He furrowed his brow in thought. "Yeah, I think so." He cropped Lachlan out of Layla's picture, added a few lines of code to his program, and set it to search. "I don't know if this is going to work. The wheels could spin for hours. Days, even. And if it does work, I have no idea how long it will take." He stood and stretched. "So I'm going to go home and re-test my blood and maybe stab myself with some insulin and get some sleep. This'll run all night. Let me know if it finds something."

He collected his backpack, threw it over his shoulder and gave us both a quick salute. "Don't get into trouble, you crazy kids."

I laughed. Lucy and I stood, and I leaned down to Lucy. "I'm going to walk him to the car. I'll be back in a minute, okay?"

"Don't be long." She pecked me on the lips. "I'll be waiting."

I walked with Davie down the stairs outside of the small apartment block. His car was parked in one of the guest spots, not far from my beat-to-shit Mazda.

Davie took a slow walk around my car, the dents looking worse under the harsh glare of the street lights. "That'll buff out, mate." He chuckled and pressed his key fob, unlocking his car. He tossed his pack in the back seat. "Call me first thing, okay? Let me know if I'm still a genius."

He shut the car door, started his car, and rolled down the driver's window. He looked up at me with a smile. 'Should I call Fiona?"

"I think you'd be stupid not to." I tapped the top of his car. "Good to see you're feeling better, Davie. Take care of yourself."

He pulled away from the kerb and I watched his tail lights disappear around a bend in the road. Time for a bit of Lucy time.

I turned and stumbled into one of the Finns. "Oh, for fucks sake." They each grabbed an arm and lifted me into the back of one of their black SUVs. Kai was behind the wheel. "Again, you fucking morons? Right in front of my place?"

Then they hit me on the side of the head.

I caught my breath as a bucket of cold water hit me square in the face. I shook my head and looked around at my familiar surroundings. I was in the stables in the Hills District again. I shouldn't have shaken my head. My brain was bouncing off the inside of my skull. Reverberating. Lucy would know I was gone. She'd call Davie. They'd work something out. I trusted them implicitly.

I blinked, squinted and hawked up a mouthful of phlegm. I shot it at Baz's feet. My phone and watch were balanced on the top of a stable door. The lights down the centre of the stable cast deep shadows. "Why am I here?"

Baz took a step backward, looking at his boots. The Finns were on either side of him. Kai must have been behind me. A couple of faces I remember from the last time I was here hung out in the shadows.

I twisted in the chair and caught a smack to the side of my already throbbing head. "Easy on. You didn't need to do that. I was just looking for Marco. How's he doing? Gotta be

279

in a bit of pain, right? That knee looked like shit when I left last time."

I was cable-tied to the arms and legs of a very stout wooden chair. No Velcro mistakes this time. And no flimsy chair that I might be able to break if I landed on it right. These guys, I've got to give them credit. They learn from their mistakes.

Baz stepped up to the chair and looked down at me. "You have unfinished business with Leung. I promised we'd keep you here until he shows." He shook a finger at me like I was a misbehaving child. "You don't take off this time, okay?"

I sniffed and tried unsuccessfully to wipe my nose on my shoulder. "Not much choice, do I?" I looked up at the camera. The little red light that indicated it was recording was unlit.

Baz followed my gaze and smiled. "We learn from our mistakes. That's disabled. We decided that operationally, we really didn't need surveillance out here. Thanks for the security seminar."

"The very least I could do." I peered into one of the corners. "Hey, that's one of the other guys I got, right? Well done for being back on the job already. You're truly tougher than you look."

Baz held a hand up to stop the man from advancing on me. "Obliged, Baz." I wriggled my wrists. "A bit unfair.

Can't put up much of a fight. Release me, though, and I'd be delighted to take you all on. One at a time, of course."

That got the big bald guy laughing out loud. "Fucking hell, mate," said Baz. "Could you just shut up and sit there?"

"What's the end game? Am I going to get chopped into bite-sized pieces and fed to the Finns?"

Baz looked confused. "The who?"

I nodded at the two big guys behind him. "Mika and Karl. The Clydesdales."

"No, no. They're vegetarians, I think. We're going to slap you around a bit. Lubricate the truth tubes so when Leung gets here, your responses are fulsome and complete."

"Wow." I tilted my head back and looked at the ceiling. "Fulsome?" I watched a spider repair a web beside a large hook fixed to the cross beam. "Another fucking hook? No imagination." I sighed. "I don't like Leung that much. Killed a good friend of mine." I looked Baz in the eyes. "I'd dearly love to pay him back for that." I looked at the ceiling again. "Is that hook new? I don't remember it from the last time."

Baz glanced at the ceiling and checked his watch. "He's on the way. About an hour out. Time to tune you up." He nodded at the Finns. "Hang him."

"What the fuck?"

Karl grabbed my shoulders from behind while Mika used clippers to snip the cable ties. I flexed my fingers, returning circulation to my hands. "Hanging is a drastic response. I'm not going to last an hour if you hang me now. Maybe wait until he's closer. A lot closer."

Mika pulled my hands in front of my body and tied them together.

"Not by the neck."

He yanked my hands above my head and looped my bound wrists over the hook. His brother helped lift me. My toes barely touched the stable's floor. Certainly didn't touch enough to take any of the weight off my wrists. "This is really uncomfortable. Could you move the chair closer? Let me stand on it?"

I swayed a bit. I rotated about ninety degrees to my left, then back to my right. Almost the whole crowd was here.

Almost.

"Where's Dom? I miss his little ponytail."

Baz grunted and punched me on the side, catching one of my floating ribs. I clenched my jaw and didn't give him the pleasure of responding. To be fair, it wasn't a very hard hit. He was toying with me. It was going to be a long hour.

I took a steadying breath. "What in the hell was that for? I'm happy to answer questions, but you haven't asked any yet. Ask. Maybe save your energy for something else."

He hit me on the other side. Same place, except the right side instead of the left, same level of impact. I was a sparring bag for him. I had to distract him. "You didn't answer. Where's Dom?"

He picked up a broom handle and smacked me across the back of my thighs. Mother FUCK, that hurt.

"I'm asking the questions."

"No, Baz, you aren't," I said through clenched teeth. "You're just hitting me. Like a half-wit sadist. Are you okay, mate?"

He poked me in the stomach, up high in the solar plexus. Just below my sternum. Great way to make a guy's diaphragm spasm. I heaved for a good minute, trying to get my breath back.

The Finns were chuckling, Mika, rubbing his fist against his open palm. Great. Unlikely they'd take it easy with me. "I'm serious. Is Dom still with Layla?"

Baz checked his swing. The broom handle stopped just short of my kneecaps. "What's that now? About Layla?"

"Her and Dom, right? A thing?"

"You're nuts. Dom spends his time running operations at the circus. They're up near Newcastle right now."

"Gosford. Don't try lying to me, Baz. I know exactly what's going on with your laundering operations. You must have more than the circus, right? You can't push enough money through the circus to cover what Leung is pulling with the drugs he's bringing in."

"Don't change the subject. Why do you think Dom and Layla are a thing?"

"Shouldn't bother you. She's your *ex*. Hasn't been in your life since the kid was a baby."

Baz pointed at Mika. "Call Dom. Tell him to get back to the main house now." He turned back to me, pushing the broomstick up under my chin. "You didn't answer me. What do you know?"

"About Dom or just general knowledge?"

He gave the bottom of my jaw, right at the point of my chin, a sharp rap with the end of the broomstick. My teeth clattered together, and I bit the side of my tongue.

I spit blood onto the floor. "That wasn't nice. Dom has been driving the kid back and forth to school every day. Driveway pick up and drop off. Or he was until a day or two ago. I'm told the kid is back at the circus, with the mother's knowledge. You didn't know about this?

He punched me in the gut this time. I swung back about a metre and swayed from my increasingly painful wrists.

"I'm asking the questions, you bell end. What do you know about this operation?"

"If you're talking about the circus, it's an incredibly clumsy attempt to launder some small amount of cash— illicit cash— no doubt from Leung's drug importation activities. If he's doing as well as he was when we thought he'd died, there either needs to be a couple of dozen other circuses running or something much bigger. Like real estate, or art, or, hey, are you guys cuckoo-smurfing?"

I saw it coming this time and managed to tense my abs before impact. It still stung, but he didn't knock the wind out of me.

"I will keep hitting you until you start answering my questions and stop asking them."

"I answered! Okay. No more questions from me."

"What do you know about Dom?"

It didn't matter what I'd say to him, he was going to hit me again. I sniffed and tried to wipe my nose on my shoulder again. "The hay in here is causing my allergies to act up. Can we go outside?"

He picked up the broom handle and cracked it across my shins.

"Son of a bitch." Have you ever tried shaking pain out of your legs when you're hanging from your wrists? Of course, you haven't. If you're ever in that situation, let me tell you now that it doesn't work. "Dom is a childhood friend of yours, through thick and thin. He's mostly thin. He has a wispy goatee and a ponytail, which is kind of funny because there's no hair on the top of his head. He seems to be stepping out with your ex and caring for your kid like he's part of their family.

I tensed, waiting for a blow.

It didn't come.

Baz took his phone out, dialled a number and glared at me while he pressed it to the side of his head. I could hear the faint thrumming of a ringing phone. Four rings, and it went to voicemail. He hung up and called another number.

Paced in front of me, phone pressed to his head, staring at me like he wanted to kill me.

Three rings, and a woman's voice answered.

"Layla, where's Dom?"

She said a lot of words or spoke extremely slowly; after a minute or so of Baz listening, he barked, "Bullshit." And stabbed the End Call button on the phone.

He stowed his phone and stood in front of me. He had to look slightly upward to look me in the eye. Despite that, I felt no dominance over him. "Where did you see Dom last, and where?"

"I didn't actually see him. It was the black SUV registered to him, and he had dropped Lachie off at the house in Vaucluse." I tipped my head sideways and looked down at him. "You're pushing a shitload of money through the sale of that house, too, aren't you?"

He scowled. "What the fuck are you talking about?"

"Her house is under offer. Almost double what it's appraised for. It's a beautiful house, but it's not worth anywhere near 20 million."

He didn't know. I could tell by the look on his face.

He punctuated his next sentence with blows from the broom handle. "What—in the fuck—are you talking about?"

Twenty-Nine

He absolutely cracked a couple of my ribs. I twisted away in a vain attempt to avoid the stick, but all I ended up doing was exposing another part of my body for a beating. "Stop, stop, stop."

He stopped, stick held high. "You going to tell me anything?"

I choked back what I wanted to say: I'd been answering his questions. It wasn't my fault he didn't like the answers. "If you kill me before Leung gets here, he's going to be pissed. I know that guy. He'll leave pieces of you all over NSW."

Baz dropped the broom handle on the stable floor and pushed my chest so I swung back and forth. A human's shoulders weren't built for this kind of abuse, and it felt like one of my arms was about to rip off.

"We'll wait." He gave me another push. "You're not going to enjoy it." He took his phone out again and made a call. It thrummed four times, and after the beep, he yelled into the phone. "Dom, fucking call me as soon as you fucking get this." He jammed the phone in his pocket, took the chair I'd been strapped to and placed it a couple of metres in front of me. He sat in it, rested his arms on the broad slabs of wood that made up the chair's arms and crossed his legs at his ankles.

"How do you know so much about money laundering?"

"You offering me a job? My dog could do better than you idiots." He started to stand. "Hey, just kidding. I'm a private investigator. My suite of skills is both broad and deep." I tried a deep breath. It was a challenge. I felt like I was being stabbed. "You're going to have to let me down, champ. I'm finding it more and more difficult to breathe." I might have been exaggerating the difficulty. "Remember, Leung wants to chat with me. Not my corpse."

Baz checked his watch again. "Thirty minutes." He leaned back in the chair and crossed his legs. "Give me a preview. Tell me everything you know about our operations."

I attempted a shrug. "I'll wait until the bossman gets here. The breathing—it's making it difficult to talk. Maybe if you lowered me, got me a cup of coffee, maybe then we could have a chat."

Baz tipped his head back and groaned. "You fucking cockroach. Mika, get this arsehole a chair and make sure he's well attached to it."

The big Finn disappeared for a second and returned with the match to the heavy chair Baz was parked in. He placed it just in front of my hanging torso. He had a half dozen thick cable ties in his back pocket. He nodded for his brother to help him. They placed themselves on either side of me and lifted with their knees. My arms dropped like bricks off an overpass, and pain rushed in right behind the blood flowing to my hands. The Finns manhandled me to the chair. Karl pulled out a knife and cut the tape around my wrists. Mika handed him a couple of cable ties, and they re-attached my ankles and wrists to the arms and front legs of the chair. I tested the arms. I wouldn't be getting out of this easily.

Baz watched all this with an amused look on his face. The Finns stepped away, and Baz tapped on the arm of his chair. "More comfortable?"

The cable ties were cutting into my wrists. "I can breathe now, but I think I might lose my hands."

"Tough fucking luck. Talk. Leung will believe me if I tell him you rushed me, and my lads had to take you out."

"Well, when you put it like that." I looked up, collecting my thoughts. The red light was on. I smiled and looked at Baz. "What's Lyla's place in your organisation? Top-level? Does she report directly to Leung, or are you the main man? She's at least in charge of the financials, right?"

He shook his head. "You're a shit detective. My ex has nothing to do with our business. Fifteen minutes. The only reason Leung is coming down here is because he wants to see the face of one of the men who killed his son as we beat him to death."

I laughed. "Beat Leung to death? You're going to beat Leung to *death*? God *damn*, I'm glad to be here."

"You, you mongrel. *You're* going to be beaten to death. It's going to take an hour or so, but you'll be begging for release long before you die."

"Oh, very melodramatic. And you're wrong about Layla. So wrong." I wiggled my fingers. "My hands are turning purple. Loosen these, would you?"

He leaned forward with his elbow on his knees. "I'm not wrong. And fuck your hands."

"You're wrong, and I don't do that so much since I got a girlfriend." I wiggled my fingers while I still could. "Layla's got half a dozen shell companies feeding just as many offshore accounts. She worked with Dom and a young attorney I know to set them up—in the Caymans, Malta, Seychelles, and a few other places I can't remember."

"This is bullshit."

"This is not bullshit."

"You've got proof of these accounts?"

I shrugged. Easier when you're not hung up by your arms. "Not on me, obviously. On my laptop. I could access some of the information from my phone." I nodded toward the stable door where my phone sat. "Are you going to give me my phone?"

Mika took a step toward it, and Baz held up his hand. "You must think I'm a moron."

"Jesus, mate. Stop feeding me straight lines. If I answer that honestly, your boys will shred me like pulled pork. Just get me the phone, and I'll—"

"Is this the prick?" Leung walked into the stable. He cleaned up in the hours since I last saw him. He wore a navy blue blazer over an open-collared white shirt and pressed denim trousers. I checked his shoes. Tan Converse Chuck Taylor low riders. Fashionable, rich dude.

He tilted his head and looked closely at me. "Dying to know how you got away."

"Talk to the brothers. Their operational security sucks."

He glanced at the Finns, narrowed his eyes and squatted in front of me. "You little prick.

"I am the prick. *You're* the prick who killed my best friend. Hey, have you sold your place yet? Nice house. Wait, wait, wait. You're going to use it to launder money, aren't you? What other—"

He stood and kicked the seat of my chair, knocking it over on its, and my, back.

Again. "You're favourite move? You're good at it.

"Shut up, prick."

I looked up at him. "How did you do it?"

He toe-punted my ribs. "Do what? Knock your chair over? Simple party trick."

"I was in the surveillance van when the warehouse blew up. A school friend was at the front of the stack and died that day. We were positive you were in there. I watched them track heat signatures. Until it exploded. We found DNA in the warehouse positively matched with yours." It was difficult presenting a strong case when you're on your back looking up while a drug kingpin circles you. "So, how did you do it?"

He toe-punted me on the side of my head, pinning my ear back.

"Son of a bitch, mate. What the fuck?" My eyes watered. That stung.

Leung rounded on Baz. "I told you I wanted him hung from his wrists. Then beat him until he shits blood."

I was running out of options. Karl lifted the chair and Mika clipped the cable ties. Karl stood behind me, pressing down on my shoulders. I tried resisting when the brother wrapped my wrists in duct tape again. Pointless. It wouldn't matter how often I went to the gym. It would be pointless.

Leung watched while they hung me up on the hook. He tapped the broomstick on the floor, anticipation on his face. "Make him swing a bit." He pounded the end of the broomstick into the ground. "I need to work on my timing."

"Wait, wait, wait. You've got to tell me how you did it." Leung was shorter than Baz. I had my chin pressed to my chest to look at him. "We found your DNA. We had you in the building when it went up."

Leung held up his hand, stopping Baz from spinning me. "If you promise to take it to your grave." He smiled. "What am I talking about? Of course you will."

"I would have thought you could afford better dental, mate. Your teeth look like shit."

That got me a jab in the stomach.

I powered through the pain. "My apologies. You look great. And I promise I'll take it to my grave." I *tried* to cross my fingers. That counts, right?

Leung sighed as he stared at me. He shrugged. "No idea why you thought I was in there. Somebody fucked up with the thermals. I'd been out for ten minutes when it blew." He leaned the broomstick against the stable wall and took off his blazer. Draped it over the chair I had been sitting in and unbuttoned the cuff on his right sleeve. He pushed it up to his elbow and showed me the inside of his arm. A jagged scar stretched from his wrist to the inside of his elbow. "This is why I left the warehouse and how you found traces of my DNA." He slid his sleeve down and buttoned the cuff. "To your grave, right?"

"Absolutely." Like fuck.

Leung nodded at Baz. "Start him up."

Baz grunted as he swung me in an arc. Leung wound up and swung at my legs.

The stable went black. Except for the single red light on the camera. I hoped to hell Davie was just watching and mounting a rescue from afar. He didn't need to be here.

Leung connected as Baz yelled, "What the fuck is going on?" A couple of the crew took out their phones and turned on the built-in torches. Noises came from outside, toward the house. A couple of long guns appeared from the stables. "Guys, I don't want to get caught in the crossfire. Let me down from this hook." Mika ran past me toward the stable doors, and I swung a kick at him. I missed, and the torsion on my arms was brutal.

A barrage of angry voices yelling things like "Armed Police" and "get on the ground" followed the criss-cross of targeted torch beams into the stable. First time I've been on the receiving end of the AFP during a takedown. It took a couple of minutes before everyone was secured. Someone got a shot off with one of the long guns and received three back in the chest. All four shots missed me. I was blessed.

Jackson looked up at me and depressed the transmit button on his radio. "We're clear in here. Turn the lights back on."

"Hey, Jackson. Think you could help me down?"

He holstered his sidearm and smiled. "Thank you."

"No worries. What are you thanking me for?"

"We got Leung."

"Sweet. Get me down, will you? My arms are seconds away from ripping off my body."

Jackson pushed a chair over. "Lift your feet. Get some core work in. And get yourself down. We're a bit tied up processing bad guys."

"*You're* tied up?" I stood on the chair and unhooked myself. Jumped off and sat. My arms were killing me, and my wrists were still bound. "Flick open your knife and cut the tape for me, would you? How did you find me?"

"Yeah, sure." He did as asked. "You get yourself into a lot of scrapes, mate."

I looked at the camera, now on. "Did you re-activate the camera?" I pointed to the small lens at the far end of the stable.

"Us? Yeah, nah. That was your mate, Davie. He's been doing some questionable things. You might want to stay clear of him for a couple of weeks."

"He's helped me get out of more scrapes than I can count. A hell of a lot more than you have."

He nodded. "Yeah, he's the one who told us where you were. We rushed the DNA on the straw and confirmed it was Leung. I called your house, and Lucy answered. Not sure what she sees in you, but she called your buddy and he tracked your phone. Told us where you were and then he got eyes on you."

"You couldn't get into the camera?"

He looked up at the lens and back at me. "We'd need a warrant, being as we're official law enforcement. I'm not putting his breach into the report, though. So get your friend to tone it down for a few weeks. You got a ride home? Because all of our vehicles are going to be full."

Thirty

"He's got a ride." Davie stepped into the stable with his iPad under his arm, Lucy right behind him. She pushed Davie out of the way and rushed over to me.

She squatted to get eye-to-eye. "You look like shit." She stood and faced Jackson. "A bit late to the party, but better late than never, I suppose."

"What are you talking about? We launched an attack as soon as you told me where he was."

"Nick fucking told you Leung was here in the country days ago, and you thought he was full of shit." She poked him in the chest. "He wouldn't have been hung from a hook if you believed him then."

I groaned as I pushed myself up from the chair. "It's okay, Luce. I'm okay."

She held me at arm's length, appraising the damage to my face and other areas where the skin was visible. "Not likely. You're going to need a doctor's visit."

Davie was holding back. He stepped to one side as Mika and Karl were ushered out, cuffed and surly. There were cops on each side. Baz was already out. Leung was sitting in a chair with four cops around him.

"Just a sec, Luce." I waved Davie over. "I owe you again." Pointed at the camera. "You did that, right?"

"Saw all of it. You need to listen to your girlfriend and get yourself to a clinic." He lifted the side of my shirt and winced when he saw the bruises. "Ouch."

I pulled it down to cover the bruises, but it was too late. Lucy saw them, and they were worse than what she'd seen in the shower. "I'm good, guys. I need to talk to Jackson first."

"Then you see a doctor." Lucy was adamant. I kinda liked adamant Lucy.

"Absolutely."

Getting Jackson's attention was easier said than done. He was busy with an on-the-spot interrogation of Leung. He wasn't getting anything from him. Leung just sat and smiled at them, maintaining silence. Jackson gave up. "Take him back and put him in a cell for the night. We'll talk to him in the morning." He bumped into me when he turned. "Why are you still here?"

"Leung isn't all of it. You picked up Barry Williams, yeah? The bald fuck. Lots of ink. Someone took him out of here a couple of minutes ago."

Jackson tapped an icon on his screen and scrolled through his notes. He nodded. "Yeah. We got him. Pretty high on the list, too. We're going to buy beers for you and your friends for a few months. We've wiped more than a few faces off our most wanted lists. What about him?"

"His ex-wife is pulling some shady shit that not even Leung knows about. With her ex-husband's best friend."

Jackson pushed me away. "I don't give a flying fuck who's banging who. We've got Leung. Many thanks for your help. Let your friends take you to a hospital. You look like shite." His team had secured Leung, still smiling and not talking. Jackson took his captor by the arm and marched him out of the stables. "Call me tomorrow to set up a time for a statement. All three of you."

I watched him leave and shook my head. "This isn't finished until we figure out what Layla is up to."

"We?"

I looked at Lucy. Shrugged. "Me and whoever wants to help."

"Whomever, I think. Tomorrow, though," she said

"I've got a full day tomorrow. I'd prefer to close this out tonight if I could."

Lucy rolled her eyes and left the stables. "I'm not driving," she called as she left.

I held out my hand. "I will."

Davie smacked my hand away. "You'll fall asleep."

"You're right." We followed Lucy out. "Hang on a sec." I ran back in and grabbed my phone and watch. I looked around the now empty, cold stables. It was surreal. I hoped to never be back.

I caught up to Davie, and we walked to his car. Lucy was leaning against it, parked between a couple of AFP vans. Agents were milling around, ignoring us. An evidence van had just arrived, and three people of indistinguishable genders in full-body bunny suits made their way to the house.

"How are you doing, anyway?"

"What, the faulty pancreas thing? It pisses me off." He pressed the key fob, and his car blurped in time with the double flash of the park lights. "But it could be worse. The insulin is magic. I feel better than I have in a long time."

"Plus Fiona."

"Mind your business," he said. But he was smiling.

Lucy grabbed the front seat, and I sprawled out in the back. "If my snoring disturbs you, tough. I can't help it."

I faded in and out for bit, head against the passenger-side window. I was absolutely knackered. By the time I was upright and mostly conscious, we were heading south back into Sydney, somewhere on the M1.

I yawned and stretched as much as I could in the car. "Where are we?"

"Coming up to the Mooney-Mooney Bridge," said Lucy. "How are your ribs?"

"The same as the rest of me. I need a hot soak." I yawned again and watched Davie and Lucy catch it.

"Davie tells me you think Layla and Dom are involved in this somehow? Are you sure?"

I cracked the window. The chill air helped me think. "I can't prove it, but I know it. Good thing I'm not a cop anymore."

"Jackson will need to prove it, which means we need to prove it." Lucy twisted in her seat, looking back at me. "How?"

"I dunno. We need to pool all of our information." I yawned again, triggering another round of yawns in the car. "But I need to rest first. Are we all okay with going back to my place?"

"That's where I was before I had to rescue you." Lucy smiled. "So, sure."

Davie nodded. "Sure." He patted a small bag on the car's console. "I've got my jabs here if I need them."

"Excellent." I looked at my watch. "We're about half an hour away. I'm closing my eyes again. Wake me when we get there."

I didn't really sleep. It was thirty minutes of drifting in and out of consciousness, random pieces of information wafting through my brain while I attempted, in vain, to stick them all in a single cohesive pile.

I had slid down into the back seat, sprawled across, my head leaning against the passenger side door and my feet under Davie's seat.

I pushed myself up when Davie turned off the ignition. "That didn't help one bit."

"You sure you want to do this now?"

"While the iron's hot, Luce." I untangled myself from the back seat and stood, stretching into the night air. "Coffee."

Davie pointed at me. "It's too late for coffee. It's not healthy."

Lucy looked at me and raised her eyebrows, a small smile on her face.

"Davie, mate, it's your pancreas that's fucked up, not your heart. I'm making coffee, and Lucy and I are consuming that coffee. If you don't want any, that's entirely up to you. Just keep your snoring to a dull roar."

"We'll need some of his tech wizardry, Nick." Lucy slipped her hand in mine. "We might have to force-feed him."

"I might let you." Davie locked his car and followed us up the outside steps to my apartment. "Extra strong."

It was just past midnight, into another day. I doubled up the pods on the coffee machine.

We took our cups and gathered in my small lounge room. Lucy and I sat on the sofa. Davie parked in the chair across from us. I held up my cup. "To all-nighters."

I didn't get a salute in response.

"Not fans?"

"Too old for this shit, mate." Davie took a sip and winced. "Too hot." He blew on the coffee. "All-nighters in uni? Sure, that was fun. This, not so much."

"I appreciate your help. Jackson and his team will close this case with Leung, but I think Layla is the real boss of the organisation."

Lucy put her cup on the coffee table. "So what do we have?"

Davie yawned. "Did you mention Layla to Leung?"

I nodded. "He didn't have a clue what I was talking about."

"So she's running a hostile takeover."

Lucy held up a finger. "And if we want to draw Layla out, we'll have to block her access to the funds."

Davie unsuccessfully tried to stifle a yawn. "You can do that, Luce?"

She stood, grabbed my laptop and sat back on the sofa. She opened the lid and held it toward me. I unlocked it with my fingerprint, and she took it back.

"You know the password, though," I said.

"This was faster." She looked at me, then Davie. "So, boys, what are we doing about the money? Are we locking her out? Stealing it? Donating it to some worthy charities?"

Thirty-One

Lucy made the changes we'd agreed to, and we crashed. Too tired to do anything but sleep, Davie and Lucy decided to head to their respective beds. They left just after one in the morning. I gathered the cups and deposited them in the sink. I ran water over them, then left them dirty in the sink. Too tired.

I had a quick shower to wash off the day and was crawling into bed when my phone started exploding. I groaned and sat on the edge of my bed, and scrolled through the messages.

All of them from Lyla.

All of them threatened me with severe bodily harm. I smiled. She'd fallen into my cunning trap. Well, credit where credit's due: Lucy's cunning trap.

I put the phone down and put my head back on my pillow. Let her stew for a bit longer.

The messages stopped and I was drifting off when the phone rang. I answered with, "Lyla, those messages are actionable. Threatening physical harm over the phone is against the law. A number of laws."

"Not Lyla, fuckwit."

I sat up and swung my feet to the floor.

"Lyla wants our money released, and I promise you if that doesn't happen immediately, I will find you and tear you to pieces."

"*Our* money, Dom? You two are taking over Leung's business, aren't you?" I can't lie. I was pleased we were right about that. Not surprised, but pleased. I was good at this.

There was a long pause. "How do you know my name?"

"Oh, I know more than that. I know you drive a late model black Range Rover, you shuttle Lachie back and forth to school, and you're schtupping Layla. Or using her. Or she's using you. Doesn't matter which. You've been setting up offshore accounts and just started removing money from Leung's operation."

"We're very happy that you've accelerated the process for us, but that end game, locking the accounts, that's not cool. And I swear to god, if you don't right this wrong, I will end you."

Trap sprung. Hook set. Any other metaphor you could come up with. "I have conditions."

"Fuck your conditions."

I chuckled. "Who has the power here, Dom? I have conditions."

He paused again. "Okay. Face-to-face. Right now."

"Are you fucking kidding? It's like two in the morning. I'm not an idiot. Tomorrow morning. Seven-ish, somewhere public."

The guy was a slow thinker. The pause was even longer this time. "There's a park in Bondi Junction. Dickerson Reserve. Seven sharp."

"Not public enough. Bondi Beach."

I was going to fall asleep waiting for his response. He finally grunted assent. "Sure. Seven. I could make that work."

I hung up. No need to drag the call out. I grabbed my laptop and crawled back into bed, sitting up against the headboard. I opened Davie's program and checked the availability of cameras around the beach. There were dozens, but most of them were inaccessible. I tagged the ones that were active and checked the angles. Most were too far from the beach to clearly identify the people, let alone pick up audio. The best location was the eastern part of the beach. A couple of houses had doorbell cameras that provided a good beach view and picked up the audio.

I sent a message to Jackson. *East end of Bondi Beach, in about 4 hours. The location of Leung's money will be revealed.*

His response was almost immediate. *I'm busy, Harding. You better be here at 11 for your trial prep and statement.*

I stared at my phone for a minute. Priorities. Trial prep was going to have to wait. Statements would have to wait.

Getting Davie and Lucy involved with this wasn't even a consideration.

I set my alarm for six and crashed.

Morning came far too fast. The insistent alarm had been going for a couple of minutes by the time I regained my senses. I was exhausted all the way down. It took me a couple of seconds to remember why, in fact, I was awakened by the alarm. It was a late night. I should be sleeping.

Then I remembered.

I cleaned my teeth, got dressed and decided to walk. The exercise would wake me up—it had to. I messaged Dom. *By the Icebergs, seven sharp.* Reverse psychology.

The Icebergs was the club at the far west end of the beach. Lots of people there. The adjoining tidal pool was a tourist draw. And Dom was not the sharpest crayon in the box. He replied almost instantly.

No way. Exact opposite end of the beach. Less people. I don't want a crowd.

I smiled. Predictable. I put up a fight. *Not comfortable with that.*

Now, his ego would kick in. *Too bad. Other end of the beach in thirty minutes.*

Perfect. And thirty minutes would be ten minutes late. He wanted to get there before me. Even more perfect. I had time to grab a coffee and still beat him there.

I walked past the skate park. Some of Lachlan's friends were there, being the unruly teenagers they were meant to be. I stopped at the pavilion and picked up a large long black, extra hot, and asked them to double-cup it. Extra hot would peel your fingerprints off if you didn't have a couple of layers of cardboard between the coffee and your hands. Even then, it was difficult to carry. I had to change hands every few steps.

I took a sip. Scalded my tongue, but the caffeine hit the parts of the brain it needed to hit. I walked along the boardwalk to the parking lot at the east end of the beach. I did a slow scan, looking for Dom's black Range Rover. Any black Range Rover, frankly. Not an exceptionally common vehicle, even in this high-rent neighbourhood.

I spotted it approaching from almost a block away. I ducked behind a shack hiring out surfboards to tourists. Thirty seconds later, he pulled into the parking lot. I watched him as he sat in the truck, scanning the beach, looking for me. Satisfied that I wasn't there, he hopped out of the truck. Three of his friends joined them. One of them I recognised from the first time I was in the stables. The other two were new to me. Battlefield promotions for the lot of them, I guess.

The three friends were dressed for the beach. They fanned out and took spots on the sand. Conspicuous when you know why they were there, but to the casual observer, just another three idiots working on their melanomas.

I needed Dom to be facing the cameras. On the outside chance the audio wasn't clear, the lip readers could fill in the gaps. I waited until he'd moved about twenty metres onto the sand. I came out from behind the surf shack and walked toward him until I was about five metres away. He was still facing away from me, expecting me to come in from the west side of the beach.

His three muscles either didn't know what I looked like or were phenomenal actors. They weren't paying me any attention. Dom looked smaller on the expanse of the beach. His ponytail was grey, and the skin on the back of his neck was sallow.

"Dom. You're fucking early." He turned. I held up my cup. "I haven't finished my coffee yet." He looked even worse from the front. Rings under his eyes. Three or four days of stubble. There were food stains on his shirt. I found it hard to believe he and Lyla were in any kind of relationship other than financial. And she'd cut him loose as soon as he delivered what she wanted.

"Release the accounts." His fists were clenched by his side. "Or—"

"Or what, Dom? You'll sic your three guys on me?" I pointed at one of them. "The beach is patrolled. You might get a few shots in, but you won't get what you want."

"We'll drag you out past the shark nets and drown you. Hard to convict when there's no corpse."

"Not fucking likely, mate." I heard a car door open as Dom glanced past me, over my shoulder. I resisted the urge to look. "You brought Layla with you?"

He chuckled. "Layla is smarter than that."

"No shit." I watched half a dozen skaters collect their boards and walk toward us. They were about 300 metres away but had just broken into a jog.

I returned my attention to Dom. "She's a fuck of a lot smarter than you." I heard footsteps close in on me from behind. "Hey, Lachie. Get around in front of me so I don't have to hurt you."

"Do it, kiddo." Dom motioned for him to stand by his side. "I'm getting tired of this, Nick. The money."

"What money?"

Dom closed his eyes and looked up at the sky. He returned to clenching his fists. "Take off your shirt and show me your phone."

I pulled off my shirt and turned my pockets inside out. "I'm not wired. And I left my phone at home." I slowly turned around, giving him a good look at my out-of-shape, heavily bruised body. "She's going to kill you." I pulled my shirt back on. I'm not good in the sun.

"Why in the hell would she kill me?"

"Tell me what money you're talking about, and I'll tell you why."

Lachie looked confused. "You told me he knew all about it." The kid looked at me with a frown on his face. "The money that my father was collecting. It belongs to us. He didn't pay any child support, and he owes us."

Well. The kid was brought in, albeit under false pretences. "Dom, you're conning the kid. You didn't tell him about the laundering activities? The drug importing that daddy's friend Leung was running?"

Lachlan's head snapped to Dom. "Drugs? What's he talking about? You said it was just circus money."

Dom shook his head while he chuckled. "Not that bright, are you, kid? No way that circus brings in the kind of money we're talking about." He pulled a knife from a sheath stuck under his belt. "I've had enough of this shit."

He lunged at me with the knife. I sidestepped and threw the cup of coffee at his face. It was still hot enough to slow him but not stop him. I danced around while Dom flailed at me.

The three thugs leapt into action, but were slowed by the skaters. Kelly, the girl I had talked to, grabbed Lachlan and pulled him away. The others looked like they were going to engage Dom's muscle, but were overwhelmed by the size of them.

The skaters were walking wounded and Dom's three friends were escorting me to the truck. Before the lifeguards reached us, Dom was behind the wheel, and I was once again the stuffing in a henchman sandwich.

"A lot more comfortable than the trucks Baz runs around in. These wheels must have set you back. Business must be good." I craned my neck to look out the back window and received a punch from the henchman on the left.

I wheezed out a breath. "She's really gonna kill you now."

"Why's that, dickhead?"

"You left her son behind." I tipped my head back and bellowed. "You can take her money, but you can never take her children!" I thought I did a good Gibson-doing-Wallace.

Henchman on the right popped me on the side of the head. He had no taste. I rubbed the side of my head and glared at him. "Where are we going?"

"Lachie is hanging out with his friends at the skatepark. Layla's cool with that. And when I deliver the source of her problems—"

"*Her* problems? I thought you two were in this together."

He shut his mouth. I could see his jaw muscles clenching. I might have bit off more than I could chew. And I had no backup.

The drive was mercifully short.

He pulled into Layla's drive and stopped. Henchman on the right opened the door, got out, then reached in and dragged me out after him.

I tried pulling my arm free. No luck. He frog-marched me into Layla's house. The other muscle walked up front. Dom brought up the rear.

Layla opened the door as we walked up the steps and quickly stood to one side. "Get the hell in here before the neighbours see."

"Fuck them," said Dom.

She held the door as we all traipsed in and then looked out the door. "Where's Lachie?" She grabbed Dom by the arm. "What the hell? Where's my son?"

Muscle guy had let go of my arm. I perched on one of the bar stool-styled chairs at her kitchen counter. "What did I tell you, Dom? You're fucked."

Layla spun toward me, her face taut and her eyes wide. "Why? What happened? Where's Lachie?"

Dom took her by the hands. "Hey, he's just hanging with his skate pals at the beach. He'll be back in a couple of hours." He nodded toward me. "And I brought this little shit stain. I'd beat the crap out of him just for fun. To get our money back? That's just a bonus."

I crossed my arms. "If it's okay with you, I've had my fair share of beatings—more than my fair share—over the roughly seventy-two hours and I think I deserve at least a week's break."

"How did you find out?" She looked pissed.

"There's all those new accounts you've set up." I listed the countries where they were established. "And the money you've been moving from Baz's accounts into those offshore accounts." I was guessing with that one. I hadn't seen evidence, but it was obvious. "And the laundering you're doing with this house? Pretty blatant."

Layla slid a knife off a magnetic holder. "Then I'll just cut you until you give it back." She advanced on me with slow, measured steps. "I'll cut your face last."

She was right in front of me, the tip of a very sharp, all-black knife resting on my chin. "Tell me where my money is."

I slowly pulled my head back. "Told ya, Dom. Where *her* money is. Not yours, hers."

Her knuckles whitened as she gripped the knife tighter. "That's right. My money." She took a swipe at my arm.

I swivelled out of the way. The tip sliced down the outside of my forearm, deeper than a scratch but not deep to the bone. It burned at first. Like fire. Then it hurt like a son of a bitch. "Jesus, you're psycho." The blood welled out of my arm and was starting to look like a serious problem. I backpedalled into the kitchen and grabbed a tea towel from the dish rack. "Fuck this. I'll take the beatings."

She backed me around the kitchen and through the dining area. I had my back up against the folding doors that opened to the patio. I reached back and fumbled with the latch and pushed the door open.

I caught a glance of Dom, a big, shit-eating grin on his face. He was standing back and letting her go at me.

I had backed out onto the patio and managed to get the dining table between us. Dom and his two 'roided out hulks were behind her, making sure I didn't get past.

To my left and right was a hip-high rock wall separating her property from her neighbours. Behind me was a knee-height rock wall, and beyond that a fifteen metre drop onto the rocks and surf.

"My money, you shit. Release the funds, or I cut you again."

"That was a lucky shot." It wasn't lucky. She knew how to handle a blade. I took another step backward. My calves were pressed up against the wall. She jumped on top of the table and then dropped in front of me.

She lunged at me with her knife arm extended. Someone to the left of me yelled, "Taser. Taser. Taser," and Layla caught two probes in the throat. I jumped backwards on top of the wall—an athletic feat only possible due to immense amounts of adrenaline coursing through my system—and almost fell backwards into the rocks.

A cop in tactical gear stopped me from taking a dive with one hand while he holstered his taser with the other. Three of his colleagues came over the wall beside her property, weapons drawn.

Dom and his pals turned to run and were met by an overwhelming force coming in through a kicked-in front door.

I sat on the rock wall and took a deep breath. My arm throbbed and blood oozed through the tea towel.

I looked up as Jackson approached. "Thanks for showing up to the party, Jackson. Better late than never, right?" I slowly stood. "Almost too late. What brings you here? I told you the beach. Don't get me wrong—I'm very appreciative—but if you'd shown up at the beach on time, I wouldn't be heading to A&E for god knows how many stitches."

Jackson grunted and pointed over his shoulder. Just beyond Layla being helped into a police wagon were Lucy and Davie, standing behind a cop who wouldn't let them pass.

I shuffled through the house and gave Lucy a big, one-armed hug. "How in the hell?"

She gave me a push. "You didn't think you should have called us before being this stupid?" She took my arm. "What happened this time?"

"I can be this stupid all on my own." I pulled her back and gave her another one-armed hug. "But I'm really glad you two figured out where I was and brought reinforcements." I took Davie by the shoulder. "How in the hell did you find me?"

He showed me his phone. His CCTV program was running, showing the video from two of the houses pointed at the beach. "Saw it all. Did you let yourself get caught, or was that a bone-headed rookie mistake?"

"Ha. I'll leave that to your imagination. You saw Dom and guessed he'd come here?"

"No guessing required. We tracked him though cameras. Real-time."

Jackson was finished with whatever cop stuff he had to do. "Jesus Christ, Harding. How do you always get involved in his shit?"

"You owe me one, Jackson. I'm going to have to put off the trial prep and statements for another day. I've got another client this morning. Not as exciting as this one, I hope."

He nodded at Lucy. "You've got a pretty decent team."

"All voluntary, mate," said Lucy.

"That's our cue," said Davie. "Let's get the hell out of here."

"Hey." Jackson called out after us. "I'll need your statements by the end of the day, okay?"

I flipped him the finger as we left the house.

Lucy threaded her fingers through mine and was nearly skipping back to the car.

"You had fun?"

"Exhilarating, Nick." She wrinkled her nose. "You need to get that arm looked at, though."

Thirty-Two

A shower with Lucy, and a strong coffee improved my frame of mind. I was more awake. I might actually last until mid-afternoon before I face-planted.

I had seven stitches down the outside of my arm. The magic painkillers were doing their job. A waterproof plaster stretched the length of the cut. I pulled on a long-sleeved shirt and headed to work.

I walked into my little office. It felt like months since I last set foot in it. I grabbed my digital notepad, set up a file for my new customer and went to her office. I rapped on the doorframe and got Maria's attention. "Hiya. Is Harry in?"

I felt a tap on my shoulder. "Right behind you."

I turned and saw Harriet for the first time. She was what people would call a handsome woman. She had curly greying hair, a wide smile and a spattering of freckles across her nose. She had what can only charitably be called British teeth. And she looked the kind of fit that ran ultra-marathons.

"My goodness. What's happened to your face?"

I touched the mouse on my cheek and smiled. "You should see the rest of me. The occasional hazards of the job. Very occasional. Is there somewhere we can talk?"

She led me to a small conference room and opened her laptop. She tapped a couple of keys, and her screen was mirrored to the flat screen on the wall.

"You're going to have to show me how you did that," I said. "I'm still getting the hang of the place."

"Claude is your guy. He's got a mousepad he'll sell you with all the shortcuts you'll ever need." She pointed at the screen on the wall. "This is the company I'd like you to check for us. And to make sure your investigation is completely independent, I'm not going to tell you anything I may have already discovered."

I wrote the company name in my electronic notepad. "PNG-based, right?"

"It is, and that's all that I'll tell you, other than the name and address." She handed me a piece of paper with those details.

"A blind test. Good call. What specific information are you looking for?"

"Financial viability, credit status, corporate reputation, history of the company and board, anything else you think I might find useful." She smiled. "Think of it as an audition. I've engaged the services of a solicitor who has drawn up an NDA we use in cases like this. His name is—"

"Ray Tennyson. Yeah, I've met him." I grimaced. "How well do you know him?"

Harry closed her laptop and sat back in her chair, looking at me. "Oh, I think you might have an opinion about him."

I contemplated how to approach this. "I have to maintain my previous client's confidentiality, though given how the case turned out, that's the least of her problems. Tennyson set up a number of offshore accounts for her that were used to hide proceeds of crime. I don't know if he knew that's what they were for or not."

"May I ask that client's name?"

I hesitated. Confidentiality should stop me from telling her. But since they knew each other, she'd find out soon enough. "You know her. At least she said she knew you. Layla Porter."

"Oh, my goodness. Yes, I know Layla. I've known her for years. An acquaintance more than a friend. We used the same legal services and have shared tea on occasion. You certainly lead an interesting life. Layla is in trouble?"

"It'll probably be in the news shortly unless she cuts a really good deal."

Harry considered this for a moment, then nodded. "Thank you for the heads up about Ray. I'll keep a close eye on him. Now," she was right back to business, "how long did you say this would take?"

We negotiated a fee and schedule, and I promised regular updates. I had a week. That week wasn't going to start today. I was stripped raw. I needed at least eighteen hours of sleep. But food first. And company.

I sent messages to Lucy and Davie. *The meeting is over, and the agreement has been signed. If you can make it, I'm buying lunch across the street from my office in fifteen minutes.*

I sent another message, this time to Jackson: *Can't get there today. Tomorrow afternoon at the earliest. I'll drop by tomorrow at lunch. You can buy.*

Claude was in his den of IT detritus. I rapped on the aluminium door frame. "Claude, mate, I'm told you sell a mouse pad with all the answers."

He looked over at me, reading glasses perched on the end of his nose. "Harding, right? Depends on the questions, but yeah." He moved folders around until he found a black neoprene mouse pad. A grid of commands covered the front, around the logo of the office centre. "This is worth at least $5000 in information alone, but I can part with it for cost. Ten bucks." He laughed. "I'll invoice you. Nobody carries cash anymore. And I know where you live." He frisbeed it across the room at me. "If you need help with anything that's not on there, let me know."

He returned to whatever he was doing, effectively dismissing me.

I left the notebook and mousepad on my desk and locked up. I'd be back when I got back. The advantage of running my own shop was taking an early mark when I felt like it. Or needed it.

Lucy met me on the sidewalk and crossed the street with me. "You're looking tired. How'd the meeting go? Agreement signed? Good money?"

"Better than I got from Layla. And hopefully not as many beatings."

She laughed. "Not possible to get beat on more than you already have. Davie going to show?"

"Davie is right behind you."

We looked over our shoulders in unison and split, and he moved in between us.

"Happy couple, how are you both?" He nudged me in the ribs with his elbow.

I shied away from the impact, gritting my teeth. "Fantastic, mate. Don't do that again until I've healed."

We sat and ate lunch. We watched Davie as he tested his glucose and then stabbed himself in the gut with a fine needle.

Lucy watched the exercise intently. "You good?"

He sighed as he stowed his medical apparatus. "Yeah, I'm resigned to the fact that this is my life. I'm building voodoo dolls for my ancestors who share this gene. And I'm doing a lot of research on insulin pumps. Picking up one of those disk things Fiona has later today. The chemist carries them."

He smiled at me. "How about you? Still hurt everywhere?"

"All over my body. I'm getting—"

"You're getting too old for this shit. Yeah, right." Lucy smiled. "Not too old yet." She looked at her watch. "I need to get back to my extremely boring office job."

"You told me it was exciting, Luce."

"Compared to what you do, it's terribly boring." She held up a finger. "Oh, before I forget, you know that flood of incoming dirty money I said we were keeping an eye out for?"

I raised my eyebrows. "No, really?"

She nodded. "Explicit link to Leung and strong inferential links to Dom and Layla."

"Did you tell the cops?"

"Nah. I'll let them know through official channels tomorrow."

"I like your style, lady. Can I be there?"

She laughed and gave me a hug. "Sure. But to work now I must go. Let's get together tonight. Real date."

Davie looked between the two of us and pointed at his chest. "So, I'm not invited?"

Lucy leaned close to him. "Call Fiona."

I was back in my office a couple of hours later, after a shower and a pastry breakfast. It was close to 11:30 a.m. The office was bustling, and I felt comfortable there. I liked the environment.

Research on the PNG company was at the top of my priority list. After days of brawn, such as it was, it was time for some brain. And I liked this kind of work. A lot of people would find this boring, but I liked the thrill of the digital hunt."

An hour in and I need to stretch my legs and refresh my coffee. The path between my office and the coffee machine passed the lift lobby. On the way back to my office, fresh coffee in hand, I was interrupted by a pair of uniforms, NSW's finest, coming off the lift.

One of them pointed at me. "We're looking for a Claude Perkins."

Huh. "I know a Claude. Don't know if he's a Perkins." I nodded toward his corner of the floor. "The IT guy in the room filled with laptops and monitors. What has he done?"

They ignored me, as they should, and headed to Claude's office as I headed to mine. I was settling back into my chair when I heard Claude strenuously objecting to his arrest. For a tubby, balding nerd, he had a lot of fight in him.

I barely had my head back into the search when a timid knock on my door preceded a small, grey-haired woman's entrance. "Mr Harding?"

I stood and pulled over the second chair. "I am. Have a seat. How can I help you?"

She folded herself in the chair, looking even smaller. "My name is Debbie Perkins. I'm the Managing Director of the company to which you pay your lease. And Claude's grandmother. He's just been arrested for doing horrible things on the internet that I just know he didn't do. I need you to prove that he's not—that way."

I opened my digital notebook and started a new file.

This place was going to be a gold mine.

About the Author

Tony McFadden is a displaced Canadian now calling Australia home. He and his wife and two children live near the beaches where he spends as much time as possible writing.

More about Tony and his writing can be found at TonyMcFadden.net/mybooks, Facebook and Twitter (Yes. I still call it Twitter)

Also by Tony McFadden:

G'Day LA • G'Day USA

Matt's War • Daly Battles: The Fall of Pyongyang • Target: Australia

Book 'Em - An Eamonn Shute Mystery • Unprotected Sax • Family Matters

Have Wormhole, Will Travel • Killing Time

Mac D: Private Investigator • A Step Too Far • Hunter/Prey

The Murder of Jeremy Brookes • Number Fifteen

Batteries Not Included • Broken • Dead Tomorrow

Tony McFadden